M000079609

I pull off my robe and toss it onto the sand. The body I expose is one I hardly recognize as my own, weak and still too skinny despite all the eating and rest they have forced on me these past couple weeks. I am stronger every day, though — this force pulsing through me is impatient and powerful. Just days ago I couldn't have made the walk all the way down to the sea on my own.

For Modesta
Happy read of!

This book is a work of fiction. Names, characters, places, and incidents either are products of the author's imagination or are used fictitiously. Any resemblance to actual events or locales or persons, living or dead, is entirely coincidental and not intended by the author.

TIDES
CHRONICLES OF THE THIRD REALM WAR: Book 2

CITY OWL PRESS
www.cityowlpress.com

All Rights reserved. Except as permitted under the U.S. Copyright Act of 1976, no part of this publication may be reproduced, distributed, or transmitted in any form or by any means, or stored in a database or retrieval system, without the prior consent and permission of the publisher.

Copyright ©2017 by E. J. Wenstrom

Cover Design by Tina Moss. All stock photos licensed appropriately. Edited by Heather McCorkle.

For information on subsidiary rights, please contact the publisher at info@cityowlpress.com.

Paperback Edition ISBN: 978-1-944728-59-5

Hardcover Edition ISBN: 978-1-944728-61-8

Printed in the United States of America

TIDES

CHRONICLES OF THE THIRD REALM WAR

E. J. WENSTROM

CITY OWL
PRESS

PRAISE FOR THE WORKS OF
E. J. WENSTROM

Royal Palm Literary Award Winner for
Book of the Year and First Place for Fantasy

"Wenstrom's debut is the catalyst for a planned series of fantasy war tales, kicked off with this thoroughly expanded retelling of the Orpheus myth...the clever use of weathered fantasy tropes and occasionally lovely turns of phrase will propel readers into book two."
  - Publishers Weekly

"MUD, I loved this book!! So unique so engaging, a Keeper and must read!!"
  - Nelsonville Public Library, Heather Bennett

"Twisting and turning, MUD won't let itself be defined or outsmarted...I'm hopelessly addicted."
- Readers Lane, Frances Carden

"Recommended For: Anyone who likes books about character journey and growth and anyone looking for a book about an uncommon, yet very human, paranormal creature. I really like books about uncommon supernatural creatures, so, when I saw MUD had a golem as the protagonist, I jumped at the chance to read it. A well-written and enjoyable read."
  - Metaphors and Moonlight, Kristen Burns

"There's something primal in MUD. It's a reverent, mythical story of supernatural beings who justify

desperate measures in their quest to feel complete. They struggle with emotions we all understand, even as they challenge the very rules that govern all of creation."
- Fantasy Author, Robert Wiesehan

"A gritty story that holds within it, a raw romance — and RAIN delivers."
- Southern Gothic and Magical Realism Author, Em Shotwell

"There is beauty in what others would consider ugly. This book shows you a deeper look into the soul of an outcast who seems terrible and unlovable on the surface. Once Wenstrom peels back his layers, slowly and meticulously, you see his brilliant core in a burst of glory. His strength far outweighs his weaknesses... I LOVED this book and will encourage my kids to read it, also. I know they will love it just as much. And I CAN'T WAIT for the next book to launch!"
                    - *Urban Fantasy Author, B. Hughes-Millman*

"Competently written, nicely paced, and intelligently plotted. Very much worth the read if you like fantasy or mythology. I'm looking forward to the next book!"
                            - *Top 1000 Reviewer, Bookwyrm*

For impossible women

... and for Christopher, always

CHAPTER 1

I DON'T WANT to be here. In this village, in this life, in this realm. But I already promised myself, I won't take the easy way out this time. I owe the realm that much.

When I sent myself to the Underworld the first time, all those ages ago, all I could think of was escape. I was willing to do whatever it took to escape what my beloved angel Kythiel had become. Watching him spiral out of control as he lost his connection to his Goddess Theia was too heartbreaking; living with the monster he grew into was too terrifying.

What I did not think, in my desperation, was what it meant to leave him roaming the realm.

Now, I'm paying the price. A force is at work within me, healing me at an inhuman rate, willing my body to fight for a life I have no interest in. I can feel it working through me, restless and hungry. My mind feels it, too, and it haunts my every moment.

My days are filled with flashbacks to the defining moments that brought me here: Adem—that *golem*—

who burst with light and disintegrated Kythiel into nothing, a power he says was gifted to him by the Goddess Theia herself.

Then, he took us to the Hunter's corpse, and his story spilled out of him — the box he is forced to protect, how these Hunters keep coming for it. It always ends the same way.

The memory still makes me shudder. Adem may not want to be a monster, but he is one. When he walks through Haven, the people step away and clear his path.

At night, my sleep is agitated and broken. Ever since I got back in this realm, restless dreams of hostile darkness wake me, over and over, leaving my heart pounding like it is going to burst free and run away without me. But once I shake my mind free of the dreams, I don't mind being awake so much. Now, before the sun is up, it's quiet. No one else is awake yet to hover over me. No one tells me to get back in bed, or tells me how weak I am, as I wait to heal. I can stretch my legs and take in some fresh air.

I am past the village and at the shore, my bare feet squishing through the mud. It's cool and soothing, like the early morning breeze that rustles through my hair. It's dark still, the only hint of morning the faintest tinge of pink on the horizon behind the village huts.

I pull off my robe and toss it onto the sand. The body I expose is one I hardly recognize as my own, weak and still too skinny despite all the eating and rest they have forced on me these past couple weeks. I am stronger every day, though — this force pulsing through me is impatient and powerful. Just days ago I couldn't have made the walk all the way down to the sea on my own.

I keep walking, right into the ocean, and let the pull of the waves draw me in as the tide comes in. When I'm deep enough, I drop to my knees and let the water rush over my head.

Its chill reminds me what it was to be alive, really alive, not this sheltered half-life they've boxed me into since I came back. It reminds me what it was to be dead too. The chill sinks deeper and fills my fingers and toes with tingling numbness.

Death, that safe, easy nothingness.

But I promised.

There is a war coming now—the Third of the Realm Wars—and it is as much my fault as it is Adem's. I didn't do what I should have before. I have to stay here and set it right this time.

The First Creatures have tried to overthrow the Gods twice before. Both times they left man's middle realm, Terath, in ruins. The second time, they almost succeeded, before the Gods locked them away in the Underworld and placed a barrier between the realms to hold them there. But now, Adem's damned attempt at heroics to save me has set them free, and now they have ages of simmering rage to fuel them. They haven't emerged yet from the gate where Adem broke the barrier when he came to drag me back, but it's only a matter of time.

The third war isn't a surprise by any means. It was foretold. The people of Haven have been preparing to fight on behalf of their Gods for generations. But not even the greatest prophets have been able to divine how it will turn out. And no one expected it so soon.

Now they all wait with bated breath for word from the Gods. Some kind of direction on what to do, now that it has finally begun.

Even Jordan, Haven's leader, who can hear the Gods the way others can sing—effortlessly, without thought—has nothing for us yet. The tension is growing thick in the air, and not even the sea breeze can push it away.

I lie back and close my eyes, let the water's current toss me.

This war is as much my fault as it is Adem's, and I hate myself for it just as much as I hate him.

If anyone had bothered to ask me, I could have told them this would happen. I would have told them to leave me in the Underworld and let me rot. I sent myself there for a reason, and it worked. I was at peace, or close enough to it.

But no one asked.

My body floats back to the surface, and I wipe the salty water away from my eyes. When I open them, there is a lean, tall figure standing over me. Loose curls of red hair blow around his head and catch in the sun rising just behind him. His face is hidden in shadow, but I can tell he is smiling by the pull of his cheeks.

By the Gods, that smile. He's always smiling.

"Jordan." It comes out with a heavy sigh. I bring myself to my feet, my dripping hair clinging to my bare shoulders and chest.

"Um..." Jordan pulls his eyes away, his face flushing red as his hair. "You weren't in your hut."

His bashful reaction to my body boils under my

skin. I stand still and tall, rejecting the impulse to cover myself.

"No, I'm not." I'm not going to give explanations for myself. They can all insist that I rest all they want, but if I want to be out, I'll go out.

"Well...I just wanted to let you know." He forces his gaze up again and makes eye contact. "Adem and I are going away for a few days. We're leaving as soon as we eat."

Both of them? I can feel the frown creases forming across my forehead. "What for?"

He pauses. "Why don't you come back up to the shore? Then we can all talk together."

I glance back toward the village and see Adem lurking at the shoreline. Resentment twists through me. "Fine."

Jordan turns and wades his way back, the hem of his robe dripping. I look out to the endless waves and take in one last moment of the sea's quiet, before following him.

Adem gives me a furtive glance as we approach, then stares back down to the sand. His shoulders are hunched in tight, as if to shut us out. The guilt has surrounded him like a storm cloud ever since the fight with Kythiel. It makes me want to shake him with all my strength until it disperses.

Jordan hands me my robe, averting his eyes. I pull it on, sand dusting over my head and sticking to my shoulders as the cool fabric falls around me. Their shoulders relax and they look at me more directly, now that my skin is covered.

"So what is all this?" I prompt.

There is a pause as they make eye contact, and then Jordan clears his throat. "Adem and I are going to another city not far from here. Ir-Nearch. We'll only be gone a few days. We just thought you'd want to know."

His tone is forcefully casual. I narrow my eyes, studying his face. His lips purse together tight, his mouth a thin line. He meets my gaze and holds it.

"What for?" I ask.

It must be awfully important, whatever it is, for Jordan to be willing to leave his village during such tense times in Haven. Or doesn't he notice? It didn't occur to me before, but he's so optimistic. Is it possible he does not see the anger and anxiety bubbling among them?

Jordan wrings his hands. He wants to lie, I can tell. But if there's one thing about Jordan, he is led by integrity, even when it is bad for him. He can't help himself.

"It's nothing. We're just talking to someone."

I huff out the air from my lungs and turn to Adem, my hands crossed over my chest.

"Adem?"

Adem isn't stuffed with integrity, like Jordan. But he means well. And his guilt for bringing me back, and all that followed, weighs on him.

He stares blankly at me a moment. It's so strange; he looks so human. But always that vacant stare gives him away. For being made of mud, I guess he does all right. I wonder if he's thinking, weighing out what he owes Jordan versus what he owes me. I'll always win in that measure. He brought me back from the dead, by the Gods, and I've been in unrest ever since.

He glances at Jordan before he speaks. "It's a prophet."

I knew it had to do with the Wars. I whip back to Jordan. "I can't believe it. We agreed."

Together. We all agreed we were in this together. And they were just going to leave me behind.

It's not just about being part of it. I was there when it all started. I saw everything fall apart the first time — even Adem is not that old. They're going to need me.

And just look at these two. Leave the fate of the realms to them? Not a chance. They were lucky Kythiel didn't obliterate them in their last misadventure.

"I'm coming."

"No, you're not!" Jordan is so insistent his voice is a high-pitched squeal. "You're still healing. If we're going to do this together, we need you strong. This is just a conversation. We don't even know if he can help yet. And it is a full two day's walk each way. You're not strong enough."

"I'm plenty strong," I snap. "And I won't get any better wilting away in that hut. I need to get out. I need to do something. I'm coming."

"There's no time," Jordan says. "We're leaving as soon as the food is ready. I just have to leave some parting instructions with Lena first."

Already the village is stirring, the morning cooks preparing everyone's breakfast around the fire.

I tip my chin up and narrow my eyes. "I'll be ready."

Jordan frowns, but he doesn't argue. I bite the corner of my lip to hold back my excitement and turn away to walk quickly back to my hut and load my pack.

Under the excitement, fear whispers to me. Reminds

me that I am still weak, like Jordan said. I feel as brittle
as a dried-out branch, as though I could snap into
pieces. But my soul craves to be out, to do something.
Maybe the exhaustion will chase away my horrible
dreams.

Can I really walk for full days, out in the sun? I hope
I've got it in me as I stuff my few belongings into a
pack.

CHAPTER 2

I FOLLOW JORDAN through the sand and into the village. Adem trails behind us.

My hair drips down my back and my robe clings to me, the breeze suddenly cold on my wet skin. But I refuse to show any hint of weakness, not now, when I am about to break free. So I fight back the urge to huddle in on myself for warmth.

The village's earliest risers are already up, pulling out the large pots they use to cook the fish-and-grain mush they call breakfast.

Jordan stops to greet them and pitch in, but I head straight for my hut. I take off my damp robe and dust the sand off of myself the best I can before putting on a dry one. The sand gets into everything here, along with its grainy irritation.

I pull together what I need for the trip and roll it into the pack they gave me when I came here. I try to work as quickly as I can without tiring, but even so when I get back the stew is hot and the village is lining up with their bowls. To the side, Jordan is talking animatedly to Lena, while Adem hovers to the side.

Adem holds out a steaming bowl when he sees me.

I walk to him. "For me?"

He hands it to me, and I take it.

My heart still hardens to even look at him, but I can't deny that he has done everything he can for me ever since he realized Kythiel had tricked him. He tended to me when I was at my weakest. He fended off Kythiel. He has looked out for my every need since then.

"Thank you." The words come out stiff. I take it from him and turn away, pushing it around the bowl with the spoon.

I know he feels terrible, but what about me? I try to be civil. But I am not ready to be nice. Regardless of his intent or anything he does to make it up to me, he ruined everything.

I shove a spoonful into my mouth and force it down. I have only been in Haven for a few weeks, but already the taste of this bland mush has become too much for me. They eat this same dish for all their meals here. It doesn't seem to bother anyone else. They aren't here for the food, after all. Some of them hardly had food before they got here, and that feeling of true, depleting hunger is not one you forget easily.

Adem is still hovering next to me. I turn back to him and stare.

"Give me your pack," he grumbles.

The pack's strap is already setting uncomfortably into my shoulder, despite its meager weight. I shift it, staring at his open hand.

"I am strong enough to carry my own pack."

He shrugs. "I do not tire. I'm carrying Jordan's too."

He gestures toward his feet, and I see another pack sitting next to him on the ground. I know it's true; Adem doesn't tire—doesn't eat, doesn't sleep, doesn't hurt. One of the few perks that come with being a golem.

I glance over to Jordan, still busy in conversation with Lena. The way his eyes flit away when I turn to him tell me this was all a ruse to keep me from exhausting myself too much on the trek.

But I can't deny it. I am already afraid of how quickly I will tire, even without it. If it makes them feel like they are looking out for me, then fine, I can play along. I slouch it from my shoulder and let it drop to Adem's hand.

To the side, Jordan is going over logistics with Lena.

"And be sure to keep a tight guard at all hours. We haven't seen anything yet, but that doesn't mean it isn't coming. With everything we've seen these past weeks." His eyes turn toward Adem and me. "We need to be ready."

Lena reaches out and puts a hand on Jordan's arm. Her long black hair streams down her back in a glossy wave. Her mouth is tense at the edges, and little lines have worn into the skin around it from years and years of this kind of strain. Jordan's shoulders relax at her touch and the worry lines between his brows smooth. Lena is the closest thing he has known to a mother since he was a small boy. She took him in and cared for him as she did her own son, Avi. Seeing him with her like that tugs at something deep inside me. I used to have these kinds of connections. In my first life.

"I agree. Go. We are all as ready as we could possibly be, for whatever comes our way here. We have been preparing for it for long before you even came to us, Jordan, and we are strong. Go. Do what must be done." She gives him a solemn nod.

Jordan hesitates, then nods back. He turns back to Adem and me. As he is about to say something, Avi leaps from the gathering villagers and shoves into Jordan. He grins, like he is only playing around, the way small boys and brothers do. But there is a hardness behind his eyes. Is it concern, or something else? I can't be sure.

Avi is taller than his brother, and broader. Thick with muscle and covered in bands of tattoos, it is easy to imagine him on the battlefield. He could have easily bowled Jordan over, but with Jordan's incredible charisma, I imagine Avi got used to deferring to his brother early in life.

Avi is Jordan's second in command, overseeing Haven's army. While we are gone, it will be up to Avi to ensure the safety of the village. The scowl that hides behind his eyes makes me think that weighs heavily on him. That maybe he is worried about Jordan's trek. Avi is not so easy to read as his brother.

"Be alert out there," Avi says. "The wasteland is where the monsters lurk."

As he speaks, his eyes wander toward Adem with sharp distrust.

Many in the village fear Adem, and I can't blame them for it. Adem is large and lurking, and none of us fully understand the magic he bears. The first time most of the village saw him, he had flung full boulders with raw, untamed magic, and banished an angel from the realm. Then, he had lugged the corpse of some kind of foreign warrior and buried it without so much as a word.

But for Avi, it seems like something more than fear. It is in the way his eyes glint as he smiles, the stiffness in his laughter. I really do believe he loves his adopted brother. But under that lurks resentment.

I can't blame him for that either.

Jordan seems to float through life without being weighed down by it. Like he can defy the pull of the world's grimness that wears down the rest of us. He loves all who come his way, and they all love him and his easy bright smile in return. Always with the right thing to say, always ready to do the right thing as if it were the easy thing. I do not terribly like it myself.

Jordan starts all over again, running through his instructions with Avi.

I try to focus on finishing my stew. Adem stands next to me, unnervingly still, unblinking. As people go through the food line and pass by us with their bowls, a few give us cautious smiles, but more look away, as if we are not there at all, or glare at us darkly.

Jordan does not appear to see it.

Usually, they bring my bowl to me in my hut, insisting that I rest. Out here among the others, my depleted too-skinny body feels exposed.

The sun is already making it a little warm for a cloak, but I pull mine tight around me anyway, like a shield, and let them all think that in my recovering state I simply get cold easily. But the truth is every move feels stiff and foreign, like my body is a puppet I am trying to maneuver from afar. Like I've been trapped in something strange and broken, and there is no way for my soul to escape it. All the eyes running over me as I stand here only make it worse.

Jordan pats Avi on the shoulder and nods. Then, he leaps onto the closest log, one of the ones Haven uses as benches for eating and gatherings that are scattered throughout the village center.

"Haven!" he calls.

The busy morning buzz of conversation dies down, and people turn to watch him.

"We are living in a time where angels fall from the sky and holes tear open between the realms. These are things we all have witnessed with our own eyes. I know that there is confusion right now. And there is fear. And there is more than enough reason for both. There is nothing wrong with having fear inside you—that is simply part of being human. But you cannot, you cannot, *you cannot* let this fear become you. We all have a battle to fight soon. And I don't just mean the one out there in the wasteland."

He gestures toward the sun rising over the blank vastness to the east.

"We have another battle to fight even before that, in our hearts. It is a battle of light and darkness, and it will define you, or it will swallow you up. I know this because I am fighting the very same battle within my own heart. But each and every one of us has what it takes to win this battle. I know this because I know each of you. As you know me. And I know this is a community strong enough to overcome whatever the darkness brings, because we are *of* the Light, and we *are* the Light, and the Light dispels the darkness, always."

He pauses here and looks over the crowd. They stare at him as if entranced. I have to admit he really is good at this. Even I feel a bit stronger, a little more confident.

"Are you the Light?" he calls.

His people respond with a swell of cheers.

"Are you," he repeats, "the Light?"

A louder swell.

"And what do we do to the dark?"

The response is an enthusiastic mix of shouts too jumbled to understand. But the spirit behind it is loud and clear. It goes on another moment, a continued build, until Jordan stretches a hand over the crowd, and they quiet again.

"Now, friends, I must leave you for a few days."

At this news there is a tangible shift in the mood. A grumble washes over the crowd.

"I would not leave you in these troubled times if it were not of the greatest importance. I am going one city over to Ir-Nearch, to do things that are critical preparations for the battle we will soon face. And then, I will be back.

"While I am gone, treat Lena as you treat me, and live by her word. Avi and the guards will keep you protected. Stay vigilant, and stay strong in your faith, in your Gods who love you, and in yourself."

At this last, my heart closes off from the inspiration of Jordan's words. *The Gods who love me?* Of all the three Gods, in all my ages of existence, none has shown love for me. I used to think they did. But all They have shown me is that when times turn dark, they will recoil from the realm they placed here, and the men they made to fill it.

Jordan steps down from his makeshift pedestal. The people pause for half a beat, then turn back to each other with urgent murmurs as they finish their morning meal.

He stands and looks over them, as if trying to assess them. His frown returns, and he bites at his lip.

"Are you sure you should come with us?" I ask. "Because they don't—"

"I am sure," he says. He is solemn as he watches his people another moment, but then he turns and looks at me, that easy smile returning to his face. "It is good for me to see Ir-Nearch's leader anyway. There are things we must discuss about what is to come. It cannot be avoided, and the sooner it is done, the sooner we can come back."

He turns to Adem and nods. "Let's go."

Adem fidgets with our packs, hesitating, anxiety scrawled over his face in small tensions.

It sends a chill down my spine, despite the day's growing warmth. I do not know who we are going to see in this distant city, but if Jordan is so determined to leave his own people in the midst of all this tension, it must be someone very, very important.

CHAPTER 3

WE SET OFF into the wasteland, the sun's rays dancing over the sea and catching on its waves.

I stretch my legs wide with each step and swing my arms. It feels amazing to stretch and move, to be out in the sun, in the open. The breeze runs over my face and the warm rays caress my skin. I feel more alive than I have since I returned.

We walk, and we walk, and we walk. All through the day. We pass through the vast, vapid destruction the First and Second Wars left behind, and for the first time, I truly understand their devastating effect.

My life was before the Wars, when this realm was in its Beginning and all was still untouched and perfect. Even near the end, when Kythiel would not leave my mind and I was falling apart, and around me, men and Firsts were feeding tinder to the rage that led to the wars, the realm itself was still mostly unscathed. On the surface, it was beautiful and at peace. Now, the only hint of that former peace is the sea, hidden from us here by the bluffs. I cling to the whispers of the waves, still audible as we make our way up the shoreline.

Out here it is clear that Terath is not just a realm that has been through war. It has been torn to pieces. It is harder to see that within the tidy limits of Haven, where a small piece of order has been carved out. But as we step beyond it, I cannot believe the devastation. Where cities used to stand, now all is nothing but rubble and big, broad, blank spaces.

The only thing out here is a great terrible nothing. No communities, no people, no animals even, for that matter. Even the plants cannot seem to bear it here, growing in withering patches, and barely even then.

Worst of all is what the war *has* left behind.

At first I don't recognize it for what it is. But with nothing to do but stare at the debris as we walk, it eventually comes into focus. Broken old spears. Pieces of destroyed roofs. Lonely tattered toys. Every step reveals traces of the life that used to thrive here. All half-buried in the wasteland sands.

Jordan and Adem do not seem to take much notice. It was all so long ago now. They know this; they have lived this truth and walked through these wastelands for years. Adem perhaps even witnessed these wars. They did not see this world as it was meant to be, as I have. It was green and vibrant and rich, once. To see it so broken and its original beauty lost shatters my heart.

This is what has the people of Haven so on edge and afraid. The terror that led to this obliteration is about to start all over again, and it is already on its way to us.

"Look out for beasts," Jordan warns. "We must stay alert and watch for anything that might be out there."

"Beasts?" I repeat dumbly.

Adem shifts uncomfortably. My hands clench into fists and I try not to look at him. If we wanted to avoid beasts, perhaps we should not have brought one with us.

Jordan ignores it. "After the wars, strange beasts were said to lurk here in the wasteland. Beasts of monstrous proportions and terrifying to behold. Beasts said to have wandered in from the Underworld with the demons who came to fight against the Gods, and were locked out when the Gods banished the First Creatures from the realm."

It was sad, in a way. All these creatures trapped here, unable to return to where they belong.

"None have been seen in many years—more years than I have been alive even. But now that the barrier between the realms is breaking, who knows what might come creeping from the abyss? We need to be ready for whatever might come our way, whether from Terath or beyond."

My hand drifts idly to the shaft of one of the two twin blades sheathed in my belt. I am glad I brought them. The idea of a fight makes me feel more alive. It surprises me, but I like this new hunger building in me. And I have a feeling I will get my fight in good time.

As the day forges on, the sun dwells above us with an unforgiving glare. Between the heat and the drudgery of the landscape, there is no sense of moving forward. The enjoyment of being out and free and moving left me hours ago. Now, each step gets harder and harder. My feet ache and my calves beg to stop; my shoulders slouch forward against my will.

The sheer redundancy of it all wears me down.

Finally, we pause for lunch. Jordan takes his pack from Adem. He pulls two wrappings from it and hands one to me, which holds a biscuit and strips of dried salted fish. I drop to the ground — carefully, but casually, trying to hide how sorely my legs need the rest — and eat. Dry and bland as it is, it is actually a welcome change from the village's mush stew. We pass the water jug between us.

The meal only half-sustains me. For the first time since I returned, I feel hollowed out by a rabid, bottomless hunger. But we must be careful of our rations, and we will be at Ir-Nearch tomorrow. I keep my stomach's rumbles to myself.

Adem steps close, casting his shadow between me and the sun. Did he do it on purpose? I want to fight the way he still shields me, but the truth is, the break from the sun is a welcome relief.

When we stand up to push on, Adem steps toward me. "I will carry you."

I stare up at him. "You absolutely will not."

"You are —"

"If you say the word 'weak' I will go off course and walk straight into the wasteland all by myself right now."

His stoic expression twitches and his eyes drop down so that he is staring at my feet. We both know I wouldn't be walking by myself if I did that. He would follow. And then Jordan would too. Gods-damn chivalry. And then when my anger burned away and all that was left was the exhaustion, the guilt would set in and we'd all turn back toward Ir-Nearch again, worn out and depleted of supplies.

"I know you want to help, but stop. I can't take it anymore." I turn away before he can respond, or his sad eyes can make me waver any more. "Are we going, or what?"

Jordan snaps to attention, looking away from us abruptly. "We're going."

"So let's, then," I snap back.

We walk on in silence.

And the walking hurts. It hurts like nothing I have felt in so, so long. It's not that there was no pain in the Underworld. Oh, there was pain, but that pain was too far away from my consciousness to matter. In the Underworld, the pain was distant, almost too far away to grasp, an intangible agony of the soul taken in through a body that did not exist.

And to be honest, it was a pain that I savored. I deserved it, after how foolish I had been. After how far out of control I let things get with Kythiel, I deserved everything that happened when it all fell apart, and so much more. I contributed to the destruction of the entire realm—all the realms. And along the way I ruined the thing I loved most: my angel, the most beautiful, most *good* thing I'd ever encountered. And then I destroyed myself too.

I treasured that pain. It was a pain I deserved. And then Adem burst through and shook me from it, and ruined it all. He brought me back here and reintroduced me to a completely new kind of pain. Or a very old kind of pain. A type of pain so old I had forgotten about it under the layers of my spirit's Underworld haze.

And this pain is so much worse. It has so many

layers, such overwhelming immediacy. And since I am fused with the corporeal again, it all ties together like an unraveled spool of thread, knotting and tangling, all of it entwined in on itself, and making it impossible to find its edges.

Like right now. Walking is simple. It should be easy. When I was alive—the first time I was alive—I walked for hours without thinking about it. But my body is not ready for this strain yet; I realize that now. My back aches, and my knees twinge, and the muscles of my thighs and calves quiver. And this is only the first day of it. I cannot bring myself to think of the walk back to Haven yet. I can focus only on the next step.

It is more than the physicality of the pain. The presence of the pain, each step, is a reminder. That I am here. That I am alive. That I've entered into this terrible mess all over again. And that pierces me on an even more agonizing level. It digs into my soul and chafes with each twinge of my body.

Yet this is what I wanted, after all, when I demanded that they bring me with them. Isn't it? I wanted to be here. I wanted to hurt and writhe and be alive in all its horror. One way or another, I will break through this weakness in my body.

Finally the sky begins to darken, tinged with pinks and oranges as the sun sets behind the sea. Jordan brings us to a halt, and it is all I can do to keep from dropping to the ground. Adem pulls out our pallets to sleep on, and Jordan gathers tinder for a fire. Too exhausted to help, I sprawl in front of the flames with my dinner of more biscuit, more dried fish strips. Nothing has ever tasted better than this simple meal.

In the twilight, the fire glows and crackles, a quiet, soothing rustle.

"How do you feel?" Jordan asks me. He scrunches up his face like he is bracing for bad news.

"Great," I say. His concern burns under my skin. I am so fed up with being treated like I am made of glass. I tip my head up and try to look strong, though every joint feels creaky and my muscles scream in protest.

He half-smiles, nodding, as if he understands. "Well, I am dog-tired."

We eat in silence. The sun disappears and the fire is the only light left.

Jordan clears his throat. "We need to put douse the fire since it's getting dark. Who knows what could be out there?"

I nod. We kick sand over the flames until they are gone. A chill sets deep into my bones.

It ends up not mattering at all, though. I am so tired I forget to dread the dreams I am trying to outrun, and I am asleep as quickly as I can lie down.

CHAPTER 4

THE DREAMS SWALLOW me up as rapidly as sleep overtakes me.

I do not know how to explain the terror of the dreams that keep coming to me. They are unlike any I ever had before in my former life. And I was a prophet in my first life, before Kythiel and I took things too far and I lost my connection to Her. She sent me some particularly strange and terrible dreams, in those times.

The dreams I have now are different. These dreams are full of darkness. And in one sense, this is all it is, really.

But this is not the kind of darkness one finds here in Terath. It is not a simple absence of light. It is a darkness without end, without the slightest hint of light. It is a darkness that eats into my soul. A possessive, angry, predatory darkness. The kind of darkness that only exists in the abyss beyond. And I am held hostage within it.

Something is hiding in this darkness. I am sure of it.

Its grumbles undulate through the darkness, are *part of* the darkness. I cannot see what is coming, but I hear the rustles and strained breathing and grunts, and I know that, whatever it is, it is trying to get to me. And I know it is great, and terrible, and very, very angry.

It is fighting to get closer to me.

My heart pounds against the cage of my ribs, and my hands grow slippery with sweat. I fumble for my blades to defend myself, but they are not in their sheaths. The fear of this creature sneaks its way into me and takes hold, wrapping its cold clammy fingers around my heart.

It is the same dream every time, so terrifying it startles me awake. I never get to see what the thing is.

Whatever it is, it is getting closer. I know this dream so well now, I know what comes next. The darkness closes in like an attack, and I awaken with a gasp.

CHAPTER 5

MY BODY SHAKES and I jerk upright. It is still dark in the wasteland, but at least this darkness is tame. The stiff cold air and the low rustle of the waves in the distance tell me I am back where I belong; the dream is over.

When I open my eyes, there is a lurking shadow towering over me, and I almost scream.

"Are you all right?"

My panic is chased with relief, then anger.

"Gods, Adem." I take a breath, trying to get my racing heart under control. "Yes. I am all right. What are you doing?"

"Keeping guard," he says. After a long uncomfortable pause, he adds, "You sounded distressed." He slouches, and turns away to face the darkness.

I sit there, letting my nerves recover from the dream. I could go back to sleep, send myself back into that place that keeps haunting me. It hardly feels right to call it "rest." Or I could get up. Face the day and my sore, tired body. There is no good choice.

I rise, and am surprised to find my body feels renewed. I hate this strange, unknown force working through me, but I am grateful for the relief from yesterday's aches.

I wrap the blanket around me and go to Adem. In the quiet of the night, the sounds of the waves are soothing, and it feels good to be up and face a darkness that I can understand.

I sit next to Adem.

"You should not sit so close," he says. "You should keep your distance from me."

I hesitate. Why does he do this? So determined to keep apart, to remain a lurking tail behind the rest of us.

But then I remember the way he pulled out that body after the battle with Kythiel. A Hunter, he called him. His neck had been snapped, and the head fallen limp. And I remember the helplessness scrawled all over Adem's face. He said he had not wanted to do it, that he had thought that all this was over.

Over? How many others had there been? What had happened? He had stood there in dismay at his own hands and the terrible work they had done. I don't know how the destroyed fragments of the box he is bound to protect control him, but he was not in control of himself in that moment.

I scoot away from him a bit more. "What are you doing?"

"Guarding," he says. "And practicing."

"Practicing?"

He nods, then gestures for me to watch his hands.

He stretches one, his fingers cautiously tense. He whispers, "*Aaeros*," and the little rocks on the ground rise unevenly up toward him, then hover under his outstretched hand.

It is the spell that he used to tear boulders from the earth and dispel Kythiel from the realm.

"Why?"

He closes his hand and the rocks drop back to the ground. He looks at me and I can see fear in the tense lines of his face.

"Because I do not have control over it. Because I do not understand it."

His eyes are wide. This time it is me who drops my gaze away, something welling up inside me for him that I do not recognize and am not prepared for.

"And because it is the only thing I can do. What if something else comes? What if casting rocks at it is not enough next time?" His hands travel up his neck and clutch around the base of his head. "I need to know. I need to be ready."

My first impulse is to reach out and wrap an arm around him. He is so earnest, and so, so hard on himself. But then, everything else comes flooding back to me: the disorientation of being ripped from the Underworld, the all-consuming pain of reliving my death and coming back to life. That he almost handed me over to Kythiel, even after I told him everything.

No.

I shut myself off and pull my arm into my chest, shift a little farther away.

"What..." He clears his throat, hesitating. "What happened in your dream?"

He stretches his hand and whispers, and the rocks float up again.

"I...it's difficult to explain. I hardly know. But it's the same thing, over and over again."

"Every time you sleep?"

"Not every time. But a lot."

"What do you see?"

I wrap the blanket tighter around me. "That is just the thing. I don't see anything. It is too dark."

He looks at me, blinking those blank dark eyes.

It is unsettling how human he is, for something so inhuman. And also how starkly not-human he is, when he is so close to being one of us.

All he is missing is that most important part — a soul. He almost got one, and at my expense. That was the deal he made: bring me back to Kythiel and gain a soul in return. Maybe I should be grateful he didn't go through with it in the end, but every hour I am living the consequences of his little quest, and I am still too filled with bitterness to express gratitude.

I break his gaze and look to the wasteland. The faintest hint of light is creeping over the horizon. The rustle of the rocks continues, knocking gently against each other as they rise, then drop, rise, then drop.

The longer we sit in silence, the more I realize how very much I want to talk about the dreams. I am so weary of carrying this on my own. I didn't tell the others in the village. They would only have fretted over me even more, and I got more than enough of that as it was, as they tried to will me into recovery.

"It's not just darkness, though, in the dreams. There is something in the darkness, or maybe the darkness is the thing itself. I don't know. But I can hear it. And I can *feel* it." I shudder, despite myself. "It is like it is hunting me."

"What does it want?" he asks.

I think on it for a minute. It is strange, the things that don't come to you in your own dreams. "I have no idea. Something awful."

He nods. But he does not try to say anything more about it.

This is the good thing about Adem. He does not talk simply to talk; he does not try to force things. We sit there, me clinging to my blanket, him drawing the rocks up to his hand over and over and over, and we watch as the sun creeps its way up and the sky transforms. His stillness sinks into me, and I have a rare moment of peace.

Finally, I find something to say.

"Who are we going all this way to see, anyway?" I ask him.

"There is a prophet there. Jordan says he is the real thing. He wants to see what this man knows about the war to come."

"But doesn't Jordan hear the Gods himself?" I ask.

Adem hesitates before he responds. "I guess they will not tell him this."

As the light grows, Jordan wakens. He rolls over and stretches and then sits up. His hair is a wild mess.

When he sees we are watching him, he grins. "Good morning!"

Neither of us responds. Even a person as cheerful as Jordan should not be so cheerful early in the morning.

He stands and stretches more, then drops

immediately back to ground on his hands and into a series of push-ups.

"Ugh." I roll my eyes and turn back to Adem. We sit and watch the sky while Jordan does his morning drills. Adem hands me the pack with the food, and I munch on some breakfast while we wait.

As we start walking, I am grateful for the unnatural recovery that came to my body in the night. When I first got back to Terath and my death wounds re-opened, I recovered with remarkable speed—unnatural speed. Ever since, it has felt as if there were something else in me, an external force willing me into life. It is uncomfortable and unwelcome. But I can't say I'm not relieved to start fresh for another full day of walking.

This day is just like the one before it. We eat our dried fish strips and our biscuits, and we walk and walk and walk up the shoreline. Though I started the day feeling renewed, my body begins to wear down all over again and goes weak on me, and again I force it to keep going anyway, ignoring the pain and the shaking of my exhausted muscles. I welcome it, hoping that maybe tonight, maybe *this* time, I will be too worn out for the dreams to return again. After last night, and the strange something that welled up in me next to Adem, I keep my distance from him as we walk. I already have too many conflicting sensations and emotions accosting me to take that on.

Finally, as the sun begins to slide away behind the sea, a cluster of old tall buildings are revealed when we come over a bluff. They look worn down from war and ages of deterioration.

"That's it," Jordan says. "That's Ir-Nearch."

CHAPTER 6

IR-NEARCH IS NOT like Haven. I can tell before we are even inside it.

I did not love Haven. But it was not Haven's fault. I hated it because I was brought there, and I had no choice in the matter.

But Haven was *good*. It held a harmony that I had forgotten a place could have. It was good in a way things were good in the Beginning. It was quiet and peaceful and full of purpose. The sea loved it and stretched its fingers through it in soft breezes.

But even though Ir-Nearch is only a little farther from the shore, the sea's presence is not in this city like it is in Haven. Moisture hangs through the air and chills against the skin with an uncomfortable stagnancy. Unlike Haven's light straw-and-wood huts, here all is made from heavy gray stone, from the tiny homes to the tall towers to the great wall that surrounds it. The wall wraps around it, shutting out the sea, along with its soothing rustle of waves and its salty smell.

As we near, I can hear voices calling from the top of the wall.

"Approaching from the South!"

"At the ready!"

"Ready!"

"Oh, it's Jordan."

The tone shifts and relaxes.

"Ho! Jordan, the great boy wonder. How fares the wondrous city of Haven?"

I peer up and see figures leaning from towers atop the wall to each side of a great gate. They are layered in full chainmail and plates of leather and metal armor, as if they are already at war.

"Come off it." Jordan laughs. "I have business with Helda. And one of your residents."

"She will be alerted to your arrival."

One of the guards leans over and turns a crank, and the gate begins to open with monstrous groans.

"Three of you this time. We almost set our arrows on you. We did not recognize you with a third."

Arrows! Just because they were not sure who we were from a distance? The thought pricks at my core.

Jordan shrugs it off. "Three of us this time."

The gates draw open, and we step into Ir-Nearch. It is bustling and dense, even as twilight sets in. In Haven, the entire village would be at its center now, quiet in meditative prayer.

But here, the people are each setting their own pace, their own schedule. As they pass each other on the bustling paths, most do not acknowledge the other, as if they do not know one another at all. They are of all kinds of races and colors, dress in more different styles than I can count, speak with a multitude of accents and even some different languages.

Scattered. Alive.

Suddenly, Haven seems bland and sheltered.

"Where have they all come from?" I ask.

"Very far," Jordan replies. "We had not seen newcomers for over a generation, until very recently. The rift began to crack open between realms when I was a boy. Something shifted. It was as if it was felt somehow, all throughout the realm. Suddenly, they started to find us again. That is when we started rebuilding some of the closest deserted cities around us." He stretches his arms, displaying Ir-Nearch to me. "It was too many for one village. We needed to spread ourselves out. Keep it harder to find us all."

"I thought you wanted people to find you," I say.

"Well, we do—"

"But we also do not," a voice with a sharp accent cuts in from behind us. We turn to it, and a tall woman stands before us. "There are people who need a place to be, people trying to escape city-states controlled by tyrannical rulers. But there are also tyrannical rulers. And those tyrants have armies."

Wild hair flies around her in knotted dreads and curling locks. A blade pokes from her belt, and her staff doubles as a spear, a flashing arrow point at its head. Her features are sharp and her expression is grim, as if the frown has burrowed permanently into her face from overuse.

She stares me down. I stare back at her, at a loss as to how to respond.

"Rona, this is Helda, leader of Ir-Nearch. Helda,

Rona."

"These people have been through things you could not imagine. The last thing they need is another war."

Her glare flits toward Jordan accusingly, and then back to me.

Jordan clears his throat. "You might be surprised, Helda, at what Rona has been through."

A swell of warmth for Jordan blossoms in my chest against my will. That's the bone he chooses to pick with this woman?

"None of us want a war," I cut in. "No one ever *wants* a war. But it's coming. Your people look strong and resilient to me."

Helda steps up so that she is uncomfortably close to me. She opens her mouth to speak. "Well —"

"Is that the Chosen One of Haven?" a voice calls from overhead.

We all look up almost in unison, completely dislodged from our tension by the voice's cheerful tone. A young guard peers at us from the wall. His skin is dark as midnight, and he seems as tall and strong as the wall itself.

"Xamson!" Jordan calls. "And here I thought they had finally gotten some reliable guards on the wall."

"I see that Haven continues to let whoever rolls in from the abyss tell them what to do," Xamson retorts.

They stare at each other, grins overtaking their faces.

Xamson jumps off the high wall, landing with ease, and strides over to Jordan. The guard wraps one arm around Jordan's shoulders, while the other cups the side of his face, and they share a long soft kiss.

I look away, a hot flush washing over me, suddenly

feeling as though I am intruding. Helda folds her arms. Her expression remains tight and stern.

Jordan never mentioned he had someone. Or maybe I just never asked. But even in the short time I have been there, it seems every single woman of Haven has thrown herself at him. No wonder he has never gone for any of them.

Does *anyone* in Haven know about Xamson?

Adem blinks, and steps away to give the couple more space.

I have never seen Jordan be quiet for so long as he is during this kiss. But when they finally part, their playful banter picks up again.

"You did not tell me you were coming to Ir-Nearch again so soon."

"You are a somewhat intelligent man. I figured you would deduce it when I got here."

Helda stares coldly at them, but it is as if they are in their own bubble, and the rest of us are not even here. She shifts her weight, then sighs and runs an impatient hand through her hair. As it pushes back, her ear is exposed—or what's left of it. The top part is ripped away, and only a jagged, raw line remains where the rest should be. Was it bitten off? Torn? Despite its crude appearance, she has decorated it proudly with a cascade of bars and rings pierced through it all down the edge.

She shifts, and I realize that she is staring at me staring at her ear.

"It was a long time ago," she says. "Back when I was still a youth. In one of those tyrannous city-states I was speaking of, before I knew there was anything else to turn to. We tried to take down an empire. The arrow only barely missed my head."

She tilts her head with fiery pride, shaking the hair back to show it off.

"Right. Sure." I don't know what to say in response. I have been through some terrible things, and in my day I trained with the greatest warriors of my city. But I have never seen battle, let alone fought in one—I sent myself to the Underworld before the real war came. But Helda brandishes her wound like a badge of pride.

"Many of my people have been in such battles, before they knew they could leave."

She gestures toward Xamson. There is a long scar down his forearm, like burn marks.

"Guard!" she calls, her voice harsh again.

"Sir, yes, sir!" Xamson whips around to face her, a boyish grin still sprawled over his face. Behind him, Jordan chuckles.

"I'm not sure how you could spot an approaching attack from your current vantage point." A twitch at the edge of her mouth flickers through her stern expression. Is she joking with him? I cannot tell. I am only glad that she is not my leader. But I do know she would put her own soul on the line to defend her city.

The grin begins to fade. "Yes, sir."

In an impressive leap, Xamson reaches for the top of the wall and grabs into the stones. He pulls himself up and with one last glance to Jordan, he disappears on top of the wall.

Helda rolls her eyes. Then, she leads us on forward.

"What brings you here this time?" she asks. "It is not time for us to convene yet."

My ears prick. I'd like to know more about this too.

Jordan is all business again, as if Xamson had not been there at all. "No. This is not about checking in on Ir-Nearch. We've come to speak to one of your residents, a prophet."

Helda raises her eyebrows. "Don't you —"

Jordan cuts her off. "We need insights into the war to come. I have heard he can seek truths from the Gods, not just receive what they share with him."

Someone who can ask the Gods, and receive answers? I have never heard of such power.

"Whatever you need, we will arrange it." Helda stops walking in front of an old, run-down shack of a house. "This is where you will stay while you are here. We do not have any houses properly prepared for you. They have been coming to us faster than we can fix them up. But this will keep you dry, at least."

"Thank you, Helda. That is hospitable, if unnecessary. You know I am fine outdoors on my pallet," Jordan says.

"Yes, well. I also know your friend here does not sleep at all. That kind of strange behavior has been what's unsettled some of our residents before. Besides, you have a third with you this time." She opens the door. "You will all stay in here in the night."

Not a hospitality. This is an order from the leader of Ir-Nearch.

"Of course, Helda," Jordan replies. "Thank you."

She nods. "Dinner is after sunset. Then we will make arrangements for your business here." With that she leaves us.

Already the sun is touching Terath's edge and sinking away. We go inside our little shack and put down our packs.

"I will stay here," Adem says.

"No, come with us," Jordan insists. "I want you to hear what the prophet says.

"You heard what she said. They fear me," he says. "They should."

"They should *not*," Jordan replies. "And we can only change that if they get used to seeing you. And I need you with me, Adem. You are the one who was there. You heard Abazel speak."

Abazel, the demon king. Adem faced him down one-on-one when he came for me, and got away with all but a single finger. In his threats, the demon king exposed some of his plans for the war to come.

Adem's shoulders slump and his eyebrows fold, his entire body pleading. "Come find me when you are ready."

"No. Besides, turning down their hospitality is rude. They won't understand. You're coming."

Jordan may be Haven's leader, but he hardly ever lays down orders like that. I decide not to mention that I was hoping to go straight to bed. Besides, if they are seeing the prophet tonight, I want to be there, no matter how much my body punishes me for pushing it further.

They are already serving the food by the time we arrive, and we head straight into the line of waiting people. Jordan hands us each a heavy clay plate. "There is a well over there, past the fire." He points across the village center to a small roofed structure. I nod.

"Jordan," Adem grumbles, pushing the plate back.

Jordan shakes his head. "Hospitality. Just take it."

Unlike Haven, Ir-Nearch uses grills instead of

cauldrons for cooking, a series of skillets over flames, with strips of fish laid over top. With it, they serve a sticky rice that is bland, but satisfying. The fish is seasoned differently, with rich spices I've never tasted before. The new flavors are a welcome, delicious change.

I sit on a bench and rabidly consume my food. As I eat, I look around at the people. They are lively in a way that Haven is not. Most of the people of Haven have been settled there for years; in some cases, for generations. The peace of the sea has settled into them. But here, there is a vibrant, restless edge to everything. A sense of transitiveness to it all.

They collect into small groups. A bonfire in the middle of the city center roars and crackles. As people finish eating, a few musicians grab instruments and start to play together, something akin to a jig. This is a people who have been through a lot, but still have a lot of fire in them. Many are decorated like Helda, in ways that celebrate their war wounds with jewelry and tattoos. They laugh into the night with boldness, as if they are daring it to try to bring something their way worse than what they have already lived through.

Do they know this trouble is already on its way? I wonder if Helda is as transparent with her people as Haven is.

Jordan slips in and out among them, a king amidst the greatest of friends, weaving among the various different cultures and tongues as if it were nothing. Always they welcome him with exclamations of enthusiasm and open arms.

He is a perfect counter to Helda, who is respected

but grim and slightly feared. I can see it in the way the others clear out of her way, and only the strongest seem to flock around her. Few smile at her, and she does not laugh with them the way Jordan does. She keeps a tight order. Jordan, on the other hand, is clearly beloved. But his leadership style would not work here like it does in Haven. Even Haven seems to be showing cracks under his hand.

It takes me a while to see where Adem has gone. He lurks at the edge of the gathering, and the people leave a gap of space around him, even when passing near him. He stares down at the food, occasionally shifting his weight from side to side, and empties his plate onto a few children's while they are turned away playing a game.

I consider going over to him, but then think better of it. He does not want my company. And I remind myself, I certainly do not want his.

I try to be social. As the people pass around me, I look up at them and try to push my face into a pleasant expression that hides my reluctance and exhaustion. But this is not a people who welcome outsiders. They have already taken in enough, perhaps. Most hardly even see me as they go about their own business. I do not mind sitting alone, and soon I stop trying to connect and just eat my food.

It is then that I realize that I am being watched.

A young girl sits opposite me through the fire. Wild curls bounce on her head, though she has tried to contain them with a band of cloth wrapped around them. She is wiry and petite, with rich dark skin, and her arms pull tightly into her with a tense energy. Her large, broad eyes watch me unflinchingly.

I glance at her and smile. She does not smile back. She gives no sign at all that she sees me watching her, as if she were in a trance. I get caught up in her stare, wondering what I could have done to draw her attention.

A bell gongs over the crowd, startling me from the girl's gaze. Everyone stops what they're doing and breaks into small groups throughout the center. Prayer time—though it looks wildly different than Haven's unified sermon led by the village's priest.

They section off into small groups and sit on the ground, each group starting their own rituals. Some take hands; others cross themselves with the Gods' symbols, or echo chants. A few men and women remain standing, walking between the groups and bestowing blessings, taking troubles to hand onto the Gods.

As the shuffle of people moving to join their groups dies down, Jordan waves to me to join him at the other side of the city center. Another man stands with him, smaller and wrapped in layers of blankets and capes and a hood pulled low over his head. Its shadow hides most of his face, but his jaw is set in a stern grimace.

Jordan spots Adem on the far side of the city's center and waves to him too.

"Rona, this is Ceil." Jordan gestures to the hooded man.

"Hello," I say.

He nods, not bothering to speak.

Adem joins us.

Jordan gestures to him. "And this is—"

But Ceil lunges at Adem before Jordan can finish,

taking Adem's robe in his fists and thrashing. Ceil's hood falls back from the sudden movement, revealing a heavily weathered face and blue-green eyes that spark with fierce emotion.

"You!" he barks at Adem. "I *told* you. *I warned you* not to cross over. I warned you that it would all lead to this."

His words are like arrowheads, flying sharp and meant to cut. Real arrows would be nothing for Adem, but this man's harshness causes him to shrink back.

"I could not understand," Adem mumbles in response.

"No, you could not. And you went forward anyway, not understanding. Now look where we are. The outcome of this has been blocked from all the prophets I can reach. None of us know where this will end, but the road is covered in blood and ash."

Adem stares at the ground, as if the blood and ash is already there.

"So...you know each other." Jordan, usually so quick with words, seems to be at a loss.

Ceil glares, chest huffing. Adem keeps his head bent low. The mounting pressure almost makes me step back.

Finally, Adem mutters, "He is from Epoh. Where Kythiel found me. He tried to stop me. I did not listen."

He looks up hesitantly and stares at me, deep lines forging into his brow.

Silence spreads between us as anger spills slowly through my soul. I do not know what to say.

Finally, Jordan gathers himself and clears his throat.

"That brings me to our reason for coming to you,

Ceil. We know everything has been broken. The Third
Realm War is coming. We need anything you can tell
us, anything that might help us stop it."

"Nothing can stop it now," Ceil says. "It is already
here."

"I have failed you," Adem mutters. He looks back
up, an unusual fire lit behind his eyes. "I know I have. I
have failed you, and Jordan, and the Hunters, and
Haven. I have failed Rona. I have failed the Gods. It is
my fault, all of it. Please, tell me what to do to fix it. I
will do anything."

Ceil says nothing, his mouth set in a stiff scowl.

Adem stretches out his hand, whispers, and floats a
few pebbles off the ground. "This is all I know. Please,
what does it mean? What do I do with it now? Tell me
what to do. I will do anything." His voice is a desperate
trembling growl.

Ceil purses his lips and brings his fingertips together
in front of him. "The Gods are not speaking like they
used to. They know what is unfolding here, and they
are afraid."

Even the Gods are afraid? I know this should make
me feel fear, but it is too big, like I cannot take it in, and
I go blank as a slab of rock.

"But come to my temple," Ceil continues. "I will tell
you what I can."

He turns away and starts walking. We follow. But
then he whips around again and glares at me. "Only the
boy and the golem. Not you."

He turns away, not waiting for me to respond, and
continues to walk. I came all this way for this? To be
shut out? Suddenly all my exhaustion hits me at once,

and I am too tired to fight anymore.

"Sorry." Jordan gives my arm a light squeeze as he passes by me to follow Ceil.

Adem gives me a sorrowful glance.

But of course. If he is trying to listen to the Gods, of course, I should not be there. I have silenced the Gods within me, and dulled them around me. Maybe I should not have come after all. I should have known the Gods would not want me there.

I nod and turn away as Jordan and Adem follow Ceil off into the side streets.

I wander thoughtlessly through the dark streets. My body is overtired, wound up and humming, and even though I ache terribly, walking is the only thing I know that can make my mind go still again. At least I have gained that from this trek.

I end up near the west gate, and just beyond, the faintest rustling whisper calls to me — the sea.

"Can I go to the water?" I call up to the guard.

He shrugs. "We can't protect you there, if anything finds you. I have to stay at my post."

I nod, my hand instinctively reaching to check for my blades in their sheaths, then push through the iron gate.

As the night breeze wraps around me and the sea's lapping waves meet my ears, my mind begins to calm. *Free.* I stretch my arms and shut my eyes, focus on the rough sand pressing into my feet and the cold water lapping over them. It seeps into the hem of my robe and chills my ankles. The moon is aggressively bright, swollen and round and throwing back at me off the sea in ripples.

I am keenly aware of my isolation out here, shut off from the walled-in city. It gives me a minor thrill, like standing at the edge of a vast cliff. Jordan and Adem would not want me out here alone, and if I am honest with myself, that is half the satisfaction of it.

But *am* I alone? A tingling pressure creeps up the back of my neck, warning me that I am being watched.

I whip around, pulling my blades free and ready for a fight. But all I find is a tiny shadow trailing me in the moonlight, a petite lithe figure with a wild head of hair. It's the girl, the one who was watching me through the fire at dinner. She stops walking, and we stand there, staring at each other through the dark, the night hanging like a wall between us.

I waver. My instinct to withdraw urges me to turn around, to keep walking and pretend she isn't there. But isn't that what made me come on this journey? I am fed up with being pinned in and locked up, fed up with being tucked into a drawer and set aside.

Something about this girl is too strange, too curious to ignore. Her diminutive figure stands in direct contrast to the boldness of her spirit, hair wild and eyes bold, her stance strong and determined. She's not trailing me out of idle curiosity.

I felt sure and strong like that, once. And I'm so very tired of feeling tired.

So I ignore my impulse and instead step toward her.

"Hello?" My voice reaches toward her, riding on the breeze. I pause and wait.

She moves closer. "You are Rona."

Goosebumps rise over my neck and down my arms. She isn't asking.

"How did you get out here?"

"How did *you* get out here?" she echoes back at me.

"The guards let children roam free by themselves at night?"

"No."

I open my mouth to speak, but confusion at her strange, simple answers holds me back.

She is right in front of me now, the moonlight gleaming off her rich dark skin, highlighting her pointed nose and sharply defined cheekbones.

"Won't your parents be worried about you?"

"Parents?" She crinkles her nose and tilts her head. "I do not have those anymore."

Again, I do not know what to say. What happened to them? How did she come to be at Ir-Nearch?

I stand and wait for her to reveal her purpose.

She glances at the sea and stares, fidgeting with her loose simple gown and rocking on her feet. When she looks back to me, all expression is washed away into a grave seriousness.

"I have a message for you. From the Gods."

Anger rushes the front of my mind and slams it closed. "The Gods have nothing for me. They have said nothing to me for a thousand years and more."

"They do. They just cannot reach you anymore."

"The *Gods* cannot reach me? *The Gods?*" My heart hardens with my words, and I can feel it, tinny and sharp, in my voice. I glimpse the sky and spread my arms wide, calling out to it. "I am right here. What is stopping you?"

The girl looks down at her hands, but she does not move.

My anger is chased with guilt. This is no way to speak to a young girl. She cannot be more than eleven or twelve. It is not her fault the Gods are using her.

I sigh and try to dial back my emotion. "What is your name?"

She glances back at me. "Nabi."

"All right. Nabi." I try to smile at her. "Give me your message. What is it the Gods want to tell me that they could not find a way to tell me themselves?"

"They say, *listen closer*." She reaches up and presses her thumb into my forehead. It's Theia's sign. "Draw out the power."

CHAPTER 7

I FEEL THAT same twisted dread now as I felt as a girl, when Theia first began to send Her messages through me.

Listen closer.

Simple words, but they are eerie and uncomfortable coming from Nabi. They are not her words. These are the words of Theia.

I don't know what I expected. I have been given messages like this one so many times before. I should have known better than to think it would make any sense.

Anger kicks up inside me like rolling clouds before a storm, and a sense of terrible smallness. Under it, though, is a secret relief that Theia still has something to say to me, after all this time, after all I have done. Even deeper down, there is a stinging resentment, that She would dare come to me and ask for something, after all that has passed.

Nabi watches me without expression as it all crashes

over me.

"Listen closer?" I say, trying to choke back the emotions. "What is that supposed to mean? Listen to what?"

The girl shrugs. "That is for you to know, not me."

"I used to be like you, you know," I say.

Now she stares blankly at me.

"They used to give me messages. In my dreams. Or Theia did, at least."

"What happened?" she asked.

What happened, indeed. "I let someone else in. The wrong one."

For a moment we just stand there, the waves lapping at our feet.

"Most of the time, I only hear Gloros," Nabi says. "I hear Her all the time. Feel the emotions coming off the people around me."

My heart softens. "That is a lot for one girl."

She peers over her shoulder to the city.

"It is like background noise. Sometimes it is stranger when it is gone." She shrugs. "I do not usually understand the messages anyway."

I laugh. Gods, when was the last time I laughed? More years ago than could be counted.

"Let's get you back inside the wall where you are safe."

"There is no safe," she says, staring past Ir-Nearch into the darkness of the wasteland. "Not tonight."

I want to ask her what she means, but I know there is no point. She is probably right though—none of us are really safe, not with the barrier down between the realms.

As we start back toward the city, a wind gusts in from the abyss of the wasteland, kicking up sand and dust in a great cloud. In its wake comes a swirling torrent, a tornado of sand and ash that barrels directly toward Ir-Nearch.

At first I cannot believe what I am seeing, and then I become too bewildered to know what to think. I place a hand on Nabi's shoulder, and we stop in our tracks as we watch, too stunned to speak.

The guards on the wall shout and bells ring in warning, but it all seems far away and pointless in the face of this terrible thing barreling toward us.

As the torrent nears, the debris begins to cluster and pull, taking shape into men, and the figures drop from the torrent's whirl one by one, slowly at first, and then in clusters. By the time it reaches the city gate, there is a vast army of them, armed with swords and arrows, spears and shields, ready for battle, approaching the main gate.

It is a horror I could only imagine encountering in the Underworld. That is where strange terrors such as this belong. But here? In Terath?

My fingers begin going cold. The bells from Ir-Nearch feel like they are bursting from inside my head, vibrating through my limbs.

Nabi shoves against my arm as if to get free. I look down and realize my knuckles are white against her shoulder. I'm gripping her too tight.

"Sorry."

I force myself to let go.

"Stay here," I instruct her, pulling my blades from their sheaths.

Then I run toward Ir-Nearch. All the innocent people within those walls. They may be a people of war, but their guard is down. I do not know how yet, but I have to help.

***

The air is thick from the torrent still, and full of sand and ash. I try to keep my breathing low and controlled as I run, to avoid taking too much in, but it is impossible. Soon I am coughing and hacking, just one among many I can hear through the haze.

"Jordan!" I cry. "Adem!"

But everyone is shouting and coughing and crying, and my voice becomes lost among them. Gods, why didn't I bother to watch where they went? They could be anywhere.

I run into a woman holding a child, fleeing toward the main gate. I grab her cloak. "No, to the back. You're running right toward them."

"No," the woman yells over the chaos. "They are already at the back gate." She tugs her arm away from me and runs forth into the cloud.

My stomach twists. *We're all going to die in here.* They have us surrounded.

Unless we kill them all first.

It's not likely, but we have to try. What else is there to do?

I haven't fought in maybe a thousand years, but instincts are funny like that. They come rushing back in an instant, and it is as if I were wielding my blades like this only yesterday.

Of course, I haven't seen a true battle like this ever. Before the First Realm War, sparring was only for sport, and for hunting. We never thought men would use it against each other for harm—we probably would not have enjoyed it half as much if we had. But back then, within the security of the Beginning, I loved it. And I was good at it.

Now, my old instincts snap into place. I creep slowly and quietly through the streets, ready for whatever might come at me from within the thick black haze.

People rush all around in a panic. The chaos is punctuated with the sounds of slicing blades and screams.

I try to listen closely to know what's ahead, but my heart pounds in my ears like a hammer, slamming at the sides of my head.

Suddenly, a soldier jumps out and knocks me to the ground. It is tall and broad, its skin caked in white, as if painted over. A helmet covers its entire head, making it faceless.

The glint of a sword swings high over the soldier's head and comes tearing down at me. The motion is stilted and stiff, but quick.

I roll to the side just in time, and swipe at his ankles. The soldier doesn't even try to dodge it. My blade swipes right through him like he is nothing more than sand, and almost as soon as I pierce him, his entire body begins to crumble away.

All that is left is a cloud of ash.

My breaths heave as I stare in shock. What are these things? Not men.

A sharp scream snaps me back to the moment— there is no time for thinking now. All that matters is that these soldiers, whatever they are, are easy to kill.

Maybe we have a chance of getting out of this after all.

The chilling *swoosh* of slicing metal makes me turn in time to duck a sword swiping at my head. I pull my blade up to guard my face and deflect the blow. With my other blade, I stab at his side. He deflects my strike with his shield, but it tips him off balance. While he stumbles, I stab into him, and like the first one, the soldier breaks apart into ash.

My body is charged up now, adrenaline surging through my veins and setting my senses on overdrive. Everything around me fades to the background, and all I can see are the enemy soldiers, their tinny helmets and their chalky white skin.

There are so many of them.

They're all around, attacking whatever they come across, slicing through bodies and knocking down walls. The dust kicked up by their arrival is settling, but smoke is rising over us. Is there a fire? Are people trapped? I stare up at it and step forward, intending to trail it to the source, but then I trip over something. I look down to find Xamson, his dark skin smeared with clumps of light ash. The way he looks now holds in stark, terrible contrast to this afternoon. His face is sickly pale and contorted into deep lines of pain, and he clasps at his side where an ominously dark puddle is growing around him.

"Xamson!" I turn around, taking a quick survey to make sure a soldier isn't coming at us, and then kneel next to him.

My hands tremble. I stretch them out to do...I do not know what. I never had reason to pay attention to matters of care and healing before.

"Oh, Xamson..." I say again. I have no idea what to do for him.

"Don't," he says. "It is not—" his eyes open wide in panic and I whip around too late, a sword is already inches from my face. At the last second, it halts, quivering, as if struggling against an invisible force.

The soldier grunts.

"Get him!" a familiar voice cries from behind me. I whip my blade through the soldier's leg and he crumbles to nothing. I turn around.

It's Nabi.

"I told you to stay put!" I scold. What just happened? How did she freeze him like that?

What powers exactly are hiding inside this little girl?

"You need me. Ir-Nearch needs me." Her face is solemn and determined. Her eyes wander to find the next soldier.

Another charges toward us, but this time I am ready. I catch his sword in my blades and deflect him, then cut into his arm. He disintegrates.

Nabi is right. This ability of hers, whatever it is, is something I need.

With Nabi standing guard, I cut a section from the bottom of my robe and push it into Xamson's wound.

"Xamson? I need you to hold this. Hold it tight." *And don't you dare bleed out.*

I guide his hand to it and press it down. He nods.

"Do you have your sword? Can you use it?"

His other hand drifts to his side and he lifts his sword.

"Good. If any of them come at you, swipe at their

ankles. It doesn't have to be a death hit. They'll break apart to nothing as soon as they're pierced." I pause, looking him over. Sweat beads along his forehead. "Got it?"

He moans.

I've done all I can here. I stand up, turn to Nabi, and nod. We have to keep going. We have to do what we can to end this.

But how, I do not know. As I survey the city streets, all I can see is a swarm of soldiers, and people of the city battling the best they can, and heavy smoke. These soldiers may be easy to kill, but how many of us will they end first?

I charge the closest one and stab it from behind, and then on to the next and the next. As each one disintegrates, more of the others begin to take notice and turn to me. Some of Ir-Nearch's people take advantage of the distraction and bring down even more, but other soldiers break away and start toward me and Nabi.

I can fight them fine, maybe even take on two or three at a time, but all of them? I brace myself for the piercing pain of a sword as they close in.

Nabi rushes in front of me and throws her hands out to her sides. Her little body quivers as if straining against a great force. The soldiers keep marching, but they don't move any closer. Like they are running against an invisible wall. I gasp and look down at Nabi. Her eyes are shut tight, her young face grimaces.

I've got work to do. And I've got to do it fast, to relieve Nabi of the burden before her strength fails.

I work my way around the soldiers, slicing and

stabbing as quickly as I can while avoiding their swiping swords. For every one I take down, two more seem to crop up in its place. Sweat beads over my face and drips down my back, my muscles scream in protest and everything aches with exhaustion. Smoke clouds my lungs and sticks in my throat.

But there is no choice but to keep going—it is fight or die, not just for me but for Nabi too, and for that I cannot bear to be responsible.

Jordan. Adem.

Their names race wildly into the walls of my mind over and over and over, a desperate call, perhaps even a plea for help.

It goes on for longer than I would have thought possible. Is it minutes? Is it hours? All my mind will hold onto is the now, the next duck, dive, and slash. The ash and smoke cake into my sweat and settle all over me, piling up on itself at the periphery of Nabi's protective ring.

Somehow, finally, the mob pares down, and I slice through the last one.

I lean forward onto my knees and gasp for air. My throat is on fire from the strain of breathing through the smoke, and my muscles shake.

Adem. Jordan.

It's not over yet. We have cleared this part of the city, but deeper in, I can still hear clashing blades and cries.

I peer down at Nabi. Her expression is set in determination.

"Can you do more of that?"

She squeezes her fists. "I can do it."

"Come on."

I hold my blades up at the ready, and we run into the smoky inner streets of Ir-Nearch.

It is impossible to see more than a couple of feet ahead in here. I force Nabi behind me and take hold of her arm to keep her close, unsure of what might lurch at us from the smoke. We weave through the rows of buildings as quietly as we can, listening for whatever might be ahead.

An ash soldier dives at us without warning, a war cry throwing from his throat. I twist to stab through him, but he freezes mid-air before he reaches us. Nabi is holding her hand from behind me. I take a beat to catch my breath, then I stab through him, and he crumbles apart to the ground.

We go on like this, weaving down the streets, searching, taking out the soldiers as we find them. The paths are strewn with sprawled bodies. Some twist in agony or pressing into wounds, others limp, staring blankly amidst red stains in the dirt.

The smoke thickens and the air grows hotter. What is burning? I thought this whole city was made of stone.

Adem. Jordan.

I don't dare to call out for them now for what else it might draw toward us. Where are they? Why did I not bother to find out where they were going? Despite everything it had felt so safe here in Ir-Nearch, with their walls and their guards. I thought I had understood what was out there, but I was wrong. I hadn't the faintest idea.

Hopefully, wherever they are, they are together, and Adem is able to protect Jordan from these creatures.

Jordan may be a born fighter, but this is something beyond us. Without Nabi, I would already be dead myself.

Something draws me from my thoughts, something sweet and strange rising over the angry smoke and the cries of battle. A woman is humming. It weaves through the smoke, a soft winding tune that tips and idles unexpectedly, and is all too at ease in the madness of this violence.

Who would be singing like that here, now? Something about it is not right. It calls to me, a sweet lure that contrasts unnervingly with the violence around me.

I stare down at Nabi, and she looks back up at me. Her wide eyes do not show any fear. Only trust and determination. She bites her lower lip.

We follow the song.

Soon we meet with others heading the same way. I almost attack, but then I realize they are not poised to fight. Instead of helmets and shields like the ash soldiers, these are robes and sandals. They are residents of Ir-Nearch.

A laugh escapes me, I am so relieved to see others have survived.

But then I notice something else, something that makes my stomach churn. They walk with a stiff lilt, and their eyes are glazed over. Though they are covered in ash and sweat and blood, they are not acting like they are in battle. They stumble along the paths as if something has taken hold of them.

The humming. But how could that be? Deep down, I feel it too. It curls gently within my chest and invites me in.

Nabi and I weave through the dazed people, the voice getting clearer and clearer as we trail after it. *What is it?* It soaks into me like a First Creature's aura, but something about it is different. It puts me almost at peace...except...if only I could be closer. If only I could reach her. As if following this voice can make everything all right. Under it, a satisfying restlessness tingles through me like a driving hunger. Wherever this humming is coming from, I want it, even as I know I should fear it.

"They want her," Nabi whispers. "They want *it.*"

Her hands are pressed against the sides of her head, as if trying to shut out something too loud.

"What is it?" I ask.

She shakes her head.

We follow with the others into a wider main road that cuts through the city's middle, gate to gate. The tune becomes louder, clearer, more urgent. Its unsettling tune sends a chill down my sweaty back despite the pressing heat of the smoke, urging me closer and warning me to stay away.

The opening is eerily empty and still. I fight against the tune's lull to stay alert, surveying first down toward the gate, then inward toward the city's center, trying to figure it out. And that is when I see it. It is the source of the hum, and whatever has the men dazed, I am sure of it.

Far down the path, a spindly figure weaves her way through the smoke in a long white robe. The men reach for her and call as she passes by. She pauses, seeming to look toward us. The humming stops. Something bright green glints at her neck. I strain my eyes, trying to make out any details I can, until ash stings my eyes and they begin to water.

The woman turns away and walks again, disappearing between the buildings. The men pick up their pace, calling and chasing after her and shoving each other in desperation.

The very strength of my desire to follow her warns me I need to keep away. I put a hand on Nabi's shoulder and stop walking, let the others flow around us and wait for them to pass.

"Wait!" I try to grab at the ones closest to us as they pass. "Something about this isn't right. It is surely a trap." But their stares are empty, and when I try to hold them back, they fight against me. I have to let them go.

They slowly disappear after her into the side streets, and the hum grows distant. Something within me still hungers to follow too, but I command myself to stay put.

Before I can think or say any more about it, Nabi glances around me and throws out her arm. "Behind you!"

I whip around with my blades up to face three soldiers charging toward us. But I am not fast enough, and as I raise my blades to block the first sword, it hits the side of my arm and slices to the bone. I scream in pain and drop my blade. Nabi catches up, throwing her arms out and holding them back with her power. Her forearms quiver from the strain. I use my other blade to slash through them as fast as I can.

As the ash settles, voices cut through the smoke. They wind from around the next corner, but they can't be very far.

I turn to Nabi. She looks up to me, still wide-eyed and calm despite the chaos. I stretch my arm to assess the damage. It throbs with a sharp pain, and blood oozes from it thickly, but I do not think it is anything serious. I take a practice swipe with my fist. I can keep fighting.

I pick up my blade, now matted in dirt and ash from its fall, nod to Nabi, and we start off through the falling ash and smoke together.

There is a mass of soldiers on the other side, but they are too distracted to notice us. They are already hording around another fighter, and behind him, there is a temple, made completely of wood, and engulfed in flames.

The fighter slices and dodges with remarkable speed and grace and strength. It is beautiful in a way, and part of me wants to stop everything and watch. But even with the fighter's exceptional skill, there are too many soldiers. They are closing in on him.

Nabi stares at me, as if waiting for a cue. I nod, and we get to work on the soldiers from the back of the horde, slicing through one and then the next, and the next. It doesn't take too long to get rid of them.

As we take out the last few, I finally look to the fighter in front of the temple. It's Jordan. He is so caked in ash and soot he is barely recognizable, a matted, slick mess of black and grey.

CHAPTER 8

"ARE YOU ALL RIGHT?" Jordan asks, surveying me. His eyes linger on the oozing blood dripping over my forearm.

"Of course," I say, suddenly indignant. "Are you?"

He nods, still panting. "Who's this?" he says, giving Nabi a concerned look.

"My new battle partner. Where's Adem?"

"Finishing up." He gestures behind him into the burning temple.

I move to run toward the action, but Jordan stretches an arm out and stops me.

"Let him, Rona. They can't hurt him."

He has a point.

"Are there more?" I turn around to survey the area as I ask. It is still and empty.

He puts his hand on my shoulder. "I think it's over."

I relax and step back from him, loosening my grip on my blades.

"I should not have let you come," Jordan sighs.

"You are lucky I *did* come," I retort. "You were about to return to the ash yourself.

The temple is beginning to lose its structure. Large sections of wood break off and fall to the ground, swallowed in flames.

Adem is in there. But Jordan is right—he is fine. The entire building could collapse, and Adem would still emerge from under it unscathed. Yet my head pounds with a high-pitched wail of anxiety anyway, and I am too fatigued to quiet it.

I take a big breath, but the air is thick and smoky, and it comes out in coughs and gags.

"It's all right. It's over," Jordan says.

I glance around. Whereas before all I could see were the attacking soldiers, now all I can see is the terrible destruction they have left behind, all the bodies limp and strewn through the streets, completely still. The dirt of Ir-Nearch's streets is marred with dark stains and puddles. Blood. Life.

"It's not. It's not okay at all." This isn't the end. This is only the beginning. My mind keeps wandering back to Xamson, the way the panic coursed behind his eyes as the blood leaked from him. Did he make it? "We need to search for survivors."

Jordan shakes his head. "We need to stick together. We'll be stronger that way. Safer."

Safer? An inhuman army just swept into the city in a massive cloud, and tore us apart in a single night. Is there any such thing as *safe* anymore?

Rage boils inside me with nowhere to go now that the fighting is over. It bleeds into everything, settles into its old familiar crevices within my mind.

Now we're stronger together? Where was this attitude when they were trying to leave me behind in Haven? And then we came all this way, and when it was time to meet with our prophet, they left me behind again.

I almost start to say as much, but then a large hulking figure crashes through the wall of the burning temple.

"Gods," I exclaim. Jordan twists around, and stumbles back a step. Nabi presses against my side.

Adem has never looked more terrible.

His hulking figure is black from head to foot, fire still crackling from the back of his robe and smoke rising around him. Light grey ash splatters over him, almost like blood. He is covered in huge gashes from their swords. Did he even try to stop them from hacking him apart? But then I suppose he has no need to. Even as I take stock of the wounds, they begin to pull themselves together and heal.

When he reaches us, all he says is, "What now?"

I have no answers for him. The question just looms, begging for an answer. But there is none. Not after something as horrific as this.

Watching Adem's wounds close up, it occurs to me to take stock of my own.

I examine my arm. The cut is deep and oozing with thick blood. I rip the sleeve of my robe from where the soldier cut through it, and wrap it around the wound. Jordan sees me struggling with the tie and takes over.

"I'm sorry," he says.

"For what?"

"For bringing you into this. You should be safe in

Haven right now."

The anger rises to a boil again. "No. I should be here. I survived, didn't I? I saved you from a whole horde of them."

Besides, turns out the Gods had a message for me too, so I needed to be here.

But I am not ready to share Theia's message yet. Not when I understand it so little myself.

I pull my arm away, his knot finished and secure. "Thanks. Are you injured at all?"

Jordan has a few cuts, but nothing serious. Nabi, amazingly, is completely unscathed.

Jordan raises his eyebrows. "You protected her well."

"Actually, she protected me." I nod at her, and she stretches her hands and gives Jordan a gentle push back with her power.

He just stares at her, eyes narrowed and strained. "Why can't I see your power?" he asks her. She looks away and draws up to my side.

There is too much else to do to worry about this. I look around. "Where is Ceil?"

Jordan glances back to Adem and an uncomfortable pause settles between us.

"They cut right through the side of the temple," Jordan says. "He didn't have a chance."

"Oh."

Gods, I can't bear to think of it. How many others went like that, an unexpected blade suddenly cutting through a wall?

"We need to make our way through the city. We need to check who else survived," I say again. Jordan raises his eyebrows. I tag on, "…if anyone."

Adem nods. "I'll do it."

He starts to turn away to go down the path, but I grab his arm to stop him.

"No," I say. "All of us. We stay together from now on."

Jordan agrees.

With Nabi in between us and Adem out front, we make our way cautiously through the streets. We check every single body we find. The pools of blood, the terrified expressions, the blankness in their eyes—it all piles up in me like rocks.

We check every house too, every possible shelter, hoping to find survivors.

The first survivor we find is Xamson—my makeshift bandage was enough to save him after all. Jordan rushes to him, dropping to his knees and cradling his head.

"Xamson, oh Xam, oh Xam…"

Xamson stutters back at him, too weak for much talking. "Sh-sh-she saved me," he says.

"Who saved you?" Jordan says. His voice is tender, almost a whisper. His hand brushes over Xamson's cheek.

He tries to lean forward and Jordan presses him down. "Shh…just tell me. You need to rest."

He points to me.

Jordan gets up again, and before I know it, I am trapped in a bear hug so fierce it strains my breathing.

I want to say that it was nothing, that what else was I going to do, leave him to die? But by the time I catch my breath, Jordan has already turned back to Xamson.

He leans over and gives him a gentle kiss on the forehead, and then another on his lips.

"You're going to be all right," he whispers, clutching Xamson's hand.

Despite his injuries, Jordan insists we bring him with us. Adem scoops him up and cradles the large man like a child.

We keep going. We find others too. Some are in their final, dying heaves, too injured to save. Others are fine—they had good weapons on them, or were protected in stone houses, or found a safe place to hide.

We collect a small group as we make our way back toward the city center. Most of the survivors are not injured. They survived because they were able to keep away from the fighting. The ones who got caught up in it—almost all of them are gone. I have never felt so lucky to be alive.

Luck. What a twisted humor it has. Here I have been wishing to be freed back to the Underworld. To see all these others with so much to fight for—futures, lovers, children—lying stiff at our feet sends a pang of guilt through me.

I glance at Nabi. Did the Gods tell her to follow me back into the city? To protect me? I would not have made it out without her.

Distant cries prick my ear. Jordan starts—he heard it too. "Let's go."

We do our best not to rush and remain cautious as we make our way around a corner and down the street toward it. But the cries are so terrible and desperate they pierce under my skin.

A man has been trapped under the stones of a

collapsed house wall, covered in rubble from the chest down. He flails to get free from it, but the stones are too great.

"Help!" he cries, when he sees us. "I must get up! I must go to them!"

His eyes are unfocused, wild, and bloodshot. He twists, despite the terrible weight of the wall on top of him.

He's going to hurt himself worse.

"Where must you go?" Jordan asks gently, taking his hand. He kneels and speaks to him while Adem and I assess the situation. "It's all right. We're going to help you. You're going to be all right."

As we start to lift the wall, the man gasps in pain, and it's easy to see why. A split pane of the window's wooden frame has stuck right through his stomach.

I glance at Adem. Jordan's comforting words are a lie—this man is not going to be all right. As soon as we lift it off of him, he's going to bleed out. Adem frowns back at me, but neither of us is willing to say it.

"I have to get to *her*, I must find *her*," he cries. "She is so beautiful! So wonderful! She is my love and we must be together!"

"He must be looking for his wife," one of the survivors says from behind us. "We already found her, a ways back. She's dead."

"Not her!" he hisses. His face is twisted, and his eyes are strangely dark. "*Her*, the one who came to us. She is the most wonderful creature I have ever…have ever…"

His burst of energy has depleted, and he sputters into a rough string of coughs, wet with blood. He has maybe minutes before he goes.

"Her? You mean the one with the soldiers?" A gut sense makes me press him. "The one who was humming?"

The man's face lights up, despite its sickly pale tone. "Yes! Her! I must go to her! Such a lovely song." He starts to hum it. The same eerie, twisty tune I heard through the smoke. It makes the hairs raise over my arms.

"Why must you go to her?" I press.

"She is my love! My only reason for being! She needs me. I must serve her."

Jordan shakes his head. "He has lost too much blood."

"No, I saw her," I say.

They all stare at me, Jordan, Adem, and the other survivors.

"He *has* lost too much blood," I concede. "But the woman was real. I saw her."

Jordan frowns. "What do you mean?"

I tell them how she seemed to almost float through the fighting untouched in that billowy white dress.

"What was she doing?" Jordan asks.

I shake my head. "I don't know. It was very strange. There was so much going on. But she was just...walking. And..." I hesitate, knowing what I am about to say will sound ridiculous. "...and she was humming."

"She was humming?" Jordan repeats. Around us, the survivors murmur to each other.

A hot swell of confusion creeps up my neck and flushes over my face. "I...I don't know. That's what it seemed like. It was dark and smoky, and hard to see, and there was so much going on... I don't really know what I saw. Or what I heard. But she was there."

Jordan offers a small smile. "I believe you, Rona. I do. It just doesn't make any sense."

I shift my weight from one foot to the other. "I know it doesn't."

The man seizes with pain and struggles against the wall pressing over him.

"They were all like this," Nabi says. "They felt just like this. It got inside them and made them want her."

Jordan stares at her, then turns to me with questioning eyes.

I shrug. "She says Gloros works through her. She senses emotions. I have seen too much to doubt her. And it fits. It was like they were in a trance."

Jordan looks back to her. "*It* got inside them? What is *it*?"

"I don't know," she says.

Adem finally weighs in. "If we move the wall, he will bleed out and die quickly. If we leave him, he will still die, slowly and in terrible pain."

I don't ask how he knows so much about humans and death.

We all exchange looks.

"We need to get the wall off of him," I say. "We can at least stay with him as he goes."

Jordan nods.

Adem lifts the wall and tips it the other way. It falls to the ground with a crash.

As soon the man is free, he twists over onto his stomach and fights to get up.

"Stop!" I cry. His face contorts in agony. How can he

bear it? I can hardly stand it, just watching.

Jordan kneels next to him. "Take it easy. Take it easy. What do you need?"

His legs won't work. When he realizes he can't stand, he starts to pull himself forward.

"I must," he huffs from the strain, "go to her. She...she...needs me."

We stay with the man until he goes. Jordan holds his clenched hand and tries to keep him from moving too much, tries to stop him from causing himself any more pain than necessary. The man spends his last gasping breaths begging us to let him go, trying to explain to us the urgency of finding the strange woman from the smoke.

Finally, he expires.

Jordan stares at the body in blank dismay. "It must have been some kind of spell."

"All the others were in some kind of trance too. I felt its pull myself." It hits me suddenly, how lucky I am to be here, to have avoided the woman's lure.

I bite my lip, overcome with the chill of fear I should have felt then.

A mess of steps comes toward us from around the corner. Those of us who have weapons raise them, ready for anything. Helda appears from around the corner, along with another group trailing behind her, almost as large as our own.

"We heard a crash," she says.

"That was us," Jordan replies. He explains about the man, and the strange woman in the smoke, and the spell he was under.

"Yes, it had to be a spell," Helda says gravely. "I

have never seen two people so in love as he and his wife. He was a good man."

Her words ring hollow, hanging idly in the musky air. No one seems to have anything to say.

At last, she says more. "We have been looking for survivors too. We've been through the full Southeastern quadrant. This is all who were left."

A full quarter of a booming city. There could be no more than twenty of them with her now.

"We've been through all of this quadrant, and most of the Northwest quadrant too," Adem says.

We all check the Northeast quadrant of the city together. There are a few more survivors to bandage up, a few more hands to hold as people die.

There are no more soldiers, only the ash they left behind. The ones we did not destroy seem to have all left at once.

We end up by the front gate, the one that seemed so great and large when we first arrived here last night. Now the great iron gates are twisted back and bent, completely destroyed.

We are cast out and vulnerable, a small group of no more than maybe a hundred of us of a city of thousands. A man or two is among us, but mostly it is women and children. Ir-Nearch is behind us, a smoking, crumbled disaster. Deeper inlaid into the wasteland, a path is torn up where the torrent barreled in, and then away again.

"Haven." Jordan looks half-wild with determination as he says it. "What if…what if…"

The silence won't let go of us. We all know what if. And the only answer is too terrible to speak.

"We have to get back to them," he says.

But I'm too full of adrenaline to just go back home. My heart throbs against my ribs and my muscles scream. My hands clench into the handles of my blades. I don't want to mend the ailing, and I certainly don't want to go back to the living prison that was my recovery there.

I feel alive. And what I want is *more*.

"They didn't go to Haven after this. And they didn't come from Haven. Look at their trail." I point to the rift the torrent left through the city and in the sand beyond it, heading out into the Wasteland; in and out again, practically in the same path.

"But we have to go back to them. We have to *know*," Jordan says. "Besides, where else could we possibly go anyway? The other cities we've set up are only farther away, most of them south of Haven, so we have to pass through there anyway."

"No." I point at the tornado's path. "We have to follow them."

Helda flashes a fierce smile that is part grimace. "I changed my mind. I like this one."

"We can't do that!" Jordan half-yells it, and then looks suddenly sheepish. "Rona, what do you want us to do? There are only a few dozen of us left. We can't fight them again, and we can't protect the wounded and the children. We have to get somewhere safe. And we have to warn the rest of our people of what happened."

"We can't just let them disappear. We have a trail we can follow. We don't even really understand what happened here. We should try to find out more about what is happening, what they're after."

"Exactly, Rona. We don't know what happened." Jordan is truly yelling now, his hands balled into fists. "We have to tell the rest of them what we do know, so they aren't blindsided like we were, if they haven't been already. We have to go back."

"She is right," Helda cuts in.

The quiet flattens the air.

Jordan steps toward her, his face a dark, ashy scowl and his hands in fists. "What?"

But Helda shrugs, as if he were a kitten swatting at a lion. "She is right. And also you are right. But she is right."

Jordan blinks blankly at her.

"So then what do you expect us to do?"

Jordan's eyes are desperate, and he begins to pace haphazardly through the sand. I have never seen him like this. I doubt he has ever been like this before in all his life. It occurs to me that he has probably never seen a real fight before. And I have never seen anyone disagree with him before.

"Look." I step in front of him to stop the pacing, raise my good arm, and put my hand on his shoulder. "We don't all need to follow them. I can go. And then, when I know more, I will come back to Haven. I can tell you where they're camped, what their plan is, their weaknesses, whatever I can find. The rest of you can get everyone settled and safe, and you can make sure the rest of your people in Haven and the other cities are safe too. You can get ready for what's next."

"But—" Jordan's frown deepens, but his voice is softer. "No, Rona. You more than anyone should be somewhere safe right now. Even without the trauma of an attack, you need to rest."

"I don't," I lie. "I'm getting stronger all the time." That part is true, at least. "This is what is best. For everyone."

"I'm coming with you," Adem grumbles.

Jordan glances at him with a look that implies betrayal, but then quickly reels it back in and covers it with an expression that tries to be stoic.

"No. No. We just agreed we aren't splitting up anymore," Jordan insists.

Adem shrugs. "She shouldn't go alone."

Jordan clears his throat. "Neither of you are going. If anyone should be putting themselves at risk like that, it should be me. But—"

"Go with them, then," Helda says.

He turns to her with betrayed eyes. "What?"

She shrugs. "I can get the rest to Haven. I can tell them what happened, and what we need to be ready for. There are enough of us, strong enough, to keep us protected. We will take weapons from what's left," she says, nodding toward the city.

Jordan thinks.

Something about the way Helda impatiently shifts her feet makes me uneasy. But of what, exactly? I do not know. Surely Jordan knows his own people better than I could.

And besides, we do need to follow the trail.

"We've got to do it, Jordan," I press. "Even if Haven is fine for now." His eyes grow wide with concern. "And I'm sure it is! But even if they're safe for now, if we all just go back there, we're an easy target. All we can do is wait for the next attack. But if we follow them, we can learn something. We can come back to Haven and be better prepared."

Jordan considers. I hardly dare to even move while he weighs the options.

Finally, he speaks, "You're right. We'll go."

CHAPTER 9

WE WALK ONCE more with the survivors through the rubble, picking up what we can of remaining food and weapons. Trying not to see the bodies strewn through the streets. We are past the point of grief now, all of us stony-faced and numb.

All I can think is that it could have been me. It should have been me, and not these proud, brave people. After all they have been through, they deserved some good in this realm, not more violence.

I deserve to go back to the Underworld. After all, it's my fault Kythiel roamed free, and my fault he was here to trick Adem.

But that ache I felt before the return there...I don't feel it quite like before. The fight made me feel alive in a new, indescribable way. It is like breaking free of a haze.

By the time we are done searching for supplies, the sun is already rising over the wasteland. It's time to go.

We turn to Helda. "Be safe out there." It sounds flimsy, but what else is there to say after a night like the one we had?

Jordan reaches out and takes Helda's arm. "Tell them what happened. But tell them not to be afraid. Remind them of all we've been training for all these years. We're ready for whatever comes. Tell them that."

Helda raises an eyebrow, studies Jordan's face lined with earnestness and deflated from exhaustion. There is a heaviness in her expression. She does not believe him. But she nods. "I'll tell them. I'll get them ready."

Perhaps she sees what I see; Jordan needs to believe that they're ready even more than he needs his people to believe it.

And then there is nothing left to do. Helda and all that is left of Ir-Nearch head off toward Haven. Xamson and a few others of the more seriously injured are carried on makeshift cots they built from sheets and poles. Nabi slips her hand into mine and gives it a soft squeeze before joining them.

We watch them, and then we turn and start to walk too, deeper into the wasteland.

The deeper we go into the wasteland, the greater its horror becomes. Even if I were one for talking much, I do not have the words to put to it.

It is really nothing more than sand and debris and piercing sun. Broken fragments of wood, cloth, shattered chunks of clay and glass. Occasionally, they are large enough to recognize what they came from. At one point I see half the face of a smiling doll, its hair torn away, buried in the sand.

There is nothing so awful about these things on their own. But each idle fragment is a reminder of Ir-Nearch. Of this thing that is out there waiting to destroy us, and the terror we saw take apart an entire bustling city in a single night. Of how this ended for those who fought back against the rebels the last time.

And the wasteland has plenty of its own horrors, even without the war starting up again. Its own monsters.

For a long time none of us speak. We trudge on in silence, too broken from the fighting, and the devastation we left behind in Ir-Nearch to do anything else.

All through the day, we find nothing. No soldiers. No beasts. No end to the torrent's path. How far could they have fled into the wasteland? Where were they heading? I begin to wonder if this was such a good idea after all. But it is too late. We're out here now, and we're going to follow it to its end.

Something far past exhaustion hums through my limbs. My muscles feel stretched thin, and my bones fight against each new step. The wound in my arm has bled through my makeshift bandage, filling it with blood and clotting over, stiff and thick. I have not felt so utterly drained since my first days back in Terath, when this force worked through me and willed me back to life.

I am bound to recover again with sleep, I tell myself. But this exhaustion is like a well that has no bottom. It keeps seeping deeper and deeper into me, and even with the unnatural way my body replenished itself before, I must rest for it to do its work, and it occurs to me only now that we did not rest last night.

I do not know that I have the will to keep fighting against it.

But a wall goes up between my mind and my body, like a shield against the ache. I have to keep walking. I cannot afford to appear weak, and I cannot stand to let the ones who wrought this atrocity over Ir-Nearch get away with this. Just keep moving forward, one foot, then the other, until the sun sets.

Jordan lacks his usual brightness, and it's not just because of the soot covering him. His hair stands oddly, pulled in strange directions. When the sweat starts to wash the soot away, it exposes dark circles under his eyes.

But the sun rises over us, and then tilts behind us on its downward bend.

"Did you see them? The way they broke apart into ash?" Jordan's question shakes me from my reflections.

"The soldiers?" I ask. But of course he means the soldiers. "Yes. I've never seen anything like it."

Adem grunts in agreement.

"They looked human, but…" He shakes his head.

"But humans don't disintegrate into ash when you pierce them," I say. "They seemed like they used to be human. Or…," I tilt my head, trying to force it into something like sense, "like they weren't alive anymore."

"The Texts refer to something like this in the old wars. The First Creatures brought back the bodies of men long dead to fight for them. A way to weaken forces or distract in battles. They used them more in the early days of the wars, before their numbers were as large. According to the Texts," Jordan says.

"Well, it appears they have chosen to do so again in the Third War."

I say it without thinking, and a deadening quiet

swells in the wake of my words. It's the first we have used that word since it happened. *War.* But it is the truth—the Third Realm War is truly here now. And after all the years of training, all the weeks of planning, we are still not ready for it. I do not know if there is such a thing as being ready for something like this.

Adem breaks the quiet. "The Texts say they are made with magic from Shael. But a manipulation of it. Dark magic."

I sigh. Even this small amount of thinking has my mind worn out. Or maybe it is just the subject.

"They were such a corruption of the Gods' power they were not even given a name." Jordan looks grim.

To be unnamed. How terrible.

After that, we simply keep treading forward. There is not anything more to say after what we saw, what we lived. My heart pounds faster thinking of it. My limbs ache with exhaustion. The wound in my arm throbs.

It is different here, in the wasteland's heart. On our way to Ir-Nearch, the shore was like a lifeline, anchoring us and tying us back to Haven. The sea whispered to us in the night in what felt like promises of protection.

But now, out here, that comfort is gone, and we have been swallowed up in endless earth from every side, directionless and untethered. When I turn around to look back, I cannot even make out the tops of Ir-Nearch's towers anymore. The wasteland stretches eerily in every direction and swallows us up.

We keep following the trail until the sun begins to set, and then we stop to make camp for the night. The day's heat gives way to a thin chill.

"Should we be worried about drawing attention in the night?"

I did not give it a second thought on our way to Ir-Nearch, but after last night, everything is different. Who knows what else lies in wait?

Adem stands, his head slightly tilted and ears perked, nostrils flared. He holds eerily still, staring blankly ahead of him. Finally he says, "There is nothing there. Rest. Stay warm. I will make sure it stays that way."

I've grown so used to him that I almost forgot— Adem is as much a monster of the wasteland as anything else that might be lurking.

We grab our pallets and stretch slices of fish we took from Ir-Nearch over a stone in the fire. Jordan and I pass the water back and forth, taking slow, careful sips.

The fire crackles, and crickets' chirps begin to rise into the twilight. With the soothing rhythmic sounds and the stars overhead, my blanket wrapped tightly around me, I almost feel safe. It is almost beautiful.

"What do the Three say about all this?" I look to Jordan.

Jordan takes another slow sip of water. He stares unseeing into the flames, and then clears his throat. Only then does he look at me.

"I don't really know what to say," he says. His eyes flit to Adem and back. "I am still trying to make sense of it myself."

A swell of resentment toward the Three rises within me. Why would They withhold from him now, of all times? How can They not send us a message, something easy and clear for once, when we are here, on the ground, chasing down those who would destroy Them?

The anger is for Jordan too, though I am ashamed to admit it. I have been the Gods' messenger before, and there is no controlling Their Will. More often than not, it is like this—inconvenient. Not at all what you are looking for from Them. But something in his eyes, the way he looked to Adem, it gives the haunting feeling that he is holding something back.

I know enough about how the Gods work to know they would not answer a direct question. But They usually have *something* to say. So what is Jordan not sharing?

I want to push him, make him say what he will not. But my whole body aches, and exhaustion sets over me like a haze. I do not have the energy for a fight.

Instead I turn away and stretch out on my pallet. Just the suggestion of sleep is a relief. The exhaustion I shoved aside all day hits me like a tidal wave, and my muscles twitch and tug in echoes of the strains of the day. The rustling of blankets tells me Jordan is settling in too.

The fire's crackling quiets my mind, and as I shut my eyes, Adem steps between us and stares into the abyss we will walk into tomorrow, still as a statue. Even after everything, there is an odd kind of comfort in his presence, here in the wasteland, in knowing he would do anything to protect us. That he is capable of almost anything. He does at least try to do the right thing, even if he sometimes falls short.

"I'm having dreams again."

The words float up toward the sky, aimless and thin. It's the first time I have said it aloud. I expected relief, but the words emerge hollow, unable to convey the terror they hold for me.

Jordan grunts in response, already almost asleep. But Adem turns and looks down at me. He does not say anything, but his mouth pulls into that grim sadness that so often sits in his face. Is that concern in his furrowed eyes? I did not expect him to be the one to understand, but I stare back at him, and we silently confess our fears to each other about the horrors to come.

Eventually, I drift off to sleep, hoping the exhaustion will keep the dreams away.

CHAPTER 10

SLEEP THROWS ME into the darkness again, and it is full of malice.

I am alone in the same terrible, vast darkness, a darkness far worse than nighttime, more terrible than the Underworld.

And there is something out there in it.

It lurks just beyond my dream's edge. I do not know what it is, but it fills me with an awful sense of foreboding that twists through me in trembling knots. I know it with a certainty one can only feel in dreams, on a deep, intuitive level that is as true as the air I breathe; whatever it is, it wants in.

Bolts of fear shoot through me. As surely as I know it is there, I know that if it breaks through, I am doomed.

I can feel it pushing and scratching and clawing against the edges of my mind, trying to find a weak spot that will allow it to break in. It cries and calls out, though the voice is too muffled to understand.

Listen closer.

Nabi's mandate from the Gods cuts through the horror and rises in my mind.

No, no, no. My fear shuts me off from it. Please, I beg to Theia, just banish this from me. Make these nightmares end.

My pleas are met only with the dreadful clawing at the edges of my mind.

Could I expect anything different? Why would the Gods listen to me now? I have not prayed to Them since long before the Underworld, and long even before that. Not since they ordered me to keep away from Kythiel, and I ignored them, and turned away from my Gift. Maybe they sent me these dreams. Maybe this is my punishment for all I have done to wrong them.

But no. Nothing is ever that simple with the Gods. They want something from me. That is the only reason they send messages.

Is this what you want? Is this what I am supposed to listen to? The dreams?

But no response comes. I do not know if they would be able to hear from in here, inside my dreams. Or if I would hear them, even if they sent me a response.

I stand as still as I can, hold my breath, and do my best to push down the fear enough to listen. I try. I truly do. I do my best to twist the scratching and muffled cries into something that makes sense.

But it makes no difference. All I can hear is the terrifying scraping that seems to come from nowhere and everywhere, rumbling through the ground beneath me and overhead. I feel as though I am going mad trying to make sense of it all.

I try to will myself awake to no avail. Finally, it becomes too much. I give up and drop to the ground of my dream, layered in marble. I curl up into a ball, and wait for it to end.

CHAPTER 11

CONSCIOUSNESS SLAMS INTO me with a lurch of panic, the restless scratching of my dream still hovering in my ears. My heart pounds and cold sweat dots my face.

I lean forward and push my hair aside, as if to make space for better air. There has never been a thing in the darkness before.

"What happened?"

The voice comes from behind me, and I jump—in the after-quakes of my chilling dream, I forgot where I am and who I am with. But it all comes back in a rush.

"Gods, Adem," I sigh. My body is sore and aching, and my mind struggles to reconcile the veil of sleep with the throbbing lot of adrenaline.

"You looked like you needed help," he grumbles.

My resentment toward him flares in a burst of hot anger.

"You would think that, wouldn't you?" I snap. "I can take care of myself."

I shut my eyes and breathe in as deep as I can. The shuffle of Adem's feet fades away, and as soon as he is gone the anger dissolves and is replaced with guilt. The truth is that I am relieved he woke me up. I hold the breath in, trying to center myself, and then release the air slowly, imagining my anger breaking away into the air in tiny particles.

My heart begins to quiet. My mind clears. Night is still thick over the sky, and Jordan is sleeping soundly, a low nasally rumble signaling his peaceful breathing. I can't bear to lie here anymore.

I tuck my blanket around me, relieved to find the strange force in me has healed yesterday's aches. I pull up the bandage on my arm and find the wound has already begun to close. I hate the invasive feel of this strange force in me, but I do not know what I would do without it out here.

Adem stands with his back to us, staring absently into the abyss in the direction we came. I can't bring myself to apologize, but I can't pretend I'm not grateful to be free of the dream either. I get up and stand next to him.

I shiver, though I don't feel the night's chill at all. That voice calling to me. It knew my name.

"Did you call to me? Right before I woke up?"

"Yes. Many times." He glances to me, then looks away again, as if to check my mood. "You looked like you needed to wake up."

"Right." A wave of relief sinks into me. Maybe that is all it was then, Adem's voice reaching into my dream world. Something in the back of my mind doesn't quite believe it, but I latch onto it anyway. "Yes."

"It was a horrible dream. One of the nightmares I mentioned last night." I try to force a laugh with the words, but it ends up being more of a shaky sigh. I keep talking to stop the terrible sound. "Every time I close my eyes, I fall into this terrible darkness. It doesn't sound so bad, I guess. But this darkness...I do not know how to explain it. It is like it is hunting me. There was something there in it this time, trying to break through to me."

He nods, the only sign that he is listening. He keeps on staring into the night.

"Anything there?" I ask.

I try to play it off like a joke, but my voice is still shaky with my tense breathing, and the threats of my dreams, scrawling and scratching to get to me, still hover around my shoulders. I tug the blanket around me tighter, an effort to shut out the sense of being hunted. It works, maybe, a little bit.

"Mmmm." Adem narrows his eyes and frowns, peering at the darkness.

A chill runs down my spine. *No*, he was supposed to say, *of course not.*

I stare at the darkness too. The moon is overhead, an abridged circle gleaming over us. But the darkness is like a wall, and I cannot see anything through it.

When my legs grow tired, I sit next to Adem on the ground. He stands guard like a stone, with only the occasional blink or twitch of a muscle to signal life. Once he turns slowly to the opposite direction, and gazes heavily into the darkness. Then, he turns around again. Anxiety prickles over my skin.

The stars shift overhead, and I suppose the time

passes. From somewhere in the wasteland, an insect hum vibrates through the chilled, humid air.

"What's it like?"

Adem speaks so little that his voice startles me here in the night, in the middle of nothing.

"What?"

"Dreaming," he says. "What is it like?"

It is an unusual and difficult question; one I've never been asked before. I've been asked what it was like to hear Theia, or to bring her words to the ones for which they are meant. Even what it was like to sleep with an angel.

But simply to dream? Never.

But then, Adem is not most people. No, he is not a person at all. I forget so quickly. There is a hunger in his voice, and his dark eyes brim with simple earnestness. I have to look away.

"It is awful."

What else can I say? My dreams have been my undoing. Theia's gift to me, if that is what I must call it, seemed a curse I could not escape. And then, it was so easily turned against me by Kythiel, who turned Theia's portal into his own way to access me, after She ordered him back to the Host. Now, perhaps I have broken it forever.

I hold my gaze down at the sand for a moment. But then guilt begins to cloud my chest, so I look back up to him. He's watching me still, with that constant blank stare of his. When we make eye contact he blinks and looks away into the darkness ahead, but not fast enough. He hungers for more. I can see it.

Something shifts inside me, and the thick layer of

resentment I have felt towards him begins to loosen. When I try to hold back my anger and see him without that tinge of rage, I am surprised to find that I am capable of it. What I see in him without it is in stark contrast to his monstrous physicality—vulnerable, pained, sad.

"Dreams are not always awful," I go on. He turns back to me. "They can be nice, too. It's just been so long since dreams have been anything good for me."

"It's hard. The way it never ends," he says.

It is an odd thing to say. But I understand what he means. When you have existed through the realms with your burdens building on you for so many years, it weighs on your shoulders so heavily you feel you will simply flatten into nothing under it all. Except that you never do, and it just keeps building against you more and more and more.

All at once, I realize he is possibly the only other being in the universe who can understand this in the same way.

The weariness of it all sinks into me, but just as I am beginning to think it is all too much, a hint of morning begins to peek over the horizon. The insect humming starts to drop away, leaving the wasteland morning quiet. The sun stretches, and for a sweet, small time, the air is filled with neither a chill nor an overwhelming heat. It is almost worth the loss of sleep, to witness this brief moment where the wasteland shifts and the realm proves that loveliness can still exist within it.

Adem sits next to me in the sand, and our arms brush against each other. It tingles my skin, but he does not seem to mind it. He whispers his spell, and the rocks rise and fall from the ground into his hand, and the rustling they make quiets my mind. My head droops and my shoulders slump, and I drift half-asleep into Adem's side, resting, just for a moment. Adem remains still as stone and equally as hard, steady, and unmoving, without even the rise and fall of breathing.

"Wow, last one up."

Jordan's voice snaps me awake, and I bolt away from Adem.

"Yes." I twist around to look at him. "We have been waiting on you for hours."

There is an unnatural strain in my voice that I do not recognize. I turn to stir the fire for breakfast.

While we eat, Jordan does the same routine he does every morning, the exhausting series of jumps and push-ups and lifts. Adem and I go about packing to start our walk. We are both all too familiar with the routine drilled into him as a child. He grins, a pink glow emanating from his face. We do our best to ignore his unreasonable, if typical, perkiness.

After we eat, we kick sand over the fire. Adem loads up with our supplies, and we begin another day of walking.

CHAPTER 12

WE WALK AND walk and walk.

We walk through sand that gives way under our bulk, straining my feet and knotting in my calves. We walk through sun so heavy and hot it is like a physical weight over my back. We walk through graveyards of crumbled memory, their city-front facades fading away from centuries ago.

One destroyed community after another, until they all begin to look the same no matter if one was made of brimstone and another of wood, if one was a small town and another a grand city. Now, they are all gone, the same debris of shattered pots and half-buried skeletons left behind.

Each one looks like Ir-Nearch. Each one looks like Haven.

Even their wells have dried up and will give us nothing, leaving us to strictly ration the bottles of water we carry, with no sense of how long they must last.

I begin to wonder what I have done to us, choosing

to follow this mystic torrent's path through the wasteland. What was I thinking? Why did they listen to me? We should have returned to Haven like Jordan wanted, and we would all be in comfort now, preparing with the others for whatever comes next.

But it is too late to turn back. We are here, and we have committed to hunting down the soldiers who destroyed our city. We have to find out what we can. We have to see if we can stop this before the Underworld's horrors break over us.

We walk through crushing heat. We walk through violent storms. We walk for days.

Then, at night, we rest. I dream my haunted dreams. Adem stands watch, and wakes me when I show distress.

My body continues its fierce fight for recovery, each day bringing me back stronger than I should be, no matter how drained I become. In fact, despite it all, I am actually getting stronger, not just healing. The deep wound in my arm from where the Unnamed soldier cut into me is gone within days. It is unsettling, this strange way my body is still not fully my own, and I do not like the creeping buzz of energy that courses through me, like an invading outside force.

I start each day surging with overwhelming energy, only to be drained at the end, feeling more like my normal self again. More like the depleted exhaustion I have grown used to in the Underworld.

This depletion was a relief in the Underworld. It is no wonder my soul was drawn there, and why I stayed there all those ages. There, the exhaustion made everything else impossible, even feeling, even thought.

And in my last days on Terath, these were my greatest enemies.

The more we wander the devastating trail the torrent left behind, the more uncertain I become that this was the right thing to do. How far did they go? What if we keep following it until we are out of water and food? What if they wanted us to follow?

But we have come too far now to turn back, and the Gods alone know what waits ahead. I have steered us all into an impossible situation.

We eat the rest of the fresh fish, and move on to more of the dried, salted strips. It is not long before these become as tiresome for me as the mushy stew of Haven. Haven—that wonder of safety and comfort on the shoreline. If I had known all the pain and disaster that lay ahead when we left, would I still have demanded that they bring me along? I like to think I am strong enough to take on struggles such as these, but if I am honest, I do not know.

Each night I lie down on my pallet so exhausted I think I may escape the dreams just this once, and too tired to fight sleep's pull. And each night, the dreams return anyway.

Whatever it is on the edges of the dream, it is persistent. Every night it scratches and claws and demands that I let it in. But I won't. I can't. I am too afraid of what it is, and what it wants from me. I lie huddled in a ball in the darkness until Adem wakes me and releases me from it.

Then we sit together until dawn, and I tell him about the horrors my dream contained.

Adem seems to be on edge too. At first he sits with

me, but after a few nights, he remains standing as I settle in next to him on the sand. He stops practicing his spell, raising the rocks from the earth, and instead he gazes into the night with sharp alertness, his elaborately jeweled blade ready in his hand. His arms flex with tension, never resting or flinching.

"What is wrong?" I finally ask.

A muscle twitches in his neck.

"Is there something out there?"

"Yes." He clenches his jaw. "I think so."

Adrenaline prickles down my back like a thousand needles. I stand up and reach for my blades.

"Where?"

He nods into the abyss in the direction we came. I peer into the darkness, waiting for it to take shape into something terrible.

It doesn't.

"I don't see it."

He gives a throaty growl in response. "It's there. I hear it. I smell it, when it gets close enough."

I swallow and shift my blade in my hand. "How close is it getting?"

"It is keeping its distance," he says. "I wasn't sure it was real at first. Still not sometimes."

"You mean it's been following us?"

For a pause we stand in silence. I strain to listen, but my heartbeat swells until it is the only thing I can hear, fast and anxious. The blades in my hands beg for action, for more of the sweet hunger and relief the fighting in Ir-Nearch brought me.

"Let's go. Let's put an end to this." My voice is sharp and cool like resting metal.

Adem studies me. Something flutters behind his eyes and he opens his mouth to speak, but whatever it is, he swallows his words. "No. I'll tell Jordan. When he wakes up. Then, we'll decide."

I sigh and gape at the darkness. The rest of the night, I spin my blades in my hands, keeping them at the ready. Every fiber of my being demands that I charge into the darkness and take it on, regardless of whether it might destroy me in the fight.

The passing time grates me, the moon passes overhead and begins to sink again, and it occurs to me that I am thankful Adem is here with us.

When Jordan wakes, Adem is good to his word.

"There is something out there." Adem points behind us. "Something following us."

Jordan frowns, looking back into the wasteland just as I did.

"What kind of thing?"

"Not sure. Something smart enough to track us for days. Something powerful enough to hide itself, even in the sunlight."

"Days?" Jordan's mouth is thinning into a tense line.

"Yes," Adem says.

A pause settles over us as we chew on the risk. I should have never have led them here.

"Little snaps of branches. Shuffles of steps. Behind us at night," Adem says. "Sometimes it gets close enough that I can hear its breathing, its heartbeat."

I try to remind myself that, with Adem's heightened senses, this does not mean what it would if I were to hear something breathing in the night. All the same, I have to fight an urge to check over my shoulder.

Jordan folds his arms. "Do you have any idea what it might be?"

"No. There was something familiar about it." Adem gives me a skittish glance. "But..."

I shift my weight and tilt my chin up, try to lie with my posture that I am not afraid. "So, what then? What do we do?"

But we all agree there is nothing to do. We can't hunt something that we can't see, can't understand. We simply go on, walking through the days and camping at night as if nothing were wrong.

But everything is wrong. Terribly so. We carry a sharp, stinging alertness with us now, and it puts us all on edge. I keep one of my blades in my hands at all times, shifting it back and forth between them all day, trading off when my fingers grow too stiff and my palm too sweaty to hold it right anymore. At night, it is under my pallet, my hand in the dirt, ready to pull the blade out at any moment, should I need it.

Sleep is harder to find than ever, my dreams more restless. The voice is getting closer, and whatever it is, it is calling my name.

Listen closer.

I try to do as Nabi told me, but every time the voice reaches me, my fear startles me awake. Was this what the Gods wanted me to hear? Was it about the creature in the wasteland? Something else entirely? How I wish I could ask.

Instead, I pour my heart out to Adem after the dreams wake me each night, hoping somehow to empty it of the terror.

I tell him about when I first started hearing the

Goddess in my mind, I was fifteen, years older than Nabi. They woke me in the night with their restless voices. Even then, I was petrified of what I heard.

So was everyone else. Life got lonelier.

Only when Kythiel came to me was I able to come to terms with it. He changed everything. First, for my gift. Then, for my heart.

The first time he came to me, it was like being pulled from the darkness and seeing the light—warm, powerful, overwhelming. He was so different in those days. Pure. A boundless river of love and peace and strength. I was lying in my father's fields with Milo, my closest friend, when he appeared before us.

Do not be afraid, Kythiel begged. I am here to help you.

He was the most beautiful thing I had ever seen. Still is, even though he's gone now. His peaceful aura coursed through me then, and I trusted him.

Once I understood the gift, as he called it, I wanted to give it back. This was no gift, I said. It was a curse. Theia turned to me when someone had to know something, but refused to listen to the signs on their own.

Still, he taught me how to understand my gift better, tried to guide me to use it more like how Nabi seems to.

But if I learned anything in those times, it was that people do not like to be told what they do not want to hear. They feared me, which meant they hated me. Only my family and Milo and Kythiel stood by me.

All this meant even more time together with Kythiel. His beauty drew me in. I knew what the Gods would say about it, but it was so easy to love him. Far easier than it would have been to stay away. When he finally confessed he felt the same...well.

Theia tried to warn me. But when the Gods' own messenger does not want to hear, who delivers the message to her? No one. I do not believe it would have stopped us anyway.

But that was all so long ago. A lifetime that has passed.

Adem considers it all in silence. Waits until every last word has poured from me.

Only when I run out of words does he speak.

"The dreams from Theia. You said they woke you?"

The question surprises me. "Yes, they were horrible."

"Sounds a lot like the dreams you have now."

I turn over the words in my mind, and slowly the words take shape into thought. They are similar, these dreams and the terrors of those first messages from Theia. Strangely so, in fact.

But after all this time, could it even be possible? Could Theia really forgive me all that has passed? Have I been fighting against Her this whole time?

Theia is supposed to be a Goddess of grace, though I have never seen it to be so before.

Listen closer.

Maybe it is time I really did.

I try harder.

Still my dreams are laced with darkness and fear, the horrifying scratching at my mind's edges. The fear rules me, and I hardly have a chance to brace myself and reach into it before adrenaline jolts me back to the alive wasteland night and Adem staring into the abyss.

Sometimes things rustle and snap in the darkness. I flinch every time, my blade ready in my sweaty palm. Adem stands.

We see some strange things, fearful things. One night, great black dog-like figures with glowing eyes wander in the distance.

"Are those..." I can't finish my thought. I am still too caught in disbelief.

Adem finishes for me. "Dark Wolves."

Dark Wolves come from the Underworld and hunt those who have escaped death. At least, that is the story. Fear cuts through me, and I am sure it is me they have come for. But they drift over us and past, finding us unworthy. Great lumbering beasts that are no more than distant shadows.

We see these and other things. Once I am sure I see the slithering tail of a dragon, though it is impossible to make out any more through the night. But we never see the thing that is following us. That remains hidden somewhere behind us. If it is there at all.

"We're seeing more beasts. I don't know why I bother saying it aloud.

Adem nods. "It was not like this before. We must be getting closer."

"Closer to what?" I ask.

He does not answer. I lean against him, my body both exhausted and wired with anxious energy, and hold my blade tight. Adem flinches against my touch, and it reminds me of his warning back in Haven, about it being better to stay away from him. But he does not pull away.

When we tell Jordan of these beasts, little creases

form around his eyes and forehead. He looks to Adem. "Ceil warned us. He said there would be rifts, now that the barrier is broken. I think we're headed toward a helmuth."

"A helmuth?" I laugh, though I do not know why. The mere idea makes my stomach twist. "You think there is a portal to the Underworld out here?"

In the Wars, the rebel Firsts opened a helmuth into the Underworld—a portal from deep within Terath's earth that barrels into the Underworld—in the emptiness somewhere. It opens when it grows hungry to release more horror onto the land, and closes only when it has had its fill. From it, all kinds of strange creatures and monsters crawl from the Underworld.

Or at least that is what they say, in low whispers between each other, in Haven, when they tell the stories from the Texts.

When I heard these things before I left, it sounded like the silly horrors children tell each other.

Now? Well. In the wasteland's vastness, the stories become easier to believe.

"And you think that's real? That there is an actual helmuth?" Even with all I have seen and experienced, I always preferred a more symbolic interpretations of the Texts' more terrible aspects.

Jordan shrugs. "I do not know what to think. I would not have thought the Dark Wolves were real. I would not have thought Unnamed were real. I would not have thought it possible to enter the Underworld and break out again, yet here you both are."

I glance to Adem and then, when our eyes meet, mine flit away again. Even after so many nights at his side, I still can't quite hold his gaze.

CHAPTER 13

JORDAN'S NEW THEORY shakes me to my core. And I am not the only one. I see it in the way the others act — alert, tense. Every shadow looks more sinister. Every rustle of the night is a potential enemy. It does not help that Adem keeps listening diligently for our follower each night, still insists something is out there. He begins practicing his spell again at night with intense focus.

We carry on as before. What else is there to do? But we all hold our shoulders more tensely and keep our hands close to our weapons.

Finally, another day comes to an end. Jordan's face is sunken and dark, his head slumped, his hair curled and matted from sweat, mirroring the fatigue that deadens every particle of my own body.

That night I stretch on my pallet, drained but so on edge I am not sure sleep is the answer.

Sure enough, I lurch awake what feels like moments later, the clawing and grumbles of my dreams still alive in my ears. My head pounds with an anxious, heavy pulse. The terrible thing in my dreams is getting worse. Closer.

Closer, closer, closer. Listen closer.

The pressure to make some sort of sense out of the darkness is depleting me. I do not want to listen closer to my dreams. I want to drown them. Burn them. Anything to silence them and make my mind numb again. If it is Theia, or a message from Her, She needs to get it together before these dreams make me lose my mind.

I sit up. Adem glances at me, rocks pausing in midair. He lowers them to the ground and sits, waiting for me to join him. The practice is paying off. His control over the pebbles he lifts has grown greatly.

We are sitting close, close enough that our arms brush against each other. His skin is neither warm nor cold, and hardly feels like skin at all. More like packed, dried clay. Something about him, his steadiness, soothes my anxious body and makes me still.

He stares into the abyss with blank obedience, but the corners of his mouth are creased with tension. *Is he afraid?* I wonder. I cannot bear to break the silence to ask.

He probably would not tell me anyway. He has become so good at being alone that he has forgotten how to connect. Or perhaps he never did know. Perhaps he was not made with those abilities.

But I do not think it is this simple. His walls of reserve have grown around him like trees, nurtured with ages of isolation and rooted deep below his surface.

I am just the same, I realize.

I have gone on too long in isolation, determined to dwell on my old mistakes. I have lived — and not lived — to punish myself for those mistakes far too long, holding myself back even when I am among others.

My soul is starved for connection.

Is his?

I look at him again. A deep sadness sets behind his eyes and in every crease of his face. It is as much a part of him as his nose.

I shift so that our arms intertwine and take his hand in mine.

My body is still wild and on edge from the horror of my dream, but as our fingers interlock, the terrible pounding of my heart begins to quiet. It feels so good to simply touch someone — a relief, like the first sips of water after a long day in hot sun. His hand is large and wraps completely around mine, his fingers folding over top of it.

A warmth begins to stretch from my hand up my arm, and nestles into my chest. This small sip is not enough to fill me. It has only made me realize how parched I am.

More, my body pleads. *More.*

Before I can think, I have snuggled up to his side and leaned my head against his shoulder. After the long nights, I have woken up like this before, pressed against his side, my head resting on him, after sleep gets the better of me as we wait out the darkness, but somehow this feels different.

He turns to look at me, and I stretch my neck to look up. His face is just inches away, and his eyes are wide, but soft. Gods, it has been painfully long since I have been so close to anyone. I lean in like there is some kind of external force pulling me, and I kiss him.

He freezes, lingering against my lips for a moment, and then he pulls away.

I kiss him again. I feel bolder now, hungry, and though he flinches with surprise, this time he does not pull away. The third time I kiss him, his lips press softly back into mine.

After that, things begin to blur. I am pressed against him and his arms squeeze around me, tight against my sore, tired muscles. But it is a safe kind of pain, the kind that reminds me that I am, indeed, alive. It makes me want to fight back and claim my life again.

We slowly drift backward until we are stretched out on the ground, and I am leaning over him with my hair cascading around us in loose waves. My lips graze the side of his neck, and my fingers drift over his large chest, slip in under his robe.

He bolts to his feet so fast I fall to the dirt.

Did I do something to hurt him? No, I immediately realize how foolish that is. But if not that, what? Does he not crave connection like I do? I am sure he does.

Perhaps just not with me.

Embarrassment seeps through me in a tepid puddle.

"Adem—"

"Shh."

His back is to me, but there is something animal about his stance, something feral. Shoulders tight, ears pricked. He turns to take in the periphery.

The back of my hands prickle. I twist and look into the darkness too.

"What is it?"

"It is out there."

He remains standing, stiff and alert. Every so often he turns his head abruptly, staring in a new direction.

"Adem..."

I do not know what I am trying to ask. But dread swells within me like a flood, and I wish I understood.

He turns to face me, though he maintains his on-edge stance.

"It is there. It is moving."

It.

Fear twists and winds through my chest like a snake and into my stomach.

"I should never have," he glances at me, "I am supposed to be *protecting*. If something happened—" He cuts himself off and turns away, to the edge of the camp. He plants his feet and stands there, his back to me, like a great stone, the most tense and guilt-wracked stone imaginable.

Now that it is over, I cannot believe it has happened. What felt so sweet and important just moments ago now seems desperate, even crazy. What came over me? I have been in the wasteland far too long.

Did he really hear something? Or maybe he simply came to his senses.

What would have happened if we had kept on?

My anger toward him for dragging me back to this damned realm may not be the raging fire it was at first anymore, but it is still a hot glowing ember within me. I poke it now to reignite it, and warm myself with its biting sparks.

Really, whatever the reason he pulled away, I should be grateful to him.

I press my lips together, trying to smother the salty warmth spreading over me from where he brushed against them.

I trail after Adem and sit on the ground near him—but not next to him—and curl into a ball, my arms wrapped around myself. Together but separate, we glare into the wasteland's darkness until the sun's rays chase it away. As it lightens, we strain to make out any kind of shape from the abyss.

We do not speak of what happened between us. We do not speak at all.

When Jordan rises and we have had our morning rations, we continue on, trudging through another day.

I keep a buffer of space between Adem and me. Something hot and ashamed courses through me, and rushes to my cheeks whenever I look toward him. It is easier to simply not.

Jordan trails to walk at my side. "Are you all right?"

"Why wouldn't I be?" I hope he doesn't know. Would Adem have told him? They are so close.

He offers a small smile. "Rona. I am not accusing you of anything."

That Gods-damned smile of his.

"Aren't you?" My eyes narrow into a sharp glare. His words are like flint, sparking against a pile of tinder I did not realize was growing within me. "From the beginning all you could do was tell me I am not fit to be here. At every turn you are against what I think we should do. And now you want to check, see how weak I'm feeling? Forget that."

"Gods." He cringes at my curse. "It is okay to have weakness. It is hard for all of us out here."

He tries to reach me, but I pull away, folding my arms over my chest. "Well I don't have any. I'm fine. Are *you* all right?"

His hand drops to his side in forfeit.

"I'm getting by." The rings around his eyes, the sagging of his shoulders, say otherwise. He's right. It is tough for all of us. "But fine. If you want to suffer alone and ignore the only people who care about you, that's fine. Great, even. Less work and grief for us."

He starts to move on ahead, but then he turns, dropping his killing blow. "You know, Rona, you go around throwing blame about how you're left out and we're not including you. But you know what? You don't have to be so alone. Alone is a choice, and you've done it to yourself. You want connection? You want trust? You need to give something first."

Regret trickles into me, but I don't know how to fix what I've broken. It is too late anyway, Jordan is already breaking away from me, back to walk with Adem.

Adem, though, seems to be the same as always. He shows no sign of embarrassment or discomfort after last night. Or interest. He simply is, trudging on, lugging our packs. Strong and steady.

No—empty.

I remind myself of what he is: nothing. And that is what he should be to me. Nothing. Less than that.

Jordan catches me staring at him.

"And what is going *on* with you two today?" he shouts to the sky.

Adem stops walking and stares back at him. My mind goes blank, struggling for an excuse he might believe. My lip trembles.

Jordan looks first to Adem, then to me, and registers our silence. "Fine. *Fine*."

None of us speak all through the rest of the day. The sun pounds down between us like a wall and we embrace the divide.

Finally, as the sun sets behind us, a blight on the horizon takes form as a large stony-black fortress up ahead, and the path of torn-up earth the Unnamed left behind leads us right toward it.

The last thing this group needs is an adventure right now. But it seems we do not have a choice.

CHAPTER 14

THE FORTRESS TOWER grows on the horizon as we inch closer through the day. By sunset, I can make it out clearly, the way it spirals up in great stony swoops, its peak a jagged point.

Night closes in around us. We come to a stop, but none of us start preparations for the evening. We just stand and stare at the tower's otherworldly grandeur.

Finally, I shatter the silence that has built between us all day. It requires deliberate force, like breaking through a panel of glass.

"We should go," I say. "Right now."

Their eyes dart to me. Adem looks away again just as quickly. I feel heat rushing to my face.

"Go where?" Jordan asks dubiously.

"*In.* Into the fortress. Where else is there to go, out here?"

The side of his mouth twitches. "That's too risky."

"Gods, if we're not going in, what are we here for?"

A beat of silence is filled by a swell of crickets as the

wasteland's nighttime begins to wake.

"We know where they're based now," he says. "We should make our way back to Haven. We're not prepared for a fight."

Maybe he isn't, but I am. A fight sounds like just the thing to work off this pent-up aggression and rouse my tired, overwrought muscles. My body craves the mindless harmony of battle, the way it forces me into the moment and silences everything else.

"It's probably better for only one of us to go anyway." I shrug. "It will be easier to slip through without being seen. Just stay here. Is that *safe* enough for you?"

I turn to go, hoping to slip away before they can react, but Jordan reaches out and grabs my arm.

"No, it's not. You are too—" I raise my eyebrows, ready to pounce at him. He pulls back, presses his lips to together to hold in what he was about to say. "Look. It is not safe for either of us in there."

"Well, what do you suggest then?" I yank my arm away from him with a glare.

"Me." Adem steps forward. "I should go. They can't hurt me."

"But that leaves us out here without your protection," Jordan says. "Besides, we don't know that. The Unnamed, sure, they weren't able to harm you. But these are creatures of the Underworld. And you were vulnerable in the Underworld. Are you sure they cannot harm you? I'm not."

Adem looks away. My eyes drift to his tightening fist, and I remember the finger missing from it, a memento of his last face-off with the Underworld.

My anger comes out in a huff. "This is not your fight. I am the one who dragged us here. I am the one who wanted to follow the trail in the first place. I am the one going in. What is the worst that happens? They kill me? My soul goes back where it should be anyway?"

"This is not my fight?" Jordan lunges at me with such ferocity I flinch away. "It was *my* people they killed. *My* city they destroyed. *My* loved ones still at risk back in Haven, and the other cities up and down the shoreline. I have drawn them all out from dictatorships across the land and told them I could offer them something better. Something safe. And now hundreds of them have been murdered. By whatever is in there. So no, Rona, this is not *your* fight."

He pushes me, and I stumble back. I have never seen him like this before. He is so friendly and personable most of the time that I would not have thought he had it in him.

"You and Adem march around like you are the only ones who can do anything. Like you have emerged from the Underworld and now you are invincible. These chosen warriors here to destroy whatever is in your path. But I have news for you, Rona. You are still only human. Just like the rest of us. Even Adem is not truly invincible, particularly when it comes to anything from the Underworld. Which, I might remind you, is what we are dealing with here. I'm a born warrior too, and I *have* been actually Chosen for this. Ever since I was a little boy, this is what I was prepared for. Don't ever forget it. This is *my* fight, and you're just tagging along."

He turns and storms toward the fortress. "We're all

going."

I glance at Adem. He shrugs, then turns and follows after him.

"But that makes no sense at all," I hiss after them into the night. It takes all my will to stop from yelling. "Then we are all at risk."

Especially with our tempers lit.

"This is a war, Rona," Jordan calls back to me. His voice is gruff and tired. "There is no 'safe' anymore."

CHAPTER 15

THE FORTRESS IS surrounded by a wall that looms much larger from up close. It is built from huge blocks of chalky black stone that matches the tower itself.

"How are we going to get up there?"

It does not seem to be guarded. A piece of luck for us. Maybe when you have crawled out of a helmuth from the Underworld, and your soldiers are already dead, guards are not necessary.

All the same, it makes my stomach twist. It is eerie, how deserted it appears to be.

From the inside, there is an unmistakable, rhythmic shuffle of marching.

"What are they doing? It's the middle of the night," Jordan says.

Maybe dead soldiers do not need to sleep.

"Let's go."

I use the uneven ledges between the stones on the wall to pull myself up.

"What are you doing?" Jordan whispers.

"Climbing over. Unless one of you has been carrying a rope I do not know about?"

I allow a dramatic pause to set in. Part of me hopes to the Gods for one of them to prove me wrong. But they do not. Adem hoists himself up next to me.

"This is a terrible idea," Jordan says. "What is the plan, once we are up there?"

I keep climbing. Jordan watches us for a moment, then follows.

The black stones still radiate with heat from the day's sun, and the warmth feels good against my chilled fingers. As I get higher, finding a grip becomes harder and more unpredictable, and in some parts it feels as though I am clinging to the wall with willpower alone, too scared of the fall to allow it to happen.

Despite the late start, Jordan passes us both ably. Finally, I reach the top, onto the wall's broad ledge next to him. I crawl to the other side and peer over.

The fortress looks even stranger up close, and not at all what I would expect any structure to look like.

The inside of the fortress is a sea of the same dark stone as the wall. The clipped sounds of marching are sharp and clear from here. Just below, row after row of soldiers march, corralled in by the fortress wall, and a second, smaller wall echoing it inside. Their bodies are caked in chalky white, and their faces are covered in iron helmets. They are the Unnamed soldiers who destroyed Ir-Nearch.

Jordan slides next to me on the wall's ledge. "They're marching in a circle. They're storing them here like cattle."

We stare at their tireless march together, waiting on

Adem.

He may be invincible, but right now he is clumsy and fumbling. His huge hands are not made for the fine grip necessary to scale the wall. He grunts and fumbles, his climb up to us painfully slow.

"You got this," Jordan whispers to him. "There, yes, take your time, get your grip. Good."

Meanwhile, I study the fortress tower, angular and twisty. It is as if the tower grew from the stones deep under the ground, rather than being built. It does not look so tall here as it did from the outside, but it gives the impression of deep roots. Like a great old tree. It is impossible to see from here how deep it might stretch.

Is that it? Is that a helmuth?

There is an undeniable *something* in the air from up here, not a smell, but more of a quivering through it. I take shallow breaths, reluctant to draw it in. As I cling to the wall's edge, I realize the stone beneath me is cool, not warm like it was on the outside.

It doesn't make any sense, I think. It should be even warmer in here, where the sun hits the most.

Adem slumps over the wall's ledge, and something holds me back from asking. Besides, it is time to focus on what's ahead.

The moon is high above us, and the night is passing by rapidly. My eyes beg to close and my body pleads to lie still and rest. All the same, my heart pounds with the thrill of action. I can hear it in my ears and feel it in my fingertips. I hunger for more.

For a pause the tension suspends between us, each of us disarmed by the strangeness of the fortress ahead of us, the clipped rhythm of the marching below. I am sure one of them will look up at us any moment and shout, alerting the others to our presence. But they don't. They just keep marching.

"We're going to have to jump." I point to the ledge lining the inside of the soldiers' path. It is wide, as if made for walking on, and somewhat lower than the one we are already on.

Will it be enough for a landing? We're going to have to find out. It is the only way in that doesn't involve wading through the Unnamed soldiers below. They may be oblivious to our presence from here, but something tells me they would not take kindly to us interrupting their march.

"Once we're in, it is going to be impossible to get out of there." Jordan leans forward, scrutinizing the wall's sides. "Do either of you see a gate or door?"

"And what do you suggest?" I ask. "Just climb back down and walk away?"

He does not respond. Part of me wishes he would. Part of me wishes he would insist we turn back right now, away from the soldiers, away from the fortress, away from this strange, terrible feeling in the air.

I look around, scouring every inch of the fortress that I can see. "No. But there has to be one. How else would they get in and out?"

"I don't know," Jordan says. "In a giant torrent of wind?"

He has a point. And what is more fortified than a fortress with no entrances?

"If we go in there, we might not make it out. There might not *be* a way out," Jordan warns.

I stand up. A small voice at the back of my mind

knows he's right, that he's just trying to look out for us all, but my anger still tremors through me, and I have had enough. His hesitation grates on me and reignites the anger from our argument earlier in the day.

Enough planning.

Enough worrying and second-guessing.

Either we will make it in, or we won't; either we will make it back out, or we won't, but we will not know until we try. And we owe that much to Helda, and Xam, and Nabi, and all the other survivors we made promises to as we parted.

I back up to the outside edge of the wall, get as much of a running start as I can, and jump. My landing is rough, my stomach slamming into the hard rock of the wall's corner, and I have to scramble to get over. It takes all my strength to fight against the downward momentum.

Once I am over, I stand up and turn around, smoothing my hair away from my face. Chilled air keeps the flush out of my cheeks.

"There. Easy," I whisper. I try to hide the way my breaths heave and my hands shake from the adrenaline. "Come on."

Jordan may not be able to hear me across the distance, but I know Adem's sharp ears can. He leans in to Jordan and I watch as his mouth moves. Jordan glances at me as he listens. His face tightens into a frown. But then, he nods.

They get to their feet. Jordan backs up, runs, and leaps. He slams right into the ledge on the new wall next to me. I stretch out a hand, and he clasps onto it. I pull him to his feet.

Jordan gains his footing and brushes himself off.

He looks back to Adem.

"Come on."

Adem responds with a short growl that rolls over the air to us.

"You can do it," Jordan whispers.

Adem looks over to him, and they both go still, something deep and important passing between them. I hate when they do this. It is as if I am on the outside, looking in.

I sigh and shift my feet. "We're going to run out of darkness, if we don't keep moving." Already the moon is starting to tip down toward the horizon. The sun won't be all that far behind.

Adem nods. He curls low into himself and explodes outward, little crumbles of stone falling to ground as he lifts off the wall and flies toward us. He crashes into the ledge next to us with a bang that makes me flinch, sure we have been exposed.

Jordan watches Adem slide over the wall's edge and fall to the ground. I lean out the other way, watching the Unnamed, my hand drifting to my blade's hilt from instinct in case they take notice of us. But the marching soldiers below keep moving forward mindlessly, paying us no attention.

I look up quizzically, and Jordan frowns back.

"It is like they're in some sort of trance," he says.

I don't know why Adem's crashes did not draw their attention, but it makes me even more uneasy than before.

"Seems safe down here." Adem is already relaxing from his fighting stance. "Come on down."

We crawl our way carefully down the other side of the wall. I would have thought going down would be easier, but it is at least as hard as going up, a constant struggle against gravity's pull to avoid falling. My heartbeat pounds in my ears, the chill of the air harsh against my fingers and neck.

Finally, my feet touch the ground. Jordan and Adem are waiting for me. This side of the second wall, all is eerily silent. No guards? No soldiers? Someone was very confident no one would make it inside this fortress.

Or maybe they don't care if we get in.

My stomach lurches with panic. Could this all be a trap? It was far too easy to get in here.

Ahead of us, the fortress holds a single opening in its side as an entrance, with a path that offers us two directions: upwards or downwards.

I dust off my hands. "Which way?"

CHAPTER 16

THE PATHS BOTH curve off into darkness. No sound is detectable except the constant marching of the soldiers behind us. It is impossible to know what lies beyond.

"Let's try this way," Jordan says, heading for the downward path.

I glance at Adem, shrug, and follow. Adem trudges alongside me. His shoulders hulk forward. His ears are perked, straining to listen for anything that might lie ahead. He places his feet carefully to the ground.

The path is cramped, and we are so close my hand brushes against his. I pull it in and slow to let him drift ahead.

The path weaves us inward and downward, the moon grows farther away, and the walls grow taller around us. The only light to guide us comes from sparse, spread out torches. The darkness that sets in between them is not unlike my dreams, strange and distorted, pregnant with predatory promises.

Listen closer.

I stop, closing my eyes and straining to try. At first I don't hear anything, just our own steps. But then, very faintly in the distance, there is a grumbling that reaches from the tunnel's depths. It holds within it a sort of uneven rhythm and draws me in. It is a pull as natural and as real as the realm's gravity, almost as if it were coming from within me.

I don't trust it. I open my eyes and free my blades.

The path leads us deeper and deeper. The fortress has swallowed us down into Terath's depths, and I begin to feel it closing in around me. Tightening.

It's more than the darkness itself. There is something familiar about it, like a dream. A chill that is more than the temperature. It is a cold that seeps into the soul.

It feels like...

"It feels like the Underworld in here," Adem says. His voice is stiff and grim.

That is exactly it. That is why this place fills me with such dread. It is the way the chill cuts through me, the darkness seeps into my soul. The desolation that sinks so easily back into my bones. It is the feeling of giving in and letting something else take over.

I was trapped in this feeling for ages, for so long it became like breathing. How could I not recognize it?

That is not what I am anymore.

The words float through my mind as if they formed on their own. It seems impossible. I was in the Underworld for ages, and have only been back in Terath for weeks. How could I change so quickly? But I have.

Gods, for how many years did I waste away in that

realm? They fell past me like raindrops, piled up until they became a sea, each individual one too small to matter.

And I am done with it. Done wasting this second chance on anger and bitterness. It should not have happened. I did not ask for it, and I did not want it. But I am done pretending the escape is not a relief.

Because it does matter. All of it. Each and every year that I lost. Each moment with my family. The life I did not take for myself among them.

And this new life I've been shrugging off — it matters too. Jordan and Adem. Haven. Whatever it is the Gods so badly want me to hear. There is a fight to be had now. A difference I can make. Something worth staying alive for.

If only I had realized it before leading us on this suicide mission. Back when I was safe in Haven, before I trekked to Ir-Nearch and took on an undead army. Before leading us all into this fortress.

Because, now that it matters, now that I recognize all I have to lose, this dark, descending path frightens me. Is it leading me right back to the Underworld? Is that even possible? Adem broke through once. Who is to say there are not other ways to slip through?

At last, we reach the bottom, and the spiraling path flattens, rounding one final corner. What I find makes me stumble back, and I trip over Jordan.

At the other side, the fortress wall fuses into a tunnel that bores even deeper into the ground. The dark stone walls hold an angry red reflection of light, emanating from deep within it, and all around the tunnel's mouth and down its throat is layer after layer of sharp jagged rock, thrust open as it if will lunge forward and eat me up.

The jagged tooth-like rocks are stained with splotchy paths of red and silver and black. As if things have been crawling and slithering out of it, over the sharp teeth.

A strange grumbling echoes from deep down its throat, along with scratching and slow, distant steps.

Something is in there.

Its horror repels me, yet something about its strangeness lures me in too. A tug. Were I to take a fall, I am not sure if I would fall down, or *in*.

In need of an anchor, I reach back and take hold of Adem's arm.

"I am not going in there," I declare.

"Don't worry, dear. You won't need to." A syrupy, too-sweet voice reaches from behind us. It is unknown to me, and it sends shoots of panic darting through me in every direction.

I whip around, and Jordan and Adem do the same, all of us with our weapons ready.

It's *her*—the tall, spindly woman whose haunting tune drew me through the Ir-Nearch streets in the midst of the fight. Her long dark hair is pinned high on her head, and a robe of gauzy white wraps around her from high around her neck and all the way to the floor, giving her a dreamy glow in contrast to the fortress' onyx and darkness. Her eyes are large and dark, empty and blank.

"I am afraid you're going to have to come with me," she says.

"And how's that?" I challenge. I shift to let the meager light flash off my blades.

She does not bear any kind of weapon or even armor. But her mouth parts in a sweet, gentle smile. The kind of smile one gives to a child who could not possibly understand.

"Oh, I assure you," she says, "that is not something you want to discover the hard way. Don't you agree, golem?"

Adem stares at her, small lines of strained thought forming over his forehead, and his lips pressed together tight. He grunts in response. How does she know what he is?

I look to Jordan, who shakes his head at me helplessly—*what we can do?*—and lowers his sword.

His willingness to give in so easily sparks a swell of burning rage within me. No, we are not giving in without a fight. I couldn't stand it. Not after coming so far. I shift my grip on my blades and swing toward her. But before I reach her, she raises her hand and suddenly, my arm slams into an invisible force that thrusts it back.

"You do not want to fight me," the woman snaps. "This is your last warning. Now come."

Then she turns and starts walking away, back up the winding path. We follow in silence, up and up and around, until the path stops at a dead end. But the woman keeps walking toward it. She waves her arm in front of her and the stone crumbles away like a stiff curtain. She walks through it, then gestures for us to follow.

I lurch to a stop, Jordan and Adem skidding to a halt behind me.

"Come, come, now, patience is not one of my

virtues," she says. As she speaks, she motions with her hand as if to urge us in, and a force pushes me from behind. A prickling panic rushes down my arms, and I jump forward into the room to escape its pressure.

Once we are all in, the stone crumbles back into place again, with no way out except the windows. Morning is coming already, and fills the room with dim, rose-tinted light. I step over to the window and peer out. We are far too high off the ground to make the jump. Only Adem would survive it.

The room lends a view far into the wasteland in every direction. She must have seen us coming from days away. Why didn't we think of that?

My heartbeat rushes into my ears, and I see a hot flush color Jordan's face. His shoulders are tense and a vein pops from his neck, but all the same he forces a small grin to flash over his face when he sees me watching him, as if to reassure me that all will be all right in the end.

Oh, Jordan, you fool. Nothing about this is all right.

CHAPTER 17

MY BLADE IS still squeezed tightly in my hand. The woman glances at it, but she shows no signs of concern, confident in her powers.

Good. Let her get comfortable. I can get to her. I know I can. I just have to wait. Eventually, her confidence will get the best of her. That very second, I need to be ready to strike with a killing blow. I'm not likely to get a second chance.

I take in a steadying breath. My mind calms, my focus sharpens. And that is when I recognize the swirling of auras twisting their way into me.

It is like nothing I have ever felt before. Separate threads of feeling, tangled and knotted together. One thread amplifies everything already within me—the anger, the fear, the hunger for the next fight, the desire to reach out for Adem—all of it loud and clamoring and urgent. The other thread is a rumbling buzz of disruption, scratchy, erratic, and anxious. The two threads writhe and fight within me.

Strongest of all is a compulsion to step closer to the woman, the same allure that drew me to her in the fight in Ir-Nearch. I can almost hear the enticing hum, almost drop my blades and go to her. It's as if I want her, even as I tell myself I do not.

But I lived among the First Creatures in my first life, and I know better than to trust an aura. I square my shoulders and exhale a breath, tightening my grip on my weapon.

The woman smiles a cool, unfeeling smile. "You can put that away. I do not intend to harm you. Not that it could stop me if I had the inclination."

"I'll keep it all the same," I snap back. Hubris. It has taken down more than one demigod.

As we settle into the room, three men rush forward from the walls and bow before the woman.

"Koreh, my sweet, how may I serve you?" they beg. I look away, disgusted by their groveling. But wait...I glance back and yes, it's true!

"These men are from Ir-Nearch!" I shout. I turn to Jordan, and his own horrified expression mirrors how I feel.

"What have you done to them?" Jordan demands. His sword is free again, and he appears as though he could throw it and tear the sky with it, the way his muscles twitch and tense.

The woman Koreh gazes at each of us in turn, empty of emotion.

"They *insisted* on coming with us, if you must know," she says. She looks Jordan over and smirks, her hand tracing along a gold chain previously hidden by her collar. "What are you going to do about it anyway? I have to admit, I am quite disappointed in your apparent powers. I thought they would be greater, from what I was told. The other two, yes, but you...," she squints, as if looking beyond Jordan to some other plane, "It is like all that is left is its shadow."

Jordan's face turns a sizzling red as his brow pulls low.

Koreh chuckles dismissively as if this closed the conversation. "But this is not why you are here."

She turns to Adem. With a sly grin, she tucks her fingers inside her robe's collar and pulls out a chain. Hanging from its end is the gleaming emerald I saw through the haze during the attack on Ir-Nearch. It is rough and unpolished but still brilliant.

As she tugs it from her robe, Adem's entire body stiffens like a board, and he steps back. I step forward, my brain flooding with anxious curiosity.

It is no typical necklace. Now that it is out, a sweet aura emanates from it that vibrates against my skin.

The necklace. It is the same necklace that was hidden in Adem's cursed box, the one he left behind when he took me from the Underworld. The one Abazel took.

Why didn't I realize it before? This is the lure I felt. This is what made the dying man in Ir-Nearch so desperate to get to Koreh, and the ones who followed her away from Ir-Nearch, and these others so dazed by her now. I am sure of it.

How is it that I felt the lure and resisted, while so many others fell into this trance?

And then, it hits me, these others are men. In fact, they were almost *all* men.

Why were some so quick to fall under the necklace's

full power, like these Ir-Nearch men now doting on her, while others evaded it? How did Adem and Jordan escape it?

Adem is easy; he is no man. But Jordan?

Then, I remember Xam.

The necklace is preying on their desire. They want her. No, they *worship* her.

"How did you get that?" I demand.

Koreh raises her eyebrows.

"I will ask the questions," she says. She turns to Adem. "Where is he?"

A burst of protective rage blusters through me like a thunderstorm. "Adem has nothing to do —"

Adem cuts me off. "Who?"

"Maelcolm. Your maker, the man who gave this to you." Koreh's mouth twitches. "Where is he?"

She is almost as tall as Adem. But as she speaks she stretches, distorting her spine and neck until she is towering over him, tension hot between them. Adem looks away.

What is this fearsome thing who has taken us captive? And who is Maelcolm?

"It was too long ago to remember," Adem says.

Koreh's eyes narrow and flash bright. "Where is he?" she demands again. She is too stretched now, and her head almost butts into the ceiling.

"It was ages ago. He is in the ground by now for sure."

"Lies," Koreh hisses. "He is somewhere. I can feel it." She shakes the necklace at him.

A creeping paranoia sneaks into my head, asking whether it is possible the necklace's luring aura could work on Adem, the way it does on the other men, or on Jordan. He may never have been close enough to it to know for sure. Perhaps in the box it could not get to him, but now it can. Is it possible he wants her, the way I felt myself moments ago? Hate blossoms, warm and inky, through my gut.

I turn away. And that is when I notice Jordan staring at me intently. When he catches my attention he gazes down at his sword, ready in his hand, and then to Koreh. *He wants us to attack her.* She is so fixated on Adem, she has all but forgotten us. I nod, shift my grip on my blades' hilts, and on Jordan's count, we attack.

We come in blades swinging, and I dig sharply into her side. Her stretched spine arches back and she lets free a terrible prolonged shriek. She whips around on us, her blank eyes glowing with rage, her distorted height making her monstrous. With a swing of her arm she casts our weapons from our hands and we are thrown back against the wall.

"I warned you," she bellows.

A wind begins to whirl through the room, and Koreh's eyes burn an ominous red. A strange pressure begins to build within me. It overtakes me from the bottom of my toes to the tips of my ears. I am sure I will explode. I wish I *would* explode as a wrenching pain comes. Next to me Jordan's skin is writhing with veins grotesquely black, and somewhere, someone is screaming. Is it me? It *must* be me, but I don't remember starting.

Just then something bursts into the room from the window, a great silver and golden something with magnificent dark wings.

Kythiel? In my unthinking agony and terror I do not know whether to be relieved or frightened more. Is it him? I cannot be sure.

Whatever, whoever, it is coos a few words and Koreh is cast to the floor. Jordan and I drop to the ground. The intense pain dissolves, followed by a new sharp ache in my side where I landed on the hard stone, but a much lesser pain than the former, and one I gladly take in trade. I've no more than noticed my blade on the floor next to me than I am lifted and soaring away from the fortress tower. The blade gets left behind.

A tidal wave of emotion overtakes me, and I do not know whether to be relieved or panicked.

CHAPTER 18

I AM SET gently to the ground as a breeze presses around me. I am alone. An intense stillness rushes over me, and then draws away.

I stand and turn to look around me. I am in the wasteland again, and the fortress is far in the distance. Then, I turn to the sky. The winged thing is already coming again, and this time it drops Jordan at my side before it turns back once more. It is large and glowing with great glistening wings of black. It is definitely an angel—a fallen one.

My core oozes with dread. We may have escaped one monster's wrath, but what is this new one we have made ties with?

"Is that... is that...?" Jordan stutters, as disoriented as I am.

"It's not Kythiel." I tell it more to myself than to Jordan. And although my body is fraught with panic set off from the familiarity of an angel's aura, I'm sure of it. It's not him.

The angel returns a third time, bringing Adem with him. This time, as he touches the ground, he lands and folds his massive wings behind him. They are so dark they seem to consume the morning sun's light. His shoulders are broad and his skin holds that same perfect smoothness, the same ethereal glow. His hair settles around his face in golden waves.

For a moment all is silent. We stand there, finding our breath, our minds catching up to what happened. The pain in my side is hot and throbbing, a bruise swelling against my ribs.

My adrenaline pumps from the strangeness of it, and the relief of getting away. A small voice in my mind is trying to remind me that this angel, whoever he is, helped us escape. But that beautiful marble skin, the fluttering dark wings, even that aura of peace he is casting out at us, it all sets off my mind's alarms. Even peace is not peaceful for me anymore. Kythiel took that away from me; he will forever be associated with that overwhelming sweet calm. It dredges up the panic and pain that swelled underneath its pulsing aura all those times he invaded my dreams after I told him to leave me.

I tighten my hands into fists. One clasps my blade, trying to stop my fingers from trembling.

Adem glances to me, and shuffles slightly closer. Somehow, he makes himself seem even larger. Jordan has his sword out, though Gods know what good it would do him in this fight. *My other blade*—I realize with a pang that it is still up in the fortress tower.

The angel lifts his hands to his sides, signifying he means no harm.

"Fear not," he says, "for I am Calipher, an angel of Thei—"

"We know all about angels," Adem grumbles.

"And we know the signs," I add, pointing at his wings with my blade. "You're no angel of Theia. You're fallen."

Calipher's face clouds, and he searches our faces, taking in our angry expressions one at a time.

"I...I helped you."

"You did," Jordan says. "But why?"

Calipher sighs, a great sigh that holds many burdens. "I am trying to make things right again."

"It was you," Adem says. He turns to me. "It was him following us all this time."

We all exchange glances. Jordan raises his sword, and my grip on my blade grows tighter.

"Why did you do it? Tell us the truth, or he will banish you from the realm like he did the last angel who tried to mess with us." I nod to Adem.

Adem grunts, curls his hands into fists.

The angel hangs his head, curls tumbling softly into his face.

"What you say is true. I have committed terrible, misguided deeds. And I have been locked out of the Host for ages in penance." He glances back up, stares me right in the eye. His are beautiful, a crystal-clear ice blue. "Please. I am trying to right what I have wronged."

"And what exactly was your 'wrong'? I take it was a little more than forgetting to say your prayers?" Jordan's voice sparks like pieces of flint rubbed together. As the sun rises above us, his hair has never shined more red, the orange in his eyes has never been so sharp. But something about the tightness at his jaw, the creases at his eyes...he is exhausted, but it is more than that.

"I created something. Something horrible," Calipher replies. I have never seen an angel wear shame, but like everything else, he wears it well. His wings tuck in tight around him as if to cover himself, emphasizing his otherworldliness. His eyes are sad, but steady. They do not hold the spiraling emptiness that drowned Kythiel's. "I didn't mean to. I just wanted some comfort for someone I loved. But I was foolish. I didn't know what the magic would do to her. What it would do to the realm."

"What did you make? What did you do?" I am surprised to find I am hungry for the rest of the story.

"I borrowed magic from Gloros. I created a necklace with a love spell in it."

"I thought angels' power came only from Theia."

"That is how it is meant to be. I broke the Order, not only then but many times over."

Jordan and I exchange a glance. *Many times over.*

Calipher sighs again, his eyes to the ground. "In the Beginning, when Theia sent us to Terath, I resented her for it. Why would I leave the Host, where all is perfect and peaceful, for the lower realm of men? But I soon learned there are many wonderful things that come from that discord. Change, and understanding. And passions."

"Oh," I say. I cringe to remember how it was at first with Kythiel. Perfect. An overflow of emotion and connection.

Calipher continues, "Her name was Riamne. I don't know what to say except that I loved her, and in my love for her, I forgot all else. I thought only of her and what I believed best for her. I forgot to think of what Theia thought best." He shakes his head. "I just wanted her never to have to be alone, after Theia called me back."

"Never alone? But that sounds awful!" It leaps from my mouth before I can think, followed by a quivering fear when I realize what I've said.

But Calipher looks to me sadly. "It was misguided."

I am still trying to understand what any of this has to do with us.

"A necklace. You mean the one Koreh has?" I ask.

"Yes."

"And you are telling us...what? There is a spell in it?"

"Yes. A love spell."

We all fall silent, staring at him. Adem blinks, and Jordan furrows his brow. My mind races as it starts to come together.

"And now she's using it as a weapon," I say.

Calipher hangs his head. "Love can be a very powerful weapon in the wrong hands."

Jordan shrugs, and looks at me hesitantly. I shrug back. Calipher doesn't sound so bad, certainly not like any sort of threat to us. But Kythiel could have explained himself similarly, all the way up to when I was driven to escape into the Underworld. All the way up to having Adem steal me back out. With angels, the problem is never the intentions. It's how unhinged their actions become because of them.

Adem steps forward, levels toe-to-toe and eye-to-eye with the angel. They are an odd pair, Calipher in all his unearthly magnificence, Adem in his utter plainness, both so large and powerful.

"Why were you following us?" he snarls.

Calipher bows his head. "I've been trapped on Terath, searching for this necklace for ages, without hope. I felt its magic being used, out in that city by the sea, and I got there as fast as I could. When I arrived it was already over, but I saw what it had done. I followed you to see if you had it, and what kind of people you were. Then, I followed because we were pursuing the same thing. It has not been used in so long."

Calipher's eyes do that thing angel's do, where they drift away from the here and now, and seem to see something I cannot.

It fuels the rage within me. I have no patience for wistfulness. Not now, after all we have suffered.

"You know what kept it so safe all that time? Adem. He was guarding your big mistake for you," I say.

Calipher's expression shifts as he digests my words and makes sense of them. His brow pulls low and his expression turns dark. He seizes Adem's robe and shoves him.

"Well, what happened? How could you let it loose?"

Adem's expression is as blank as ever, the only hint of emotion the small line of tension that forms in his forehead between his eyes. He slowly digs his fingers into Calipher's hands and pries them away.

"I carried your burden for ages and kept it safe, though I did not even know what it was," Adem snarls. "Here I am invincible, and none could take it from me.

But it was taken from me in the Underworld."

Calipher's mouth twists with tension. "The Underworld? My necklace? How has such a low creature as you become entangled in such great power and consequence? You are in over your head, golem."

Adem's head droops. My skin burns with anger.

"I have a better question," I snap, stepping between them. "If your intentions are so noble, what were you doing following after us? Why didn't you approach us sooner?" Calipher's mouth drops open. He stares at me, then at Jordan, then Adem.

"I would have preferred not to approach you at all. But you were in trouble. I felt I no longer had a choice. I had to help you."

I turn to Jordan and Adem, hoping one of them knows what we should do. They stare back.

I frown. My body is still sounding all its alarms, fighting to keep panic at bay. But if I separate what my body screams at me, set aside Kythiel and all that is past, and focus only on what is in front of me, I can find no reason to be afraid.

"He did save us," I offer. "And he could have come after us at any point, this whole time. He didn't."

Jordan nods. "That woman. Koreh. He was the only one of us with a fighting chance against her. He could be a useful ally."

Besides, what else can we do? Fighting an angel is no easy thing. Adem has done it before, but we all know how much luck was involved.

Adem snarls, but says nothing.

We decide to keep the angel.

CHAPTER 19

EVEN WITH CALIPHER, we are in no position to take on Koreh again right now. We have done what we came to do. We know where the enemy is and a lot more about them.

But now, we need a plan. We need more fighters. We need to return to Haven.

As we trudge back again, shifting our course southward to move toward the village instead of Ir-Nearch in our return, we try to carry on as before. But things are different. Calipher questions everything, as if everything he does not understand about us has been pent up in him all the time he has followed us.

Why does the boy do these exercises each morning?

Why do you not sleep?

Why does this glow of magic surround you?

This last question I hate the most. I dread every time his mouth opens, exposing our group's oddities and cracks, but this one makes me flinch. I do not want the Gods' magic on me anymore. I never did.

I do my best to ignore his questions. I focus instead on the next step in front of me, the way my muscles tug and strain as the day wears on. But I do not drain like I did when we set out on our way to Ir-Nearch. I'm stronger than I was when we started.

But Jordan is too eager. He answers each question as thoroughly as he can. He wants Calipher to understand. As if each word can build a bridge between us and ensure the angel's loyalty.

Adem grits his teeth and trudges on, always just ahead of the rest of us, always a little apart.

Calipher's aura is an unceasing presence, ever seeping into me, ever battling with an instinct that tells me to fight, to run. It keeps my mind unsettled, like clouded water after something kicks up the sand beneath.

We don't talk about what happened at the fortress. Or Koreh, whatever she is. Or what we will do after we get to Haven. We don't *know* what to think, what to do. The fear spills from us into the silence.

On top of the fear instilled by the encounter with Koreh and our helplessness against her, we are beginning to run out of food and water. Each day I am sure we are at the last of it. Each day, somehow, we manage to get just a little bit more from what we have left.

And if the days are tense, the nights are even worse. Jordan and I settle onto our pallets, Calipher and Adem standing over us, the air thick and pulpy between them. They turn out back to back to watch the wasteland, and utter not a single word to each other.

I try to shut it from my mind, to turn inward, to

reach deep into my dreams, like Adem suggested. But they come at me like the edge of a waterfall, churning and chaotic, and I could no more reach out and pluck their meaning than I could separate a single thread of a river's current.

Night after night, I wake.

I can't bring myself to go to Adem again. Not after what happened that last night before the fortress. So instead, I end up next to Calipher.

"Why can you not sleep?"

A huff of frustration escapes me. I tug my blanket tighter against the frigid night air.

"I get strange dreams."

He considers, his eyes unfocused and staring past me in that way only angels can look. "What kind of dreams?"

I bite my lip. The terror of tonight's dream is still too fresh in my mind. I'll talk about anything else, but not this. Not with him.

I snag at the first topic I find, something that has been weighing on me, something Koreh said that I cannot let go.

"You said you could see magic around me."

Calipher tilts his head, studies me a moment. "I did. It hums all around you."

"And you can see it around Adem?"

He blinks, a slow, deliberate motion. "It bursts from him like an earthquake. Potent and uncontrolled."

"And what...," I swallow a seed of guilt. I can't help the feeling that I am prying into something that is not mine to know. But if it is true, it could affect all of us. "What about Jordan?"

Calipher frowns. "What about him?"

A sense of betrayal squirms in my chest.

"Do you see any magic coming from him?"

"No."

Koreh was telling the truth.

"Are you sure? Maybe it is a different kind of magic. Maybe..." I know it is not so. Angels can see all that flows from the Gods into this realm. If Jordan held a direct line to them, wouldn't it show?

He shakes his head. "There is no magic in him."

He always said the gift was not his, that it was the Gods', and they simply worked through him. But if they left him, he would tell us. Wouldn't he?

I twist around to look to Adem, and he is already looking back at me. He heard. The lines of his face are deeper than usual, his mouth a thin, tense line. The moonlight catches his features and shadows cast anxiously across his face.

Fear hollows me out. Just how far have the Gods recoiled from this realm?

I watch Jordan as he wakes the next morning, stretching slowly and then pushing back his mess of hair. The joy he used to have, that cheerfulness that irritated me so much...it is gone. I had not though about it before, assumed it was the weariness of the journey. But now? Well, perhaps it is more than that.

I do not bring it up. It seems too personal.

Instead, I turn inward. I reach even harder into my dreams than ever, as if I could grab Theia and drag her back to Terath with me. Somehow I wish I could force the Gods to stay here with us and face the discord they have left behind.

I feel unanchored, tossed about in the storm. I need to quiet it. No matter what the dreams' truth holds for me, I need to find it. Perhaps it will bring answers.

So I listen closer. Try to stay in the dreams longer.

And it works...slowly.

Over the nights the voice begins to take shape. Just a murmur, like it is searching for something to cling to.

I push to my feet and strain, looking for it. Before I know it I am in the void of the dream, wandering in search for it. As I meander, the void begins to take form around me. At first, it is only a floor beneath me, a magnificent spread of gleaming marble below my feet, if aged and cracked.

But night after night, I dare go farther in my search as the muffled voice stretches before me. The marble grows into magnificent columns. And then, at the end of a grand parlor, I find three glorious, giant thrones.

The Host. Somehow I have slipped right out of the in-between and into the Gods' home realm. There is no one and no thing to tell me this, but within the dream I know it as surely as I know my own name. Their presence sparks from every inch of this place.

But where are They? Why are the thrones empty? Despite its glory, the Host seems broken and abandoned. Tiles of the floor are cracked, and fragments from the columns crumble to the floor. Weeds stretch over the thrones. Where are the Gods?

Despite the nearing voice, these questions dart through me with dread.

But then, finally, the voice becomes clear, and I catch it. Just a fragment, three small words. But oh, what words they are.

I am coming.

I awaken with a jolt, its syllables still alive in my ear. My heart races. My face is dotted in cold sweat.

I am coming.

Does it mean what I think it means? My heartbeat pounds in my ears, and my chest flutters erratically. I forget all that has passed and go to Adam.

"I heard it. The voice. It said, *I am coming*."

He turns his head and blinks at me. "What does it mean?"

I laugh, giddy and lightheaded, and shake my head. "I don't know. Not yet. But it's Theia. It has to be. She is the only one who ever sent me dreams."

I can't believe it. I can't believe the Goddess has come back to me, or how truly elated I am over it. Theia's messages were always an awful burden on me, but somehow Her return feels like a light of hope. Everything has been so terribly wrong, for so, so long. At last, it feels as though something is setting itself right again.

If Theia is coming, it won't be on us to take on Koreh and protect the realm. The Goddess will save us. All we have to do is wait, and trust Her.

The sun is already coming up on a new day. I slept through almost the entire night for once. Light breaks through the clouds in golden bursts, cascading ethereal beams over the wasteland.

CHAPTER 20

"WHAT DO I tell him?" I look to Adem, nodding back to Jordan.

The question sits between us like a loaded bow, poised to strike. At what, I am not sure.

Neither of us answers. We just stare at the endless sand. The sun glistens over it from behind us. It feels too soon. Having slept through more of the night than I am used to, I am not ready for this new day.

"The truth." Calipher's velvety voice reaches forth, and he steps to my side. "There are enough secrets here already."

"The truth about what?"

Jordan's voice is groggy and sluggish with sleep. We all turn to face him. My body is still wild with excitement from my dream's revelation. All the same, a lump wells up in my throat, an inexplicable resistance to what I have to tell him.

"My dreams, the ones that have been waking me in the night," I start.

"The ones that have been terrifying you each night," he jumps in.

"Yes, those." Something about his tone feels accusatory. And he is right. It is strange that I have been so frightened of Her. It is a fear that, to some degree, has always defined my relationship to Her. To all the Gods. "I was wrong. There is nothing to fear in them at all. I just couldn't understand them. It's Theia. She is coming."

"Coming?" Jordan tilts his head. "Coming how?"

I shake my head, my hair flying around me. "I do not know. I have to keep listening, keep trying to understand more. But that is what She said." My soul feels like it is flying. My words tumble over each other, too eager to spill out. "All this time. I've been so afraid. But it's all going to be all right. Theia is coming. We're not alone in this anymore. Never were, I guess."

Jordan's face goes pale, his eyes hollow with…is that longing? Sadness?

"That's wonderful." His words are small, but it is clear he wants to mean them.

I turn in the direction of Haven. "How much longer do we have to go?"

"We will reach Haven by nightfall."

My heart wants to race ahead and go splashing through the waves, lie back into them, let them swell around me.

Jordan looks like he would rather stay here in the wasteland.

"Well, then, let's get going," Calipher says.

Jordan nods, then jumps to the ground to start his training rituals.

We divide up more of the bread and water between us. Still, somehow, thankfully, there is enough left to sustain us. And then we go.

We do not mention my dream again, but it is there, hanging among us. Jordan will not look at me. Guilt builds up on my shoulders. And yet what have I done? Only listen. Only what I should have done from the beginning. It is not my fault I have found something in me that he seems to have possibly lost.

So why do I feel as though I have stolen something from him?

I have had enough of this, the strain between us. I have had enough of walking. Of adventure. Enough to last me a lifetime.

It feels good to be almost home. It feels good to *have* a home. For in spite of it all, this is what Haven has become for me.

Finally, we can stop walking and find some rest, for a time. Soon, we can turn our burdens over to Theia.

CHAPTER 21

I KNEW WE were close, but all the same, Haven sneaks up on me. Hidden behind the bluffs, all of a sudden I can feel it before I see it. Its salty breezes wrap around me, the sea's whisper over the shore calling for me.

I never realized how truly hidden Haven was. Had we not known exactly where it was, it would have taken a miracle to stumble across it.

As we make our way over and down the bluff, Jordan sighs in deep relief. "Thanks be to the Gods."

The village is as we left it, strong and thriving and alive. No ambush has attacked here. Around its edges tents have been cast up. The rest of Ir-Nearch made it here safely too.

As we make our way down the bluff, villagers stop and look to us. I expect to see the warm smiles I grew used to here, but they do not come. In fact, the people do not seem happy to see us at all. Their expressions drop away to sobriety, solemn and wide-eyed.

Is it because we have yet again brought a powerful

stranger among them?

"Calipher, maybe you should stay back, for now," I suggest.

They have as much reason to be wary of another angel as we did. They all saw what Kythiel had become.

Calipher nods and turns back to the top of the bluff. But as we continue to approach without him, the villagers' expressions only grow more serious.

Haven may not have been attacked, but something has gone terribly wrong.

Jordan doesn't see it. He rushes in, beaming, too overjoyed to see Haven unharmed to notice.

"You're here! You're safe!" He doles out hugs to the villagers closest to him. "I was so afraid another disaster would strike before I made it back."

At the word *disaster*, the villagers' eyes drop away from him.

Jordan's smile fades. He looks around at them. "What is it? What has happened?"

They look at each other. They do not say anything. My stomach tosses.

Jordan frowns, the mood of the village finally sinking into him.

"It is not yet sunset. You all should be in training right now. Why aren't you training?"

None of them respond.

Jordan presses further. "Where is Avi? And Lena? And Helda?"

I slowly pull my blade from its sheath. Behind me, Adem releases a throaty growl.

A woman steps forward and puts her hands over Jordan's. "A lot of us still support you. We still believe in you. But they were our own people. We were not prepared for it, and they were willing to turn it into a battle if they had to. Our choices were to let them take over in peace or destroy our own brothers. They threatened to hold us captive in the cave."

It is like sinking, the slow submergence into understanding. When Helda brought her people here, she did not have only refuge in mind. She wanted power.

"What, you think they could fit all of you in there?" I snap.

"We did not know if you would even come back. They said you wouldn't," the woman replies.

"They?" I prompt.

The woman tugs at her sleeve. "Helda. And Avi. They brought their forces together, all who they knew openly supported them."

But Jordan has other things on his mind. "Where is Lena?" he demands.

The villagers fidget. None will speak up.

"Rachel." Jordan's voice is hard and flinty, suddenly focused. The young woman's eyes dilate wide. "Where is she?"

"I am so sorry, Jordan." The woman's lip trembles. "She would not relent. She would not stand down."

Something within Jordan shifts, casting shadows over his face, hardening and sharpening it. He pulls out his sword.

"Avi!" Jordan bursts through the gathering villagers as he bellows his brother's name, marching toward Haven's center. "Avi! Come out here and face me!"

The boy I have seen in Jordan — the joyful, innocent

thing with that constant, irritating smile — is gone. If he still lives in the furious man storming the village now, he is buried deep. I would not have thought it possible for him to be so furious, so fierce, but it is like the joy that usually floats around him has burned away, leaving only the warrior that was hidden underneath.

"Get out here!" he cries. His voice crackles with emotion.

A crowd is growing around the village center, curious to see what will happen next. Guards in Ir-Nearch armor are stationed throughout the village, but they do nothing to respond to Jordan's shouts. How many of them are stationed willingly, and how many sought simply to avoid violence with Helda and Avi?

A door opens to one of the huts along the center's rim, and Avi steps out. Helda emerges behind him.

They look calm.

No, they look *smug*.

A burst of protective rage burns within me for Jordan. How could anyone muster such hate, such *lowness*, as to cut in behind Jordan's back in this way? To so deliberately sneak and plan, wait for just the right moment to strike?

And the people. They have hardly tried to fight back at all, from what I can tell. These people who have pledged their allegiance, who have loved him and followed him. These people who are supposed to be our greatest warriors in the war ahead could hardly face their own neighbors.

Under the rage, guilt riddles my chest. *I knew.* I saw the dissension in Avi before we left. I felt the rumbles of discontent reverberating through Haven, and I did nothing. I pulled Jordan away for days and days, chasing mysteries into the wasteland, kept him from his responsibilities here. And all the while, I said nothing to him about it.

I let this happen as much as the rest of them.

Avi steps to the village center to face Jordan. The Ir-Nearch guards fill in around them.

"Drop your weapon, Jordan." The words are over-easy and comfortable. Too pleased with themselves.

Jordan slowly lifts his sword out to his side and leans down to place it on the ground. "There is no need for this, brother."

Avi ignores him. He looks back to Adem and me. "You too."

"No!" I cry.

Jordan turns to me and nods. *Just do it.*

I huff in frustration, but I hold out my one beloved, remaining blade and place it on the ground in front of me. The bruise along my side stretches and pinches as I bend. Koreh has not left me in my best fighting condition, and my muscles ache for rest. The force that healed me so quickly after the fight in Ir-Nearch finally seems to be leaving me. All the same, right now my body craves the satisfaction of my knuckles in Avi's face.

"What is this, brother?" Jordan's words are calm, though something hidden quivers underneath them.

Avi shakes his head. "Brother? No. You are no brother of mine. You are an intruder who stumbled upon us by luck, and weaseled your way into half of all that was mine. Half my bed. Half my toys. Half my mother's affection. The whole village's."

He kicks at the sand.

"You didn't earn any of this. You charmed your way into it with that pretty little smile and your special, direct connection to the Gods."

The muscles along Jordan's shoulders tense.

"Avi, come now. We have always been friends."

"We were, yes. But then we got older. You always had to be better, a little ahead. With me always somewhere in your shadow. I can lead as well as you can, Jordan. Better, maybe. But I never got a chance."

"I never meant to overshadow you. Not once. I just wanted you there with me." Jordan frowns, his eyes lost as he adjusts to seeing Avi in this new light.

"Well, it doesn't matter now," Avi sneers. "You finally went too far, dragging us all with you into this Third Realm War you say you have been chosen for."

Avi steps aggressively close to Jordan. He is taller and larger, muscles bulging from his shoulders and chest. If someone were to pick a leader from just looking at them, they would pick Avi. But Jordan is calm under Avi's glare. He looks back with his own steady burning gaze.

Adem rushes past me to Jordan's side, fists ready.

Jordan stretches out a hand, not bothering to look back. "Adem. It's okay."

Avi continues.

"So tell us, *Chosen One*, where were the Gods when the First Creatures broke free? Where were the Gods when their wars tore our realm apart? When our land's cities closed up and turned into tyrannies like the one you, yourself, fled from? And now you want us to fight for them, risk our lives, when They have never fought for us? No, Jordan. No. It stops here. I'm stopping you."

Helda whoops in support. I turn in response, and realize the crowd around us is growing. Weaving through them are Ir-Nearch's guards in full armor and brandishing spears. They are spread out, inching in from all sides.

At this, Avi folds his arms over his chest, an ugly smirk spreading over his lips.

"What are the Gods telling you now, Jordan? Do they still speak to you in these dark days?"

He waits. Jordan is silent, his lips pressed together so tight they are turning white.

"Could you ever even hear them at all?"

The words ooze out of Avi like venom, seeping into the air, into Jordan.

I want to run to him, to shield him from this ugliness, the rotten silence that sets in over the village.

"Jordan—" I start.

He holds out a hand to silence me, but his eyes stay on Avi.

"Where is Lena, Avi?"

Avi's smile fades, but a satisfied glint still shines in his eyes.

"As it happens, we were about to take you to her."

Four guards lead Calipher to join us. More guards come forth from the crowd and move into formation around us. They lead us through the village and down the shore.

They are leading us to the cave.

This is where Adem first brought me, when I was still too dazed from the Underworld to understand what had happened, and thought I was reliving my death all over again.

I spent days pent up here, floating in and out of consciousness, watching the sun's and moon's reflections twist on the water, too weak to move.

I have avoided the cave ever since. Even looking at it, even thinking about it makes me feel desperate and queasy again, like I am fighting for my life.

Another set of guards pulls up behind us, spears out, leading Calipher to the cave with us. Calipher looks to us with questioning eyes. Jordan shakes his head.

Why won't he let us do anything? We could stop this between the four of us. We could stop it all right now.

"Jordan!" It calls out from behind us, and we all turn in spite of ourselves. The deep voice resonates with such great desperation.

Xamson is running toward us, flinging aside his helmet. He ignores the guards and bursts through them, throwing his arms around Jordan and planting a kiss on him.

"Thank the Gods you are alive," he mutters, pressing into him again.

Jordan hugs him back halfheartedly, a deep flush spreading over his face.

Avi's face tightens, a knot pulling at his jaw. He blinks. Then he smirks, his eyes sharp.

"Well. No wonder you never took on any of the girls that threw themselves at you over the years. Here I thought you had no warrior's spirit, but it turns out you have been conquesting... *elsewhere*. How long have you kept *this* secret?"

Jordan glances to Avi. He closes his eyes as if to shut the world away, and pulls Xamson closer, gently placing his hands around Xamson's face.

"You didn't tell them," Xamson says. His voice is sad, but gentle.

"I'm sorry," Jordan replies. "I did not know how."

A soft murmur makes my eyes drift from Jordan to the guards behind them. They look not at Jordan while they talk, but Avi. Are they displeased with his slurs?

No one seemed to have a problem with Jordan when they were in Ir-Nearch. No one had a problem with his relationship with Xamson. They were loved. Respected.

Xamson shakes his head. "It doesn't matter. Not now."

Jordan stretches up and gives Xamson another small kiss. "Go. You're going to get yourself into trouble."

But Xamson only hugs him tighter. He whispers something into Jordan's ear. He goes on and on, whispering too low for anyone else to hear, his eyes hard and focused, his words fast and fevered. Jordan listens, nodding soberly. When he is finally done, Jordan pulls him close by the belt slung around his waist that bears his sword, and kisses him passionately.

When he pulls away again, emotion flickers over his face in small constrained ripples. "Now really. Go."

Xamson runs his hands down Jordan's arms and squeezes his hands. He nods, then turns to go. As Xamson turns away, I see a glint of something metallic flash in Jordan's hand.

My heart leaps. And then I step closer to him, trying to block the guards from seeing what I have seen.

Xamson goes to leave. Avi steps in front of him, cutting him off.

"Oh, no, I can't have some *consort* of our former

leader walking around my village. You're staying here,"
Avi says. He motions to the guards. "Lock them up."

The guards hesitate, looking to each other.

Dissension. They don't like this, being told to
imprison one of their own.

"I said do it," Avi snaps.

The one in front nods. "As you command."

They usher us into the cave, swords drawn.

Do the guards believe in what Avi and Helda are
doing, or are they just following orders? I couldn't
blame them for being afraid. I'm afraid. We all are. But
to go along with this? Have they been secretly resenting
Jordan's leadership for as long as Haven? I search my
memories for any sign of distrust from them. I find
nothing.

The senselessness of it all bursts inside me, an anger
so hot it hurts.

"You think you can hold us if we do not allow you
to?" I shout. My voice echoes, trapped in the cave.
"Don't count on it. You may be soldiers, but we are
born warriors. Chosen warriors. You think you can keep
an angel in your control? A golem? You may not have
seen what Adem is capable of yourself, but I know you
have heard the stories. I warn you now, they are all
true."

I am surprised by the venom in my voice, the way
the words splinter as they leave me.

"Ungrateful. *Worthless.* All of you. We helped you.
We protected you. And this is how you thank us? We
fought side by side with you against an undead army as
it burned your city to the ground. We are your only
hope for setting things right again."

"Rona." Jordan flashes me a chiding look, as if to say, *Don't be so hard on them. It isn't their fault.* I glare back at him. I don't feel bad about it at all.

Adem places a hand on my shoulder. I shake it off, setting my rage loose on him.

"How can you be so calm!" I shriek. "Nothing about this is okay!"

The four guards settle back into place at the cave's mouth, turning away from us. We turn inward to face our prison.

A figure stands at the back of the cave.

"Lena?" Jordan rushes to her side. "Gods, what did they do to you?"

We settle into our prison. Calipher's glow lends some better lighting to the back. Jordan brushes aside Lena's hair, exposing black bruises along the side of her head and caked blood.

We try to allow Jordan and Lena some space to reunite in privacy, but it is tight with so many of us crammed in. The damp musty air presses into my skin with an irritating hum.

"You should not have had anything to do with this," Jordan chides Lena.

"Just let them take over the village and spread lies about my boy? Hardly," she huffs, stepping back and settling the hair over the bruise again.

"Avi is your boy too."

"He was raised better." Lena's eyes are stern. "But what has happened? Where did you go?"

"The Third War. It has begun." Jordan explains to her about the Unnamed, the fight at Ir-Nearch, the trek into the wasteland, Koreh.

I shut out their conversation and try to think. Try to listen.

What now? Please, Theia, please, give me something.

We have an angel and a golem in here, two beings that are all but living weapons. Not to mention the blade Xamson slipped to Jordan. We are all warriors here, even Lena. We can bust ourselves out whenever we like.

And oh, how I would like to. The cave's musty darkness closes around me and strains my breathing, chokes at my memory. I have fought for my life once in this claustrophobic space already. Must I do it again now? What will happen if we wait here?

I scoot myself closer to Calipher. He is too large to stand in here, and has taken a seat against the wall.

"Let's get out of here."

Calipher nods. "I would. But…"

Not him, too. What is this hesitation? Why will none of them fight with me? "But what?"

"I don't think Jordan wants me to."

I look over. Jordan is fiercely focused on Lena, tending to the wound on her head. They talk softly as he checks her over, using the sleeve of his robe and some spit to clean the wound. He smiles as he does it, and says something that makes her laugh.

Always the golden child. Always beloved. It comes so easy to him, these connections.

Jealousy cuts like a blade through my heart. Suddenly I see it all so clearly.

Adem has his freedom to fight for. Jordan has his family, his people. Even Calipher has a reason to be here. He is trying to fix what he has broken, to do right by someone he loved.

And me?

I have nothing in this fight. Or any fight. And without anything to fight for, what is the point of being here at all? No wonder I've been so willing to put my life on the line time after time. No wonder I am so comfortable going back to the Underworld.

What is the difference, really, without anything to anchor me here?

The realization is abrupt and terrible. A sudden, violent storm crashing over me.

I give in to the pull, curling into a tight ball on the sandy, rocky ground.

Let one of the others fight for a while. Someone with a reason to.

CHAPTER 22

AS EVENING SETS in, the rest of them fall quiet too. Adem rarely is anything else, and Calipher has little to add to the situation. Eventually, even Jordan runs out of encouragement for Lena and Xamson, and the only sound that is left for a long period is the waves on the shore, lapping in past the guards at the cave's mouth.

Jordan is the one to break the silence. "Avi isn't wrong."

"Of course Avi is wrong," I snap. "Everything about this is wrong."

But Xamson is watching him more carefully. "What do you mean?"

Jordan sighs, slouching forward and digging his fingers through his hair.

"I have to make a confession. Something I have not told any of you, have barely been able to admit to myself." He looks up, makes eye contact with each of us in turn. "I can't hear the Gods."

No one speaks. I weigh it out, considering what kind

of reaction I should be having.

He continues, "I could. Most of my life they hummed around me like the heat that comes off of a fire."

He stretches his hand as if to feel the warmth.

"I couldn't see it, but I could feel it as sure as I can feel the sand between my toes. I didn't even have to think about it. Listening to their presence in the realm was like breathing. Then, in recent years, they started to grow too loud. Instead of a warming hearth, they became more like a house burning to the ground."

He stares blankly in front of him, lost in his own bewilderment.

"And then... it changed. After Adem came back and Kythiel was banished, the Gods went silent. They were just gone. I have no idea where they went. But I do not think I lost my ability to hear them. I think they're gone from Terath."

He stares at us again. His eyes are desperate.

Adem shifts, glances away uncomfortably.

"It is not your fault, Adem. Even if it was because of the rift between the realms, you couldn't have known."

"I still did it," Adem grumbles. "It was still because of me."

It unsettles me, to see how unsettled Jordan is. Jordan's ability to hear the Gods seemed to be so much a part of who he is. As a person, as a fighter, as a leader.

No wonder the people of Haven have been shaken up.

"Does anyone else know?" I ask.

"No," he says. "At least, I have not told anyone. They couldn't know it for sure. But...well. If Avi has noticed, he is probably not the only one."

"Koreh knew. Somehow," Adem says.

"I knew too," Calipher adds. "Well, not all of it. But I can see that any magic you may have held...it is no longer there. Any First Creature would be able to see this."

"We all kind of knew," I confess. "After what Koreh said. It wasn't hard to connect the dots. It had been a while since you had shared anything from the Gods."

I remember what it felt like when I first realized Theia would no longer speak to me. Back when Kythiel had figured out how to inhabit my dream life and broke into my mind from the Host.

It was terrifying, like being lost out at sea on a small raft with nothing to show which direction to head.

"You get used to it." I try to smile at him over the fire, but we both know that it is a lie. I have never been good at comforting people.

Jordan nods into his chest. His entire body seems to sag.

"What matters now is what happens next," Xamson cuts in, picking up the conversation. He leans in and gestures for us to come closer. We scoot towards him. When he speaks again, it is in a low whisper. "What I was trying to tell Jordan when I cut through the guards is, we have a plan. Some of the guards have been lying low, waiting for the right time. We knew you would be back, and we are ready for it."

He takes us through the plan. It's simple enough. He and a few others put it together as soon as Avi and Helda swooped in to take over. They will organize, and when they can, they will come free us. Then, in the night, we will take Avi and Helda hostage and set things right again.

All we have to do is wait.

Waiting is the thing I am least prepared to do.

"Why would we do that? We have all we need to break free. There are only two guards out there. What are we waiting for?" I demand.

Jordan shakes his head. "No, Rona. Let it be. We could all use some time to regain our strength anyway. The guards on the outside know what is going on in the village. They will know when the time is optimal. I will not allow any more bloodshed over this. I cannot regain leadership with sheer force. If they want me, this has to come from the people, or it will only happen again. We will trust them. We will wait."

I huff my frustration and drop back against the cool side of the cave. Guess I had better get comfortable.

CHAPTER 23

OTHER THAN THE waves and an idle dripping sound within the cave, it is silent and dark.

The sun sets over the water, leaving only Calipher's glow and the moon's reflection on the waves for light, and we have all settled into a restless quiet. I wish Xamson's friends would hurry up.

We could use the rest, but no one sleeps.

Adem alone is still standing, still as a stone and staring out to the sea.

I am too restless to sit, so I get up and stand next to Adem. With our backs to the cave and the glistening moon over the sea in front of us, it is easy to imagine we are alone. Even the guards outside the cave have gone quiet and still.

The waves brush over the sand in soothing sighs.

It feels almost normal again, standing next to him. Like it was before I messed it all up. I can almost pretend it never happened at all. Maybe it is better that I am not quite so comfortable with him anyway. I glance over at him, his large body still and stoic, his eyes blank and his face emotionless.

"What does Theia say?" he asks.

The one thing I am good for in this group, and I have no answer. I am too anxious to sleep, locked in this place. And if I cannot sleep, I cannot listen.

I shrug and shake my head.

My hand drifts idly to my side for my blade. When it is not there, I drop my hand and tap anxiously at my leg.

"We need to get out of here."

Adem shuffles his feet, pushing the sand between them. "Then what?"

The question drops on me like a brick. "What?"

"After we get out of the cave. What's next?"

I had not thought that far yet.

"He won't cast out Avi and Helda," Adem continues. "Jordan won't do that. I do not know what to do."

And so he stands here and stares at the sea.

He is right. So what if we were to break free? Maybe we manage to take Haven back. What then? What would we do about Avi and Helda to put an end to this? What about all the people who let it happen? This may be a village of trained warriors, but right now they are scared and angry and though they may love Jordan, they no longer trust him to lead them.

As I stop to truly examine the mess we are in, I see all kinds of tangles and snares hidden within it.

Jordan was right. The abrupt realization is like a swift hit to the chest, knocking the wind out of me. This is not about fighting our way free. With Adem and Calipher on our side, we can do that whenever we like. This is about winning back hearts. Something I know nothing about.

Adem clears his throat, pulling me from my sinking thoughts.

"I am sorry," he says.

His words are darts, piercing my heart. My ears grow hot.

"What?" My mind scrambles to catch up. I turn to study his face, trying to understand. "For the other night? No. That was my fault."

"No. Not for...that." He gazes down at his hands, refusing to look at me. "For bringing you back."

The air flattens. My heart pounds loud and fast and thick at the back of my head. I am not prepared, not to talk about *this*.

But he keeps going.

"For not believing you. For putting you in so much danger. I...I almost handed you right over to him." We both know who he is referring to. "For bringing you back to *this*. For not asking more questions. For not...for not knowing. For..."

His face is hidden in the shadow from the moon, but his hands wring around each other fervently. I watch them, my eyes fixing on the rough stub left behind where the demon bit his finger off.

Gods help us, he really thought he was saving me. He really thought he was going to be the hero, and then turn around and be rewarded with a soul.

The weight of the truth is crushing him.

"Stop, stop." I put my hand over his fidgeting ones. They are rough and chalky, like thirsty earth, and go still under my touch. I slip my hand between them and he wraps his large hands around mine like the gentle giant he is. "You *didn't* know. You couldn't have."

"I still did it. Even when you told me, I almost did it."

I sigh. One misdeed. So much burden. For both of us.

"Let's just put it behind us."

A memory rises like a wave on the shore in my mind. Something I have never dared to tell anyone. Do I dare to confess it now?

The words start pouring out of me before I am sure I should, and I cannot stop them. As if I have been waiting for someone to unload it onto. Like water bursting through a broken dam.

"He tricked me too, all those years ago. He was so easy to trust. Who would have thought that an angel could be so deceptive, so manipulative? *An angel.* Back then, we did not even know they could fall. *I* am the one who let him in, *I* am the one who was too naive to see what it was turning him into."

I gaze at the moon's rippling reflection as I talk. I do not know that I could bear Adem's sympathy right now, behind those blank eyes.

"Gods, even after it should have been over, when Theia had ordered him out of Terath, I traded Theia's true voice to let him reach me from Her way to me inside my mind."

My voice quivers, tears threatening at the back of my throat. I take a breath and look up to the stars. Adem remains mercifully silent, waiting for me to finish.

"I never wanted Theia's voice in me. I never wanted

the burden of delivering Her word to those who did not want to hear it. But it was a privilege too. A gift. Like having a small piece of Her with me all the time. I did not even know I possessed it until it was gone, and all that was left was the fear of what Kythiel had become, and when he would show up next."

Adem presses his hands over mine tightly, and I realize I am shaking. I squeeze my other hand, loose and trembling at my side, into a fist to try to stop it, but it is no use.

"Look, all that, it is over now. And that's because of you too. I did what I had to, to escape him. I didn't even think of finding a way to stop him for good, I was too undone. It is my fault he was even out there to use you in the first place."

It is only after I say it that I realize this has been the irritating grain at the heart of my rage this whole time. I should have done it myself, destroyed Kythiel, and the rest would never have happened. Getting the words out, finally staring it in the face, is like removing a great weight.

"Please. Just forgive me," he mumbles.

I turn and study him. He will not even look at me. His head hunches forward as if the guilt were a physical presence bearing over him.

"I do. I forgive you."

In the calm pause that follows, the whisper of the waves is almost a physical presence brushing over me. My trembling stops. The moon's glistening reflection is milky and sweet.

Adem's hands go still. He smooths out my hand and presses his flat against it on either side, then he presses them together against his chest. Almost like praying. His touch sends a sweet, tingling warmth up my arm.

I pull my hand away.

"Let's just forget all about it. We have enough to deal with right now as it is."

He clears his throat in response and straightens, edging slightly away from me on the dirt.

Secretly, it is like a cage that had seized too tight around my heart has torn open. He apologized. And I have forgiven him. I did a while ago, I realize now. For a moment, I bask in it, this newfound peace that was so hard to earn.

There is so much still wrong, so many bigger things ahead that we must figure out. But this one small thing, at least, has truly been set right.

I close my eyes, let Haven's natural, deep-set calm settle into me. Push the memories of Kythiel out, and the sour memories of this cave. Push aside the coup and Koreh and the war. Just for the moment.

We might be here for a while. And maybe that is okay.

I let myself take it all in and breathe.

Calipher's aura fills the entire cave with an overwhelming peacefulness. For once I invite it in, let it drown out the anxiety this place fills me with, let it quiet the impulse to fight. Just take a deep breath and let my mind go still.

I have a feeling I had better enjoy the stillness while it lasts, because something big, good or bad, is sure to happen soon.

My hand still tingles where Adem's wrapped around it. Maybe I should nestle it into his again.

Before I can decide, I hear a dull but distinct *thud*, and I open my eyes just in time to see one of the guards slump to the ground.

CHAPTER 24

A SHADOW RUSHES past the cave's mouth. Another *thud*, and the other guard drops. Then, a hooded figure fills the mouth of the cave. In his hand is a large blade, moonlight glinting off its meticulously jeweled handle.

I bolt to my feet, reaching to my waist for my own blade that is not there. My hands fold instinctively into fists, and my heart's pounding floods my ears.

Calipher is up too, with Jordan, Xamson, and Lena just behind him. His glow casts light over the figure, revealing a deep red robe and a menacing grimace.

Adem bristles and a low growl rises from him. His head droops into his chest.

"Don't do this," he grumbles to the night. "It will not matter."

The hooded figure takes a step closer. Calipher's glow illuminates him to reveal a brooding glare with thick eyebrows and a wiry beard.

"Hand it over, and I will let you go in peace," the stranger declares.

"Hand what over?" I snap back. It is all happening too fast. It makes no sense, some stranger appears out of the night and frees us, only to hold us captive himself?

Adem turns to me and places a heavy hand on my shoulder. "This is not your fight," he says.

"This is not anyone's fight," I retort. "This is a lone rogue who picked the wrong group to stalk out of the wasteland."

"Rona...," Adem pleads.

My pulse throbs in my fingertips. The adrenaline, the urge to *act*, feels satisfying after so long cooped up and helpless. I bend to the ground and pick up a rock about the size of my fist. It is no blade, but it could do some damage.

"This one knows what I am here for." The hooded stranger gestures to Adem with his blade.

I stare at him, then at Adem, and back again. His eyes are full of a thousand years of burden.

A soft hand squeezes my shoulder from behind, and I jump, but it is only Jordan. "He is like the other one that came here after the Underworld. He is one of Adem's Hunters," he says.

"The Hunters?" I study the figure in front of us again, registering all the little familiarities I did not take time to understand at first.

As it all pieces together, my chest contracts and my heart hardens. I lunge at the Hunter, swinging the rock, a warning strike. "We buried the last of you in the ground, and we will do the same to you, if you make us."

Adem shuffles back, putting more distance between himself and the Hunter.

But the Hunter leans in, meeting me step for step. "Hunters? I am from the brotherhood of Shael's Sworn, and I am here to destroy the magic you are carrying. Do what you must, but I am taking it with me."

"You can't," Adem says. I have never head his voice so flat and defeated. "Turn away. Go back to your brotherhood. If you force this, you will die, and there will be nothing I can do to stop it."

The Hunter settles into a fighting stance, his blade poised to strike. "I must have the object. I cannot leave without it."

"I cannot give it to you."

They level each other with heated stares. The Hunter steps forward, ready to fight, and I can see the burden settling heavily across Adem's shoulders.

"Stop."

They freeze and stare at me. Adem shakes his head, his forehead pulled into a frown. Is he angry at me? I have never seen him angry before.

But the last Hunter in the other robe is seared into my memory. The way the mangled body froze, staring blankly at nothing. The way it destroyed Adem that he had done it, adding to this burden that tortures him and is ever present in his eyes.

It is a cycle that seems to never end. It can't keep happening like this. I can't bear to let it.

I step between them and face the Hunter. "He does not kill anymore. But if you try to fight him, he will kill you."

The Hunter does not speak. Whether from shock or curiosity or complete disinterest, I cannot tell. But I do not care.

"So you do not get to fight him. You can fight me. You can fight Jordan. You can fight Calipher. But you cannot fight Adem."

The Hunter glares at me. The shadows of the night hide his face and make it impossible to read his thoughts. He raises his blade. A rush shuts down my mind and I shift my grip on the rock, ready to use it.

But before I can, a hand drops on my shoulder, and Jordan wedges between us. "What is your name, friend?"

The lines of the Hunter's frown grow deeper. Does he have any other expression? But he seems to be considering.

"Thane."

"I am Jordan." He nods in greeting, as if this were a friendly gathering, rather than a midnight ambush. "We have no interest in fighting you, if we do not have to. Why don't you lower your blade, and we can discuss what it is you have come for? We will even show it to you."

Adem emits a displeased snarl. Jordan reaches back and squeezes his wrist, but does not look away from the Hunter—from *Thane*.

"Come now. All these ages of coming for this magic, and this fighting has gotten your Brotherhood nowhere." Jordan presses his lips together, allowing Thane time to consider. "If you would pause long enough to understand, you would know why fighting him will not help you gain what he carries, and you would know how to acquire it."

Thane hesitates, turning to look at each of us in turn.

Enough already.

"You can fight Adem now and die, or you can talk to us," I sigh. "If we get to the end of our talking, and you still think that fighting Adem for the box is the right thing to do, go ahead. We are not going anywhere."

From the corner of my eye, I can see Adem shift uncomfortably at the last part of my statement, but I hold my gaze on the Hunter and wait.

He looks to Adem and eyes him carefully, then back to me, and then to Calipher behind us. Jordan turns to me and nods to the rock. I hold it out, and carefully set it on the ground.

Thane loosens his grip on his blade and tucks in into its sheath in his belt.

"Fine. Tell me what it is that I am not understanding," he says.

A laugh escapes me. I am not sure what I expected, but not for him to go along. I just could not bear to stand by as Adem took on yet another burden. Only Jordan. He is the only one with this kind of influence over people. I can't believe that it worked.

For now, at least.

"Sit down." Jordan points. Then, he looks to Adem. "Show him."

Adem holds Jordan's eyes an extra moment, but then he nods. He sits, and the rest of us follow, settling onto the cool sand. All but Calipher, who moves around us to stand behind Thane, tall and stern. He checks each of the guards. He nods. They must be alive still, just unconscious.

Adem pulls a swatch of fabric from an inner pocket of his robe, and sighs, holding it close to his chest and staring at Thane.

"He has to know. He has to understand if any of this is going to change," I urge him.

And then I turn to Thane. "You have to understand. You are not to touch it. What he is about to show you...He will kill you. He won't have a choice."

Thane rolls his eyes and holds his hands up in surrender.

Adem places the fabric on the ground and unfolds it. In it, there is a pile of splinters and wooden chunks.

"It was a box. This is all that is left of it," he says.

Thane leans in, and Adem flinches, his hand wrapping back over the fragments.

Thane studies him, waiting. Adem opens his hand again, slowly.

Goosebumps rise over the skin of Adem's arms. The edge of his eye twitches. "I can't leave it. It will hold me back. And I can't let someone else have it. If I do, it makes me destroy them."

Adem looks up, the muscles over his back tensing. Thane frowns.

"It was locked. For a long, long time, I did not know what was in it. But when I was in the Underworld –"

"When you were...," Thane tenses, "You mean you broke through the realms? This is all your doing?" He waves to the air.

Adem stares at the ground and releases a heavy sigh. "Yes."

Thane's eyes go wide: half-awe, half-dread. "How powerful are you?"

Adem shrugs.

I jump in with, "He is essentially indestructible. In Terath, at least. His Maker, whoever he was, was powerful. That magic has been compounding in him for ages. Show him."

I nod to Adem. He glares at me like I have asked him to step on a mouse.

Adem hesitates. "I still don't even know how to control it."

"You do, though. I have seen it," I say. "He should know, if he is going to hunt us down in the night and try to tell us what we should be doing."

Adem sighs and shakes his head, a solemnity settling over him. He puts his hand toward the ground and stretches his fingers.

"Aaeros."

The pebbles and small stones roll and stumble toward him, then float upwards to him. It is still unsettling to me, even after watching him do it so many times as we idle away the nights. It still takes me back to that brawl on this very sand, a fight for my fate, and a tremor of that night's terror stings through me.

Thane leans away a little, and watches with sharp, suspicious eyes.

"Adem is a powerful ally," I say. "And a powerful enemy."

"No one wants to make enemies here," Jordan quickly inserts.

Adem waits to see what else Thane has to say. But Thane just squints at him, head tilted, mouth open.

"You can see, on some of the pieces, there was script around its sides." Adem pushes them around in his palm to show Thane. "The last one of you who came, he said it was a charm."

Thane leans in to examine them. "Looks like it. I'd

need to see it all together to know for sure."

Adem drops the pieces onto the sand and starts pushing them around into order.

"When I was in the Underworld," Adem says. "The charm didn't work anymore. I couldn't protect it like I do here. It broke open." He holds the pieces out again. "And I finally saw what was inside."

"What was it?" Thane is like a child at bedtime, transfixed by the suspense.

"A necklace."

The Hunter's head tilts. "All that for a piece of jewelry? Why?"

Calipher cuts in. "Because it holds magic stolen from Gloros. Magic I stole."

Thane twists to look at Calipher. "You...you stole...from the Goddess?" He looks as impressed as he is horrified.

"And now Koreh has it," I add. We have all made mistakes here. Dwelling on them has gotten us nowhere. We need to look forward.

A deadening weight spreads over the circle.

"When was this?" Thane asks. "Who is Koreh?"

"All we know is that she is more than human, and that she must have some tie to Abazel, to be in possession of the necklace."

Thane's eyes widen. "More than human?"

"We saw it with our own eyes. She can't just *do* magic. Her will *is* the magic. And that is all we know."

"We know more." Calipher stops pacing and joins our circle. "I know who Koreh is. And what."

CHAPTER 25

CALIPHER'S WINGS SLUMP over his shoulders and tuck into his sides tight. He runs his hands through his golden hair, pushing the loose waves back and awry. Everything about him is in discordance with the calming aura he emits.

"Tell us," Jordan prompts.

Calipher huffs a great breath out and nods. "Yes, I will tell you. I will tell you everything."

Gods, how much is there to know? What has he been holding back from us? A knot tightens in the pit of my stomach.

"I knew Riamne's touch even before I noticed her. Riamne—Nia—was only a girl when I came to her town. Her family were followers of Gloros, It was easy to see she was sad, but she was not mine to comfort. That was for the sprites. I had others to tend. Before her, I did as Theia commanded and nothing more." He hesitates, drawing in a breath. "But one day in the market, Nia reached out and touched me. Her touch woke me up, or so it felt then. For the first time, I tasted what it was like to have one's own will. I wanted more. I wanted to have that feeling all of the time."

Kythiel's face rises to the forefront of my mind. The way he used to look at me. It was more than love. It was this same hollow hunger behind Calipher's eyes right now.

"In my hubris, I made myself believe I could have both—bask in Theia's light and power, and also steal my freedom through Nia. I used her terribly."

His wings pull in as if to cover his shame.

Good, I think, my heart hardening. *He should be ashamed.*

"I used her terribly. But I cared about her; I truly did. Nia was bold, strong, a survivor. Like a lone wildflower that springs up in a drought where nothing else will grow. There was beauty in that determination, a ferocity I did not have myself, and never saw before or since." The wistful look in his eyes only fuels my anger more. My teeth grind together, holding back words. I need to hear the rest of his story.

"She seemed more like a Goddess to me than a girl. She *was* my Goddess, and in my ecstasy, I forgot her humanity. And I forgot my true Goddess."

He pauses, emotion twisting his mouth. We wait for him to continue in silence.

"So Theia ordered me back to the Host. I panicked. I knew I had no choice but to go, but I resisted long enough to leave Nia with a gift. Something to remember me by. Something to protect her, or so I thought."

His gaze drops down to his feet, and a hint of pink tinges his perfect pale cheeks.

"The necklace," Jordan prompts.

He nods. The red in his cheeks grows deeper.

"I went to Gloros' temple and *drew* from Her magic there. This was a gift of love, a gift of passions, and Theia's magic would not do. I made the necklace into a vessel for what I took from Her. So that Nia could carry a piece of me, and our passion, with her always."

Calipher looks up and catches my gaze with his own, pleading, as if it is me he needs forgiveness from. "Nia seemed so strong. I forgot how fragile men are."

When I don't respond, he goes on. "I gave it to her. And then I gave in to Theia's growing pull and returned to the Host."

Just the mention of Host throws me back into my dreams. I cannot imagine anyone ever resisting such a perfect place.

"But it was not enough. I had already drifted too far, and the loss of my perceived freedom was too much to bear. It was like anchoring a boat in a storm. I rocked and tossed in the waves, until finally the line broke, and I snapped free again. I rushed right to Nia. But time had passed too quickly in Terath. The magic of the necklace kept her from aging, but the similarities of her physical beauty only exposed how terribly her soul had changed. She was no longer mine. And it was my own fault."

I can't argue with him there. No one speaks to try. Calipher presses his lips together, then goes on.

"Nia's girl was already gone and grown by then, but I heard rumors of her. Nia named her Varya. For a long time, I thought she was mine...but it seems her superhuman power came from a demon, not an angel."

At the cave's opening, one of the guards begins to

stir. Adem goes to him and hits him. He goes limp again.

Thane pounds his fist into his hand. "We do not have time for this. What does this have to do with Koreh?"

"Koreh is Varya's daughter. Nia's granddaughter."

The words are like a vase shattering to the ground. None of us know how to respond.

"But surely—you met Nia in the Beginning. That was a few thousand years ago," I say. "Koreh is hardly an adult. It is not possible."

Calipher nods somberly.

"With the power in the necklace, Nia lived far past her natural life. And—"

"And her descendants have First blood in them. They are human enough to age, but Halves do so far slower than true men," the Thane finishes for him. "They can walk Terath for hundreds of years."

Calipher nods. "And not only Terath. Halves have been known to be able to cross over into the other realms, sometimes. Before the Gods put the barrier in place to hold back the rebels."

A quiet settles over us.

My mind churns, trying to piece together what Calipher is telling us with all we have seen.

"So that is how she got the necklace. Now that the barrier is broken, she must have gone to the Underworld." And then more truths crash over me as I register the rest of what he said. He thought she might be his own descendent? "You weren't trying to save us when you took us from the tower. You were protecting *her*."

"I did that for *all* of you," he says. His hands fly out to his sides as if deflecting an attack. "You think, with all her power, she needs my protection from you? You would never have overcome her. But I did not want to see you destroyed, and the last thing Koreh needs is for the necklace's power to seep deeper into her. It is the last thing any of us needs. As long as she has it, the whole realm is threatened." His expression softens. "But I confess, my love for Nia has fed a great attachment to her. Even now, my heart is unable to turn away from Nia, though I realize she is not mine. I know my heart, and it is hers forever."

Calipher keeps going, as if he can't stand the silence. "The sprites protected Varya, and they had possession of the necklace, for a time. I am not sure what happened from there. But somehow it ended up with you, Adem, and then Abazel stole it away. And Koreh must have been in the Underworld, for some reason."

"But," Jordan tilts his head, eyes narrowed and focused intensely on the sand. "What does any of this matter?"

Calipher's wings bristle. "I started following the necklace—following all of you—because I thought Koreh was mine. I thought I could help her destroy the necklace, set things right again, break this terrible cycle I have set in motion. Perhaps then Theia would let me come back to the Host."

I scoff. Yet again, it all comes back to him. Not so angelic. But very much in line with my own experience with angels.

He looks down, and golden curls tumble forward, covering his face.

"Though I realize she isn't mine now, my heart is already too deep in this. You know what it is for an angel's heart to change." He looks up to me, and only me, begging for understanding. "You know. And every time, it is harder than the last. I must see this through."

I step back, uncomfortable with this role of pardoner he is searching for in me. But he steps forward and takes my hand. A rush of peacefulness overtakes me.

"Please," he begs. "What is best for her is best for you too. We all want the same thing. No matter what I feel about Koreh, or about Nia, she has to be stopped. Don't force me out."

CHAPTER 26

THE ENTIRE CAVE stills. A whirl of emotions play tug of war inside me. Anger hums through my sides, sympathy softens in my chest, and a hot thirst to obliterate Koreh pulses in my veins.

"Of course we won't force you out." Jordan steps forward and reaches up to put a comforting hand on Calipher's shoulder. As if he were anyone else, and not one of the Gods' First Creatures. "The Third Realm War has started. We need to work together. All of us."

He stares pointedly at Thane. We all do.

Adem clears his throat. He is still sitting on the ground. I gaze down at him. While Calipher told his story, Adem put together the box's pieces as best he could. They settle into the sand, pushed roughly against each other, shards missing here and there in a cluster at one corner.

Thane settles onto the ground next to him, lips moving as he reads the symbols.

"It's angelic. It is impossible to translate exactly." He

glances up to Calipher. "It's a very strong, very difficult spell. It is no wonder you have been trapped by it all this time."

"What does it mean?" Adem asks. He leans in to peer at it with Thane. He is so absorbed he forgets to flinch when Thane shifts his weight.

"It is a binding spell, paired with charms to make it unbreakable and unopenable. Quite complex," Calipher says. "It requires great magic strength and skill, more than I have ever seen in a human. It almost had to be the same person who made Adem."

Adem nods. The pieces begin falling into place.

"What does the fourth side say?" I ask, leaning over them.

Calipher jumps in with, "That is not part of the charm. The fourth side is a warning. It says, 'death'."

"The charms themselves are quite simple," Calipher says. He tilts away from the box's pieces, frowning. "But for them to hold so strongly, for so long, the individual who carved this must have been very powerful indeed. A power rarely seen outside the Firsts."

I scoot closer, awed by the power splayed into shards on the sand in front of us. The others crowd in closer around it too.

"So," I start after a pause. "What happens now?"

"I go," Thane says.

"Really?" Adem's voice is rough and sharp, but his shoulders loosen visibly with relief.

"Whatever this is, it is clear you are right. The necklace needs to be the priority, not this." Thane waves his hand at the box. "I will come back. I will bring an army from the Sworn with me. We will fight with you. We will stop this. We have to."

The other guard begins to sluggishly shift. Thane gives us a grave nod, then delivers the guard a firm kick to the head as he exits into the shadows of sunrise, putting the man out again.

My thoughts drift back to the shards of the box, and then to Adem. He slowly sinks from kneeling stance until he reaches the ground, and then it is like his shoulders, his spine, keep sinking. Like all the weight of the box's burden is melting off of him. He stares at it, blinking his eyes rapidly—can Adem cry?—and finally glances up to me. I am so startled to be caught watching him, I jump, but before I can say anything, he tucks his head so that I cannot see and starts carefully picking up all the pieces.

I force myself to look away.

Here we are, a band of Firsts and creatures and warriors, standing in a prison with no guards.

"We need to go."

My blood is pumping and after this strange night, I am hungrier than ever to take these betrayers down. There is nothing I would love more. Sure, Jordan is not perfect; no one is, but his heart is always well-intentioned. This was no way to fall. There was simply no point to it. This isn't about political differences, not really. It's about power. And jealousy.

If I am honest, Helda and Avi's betrayal frightens me more than anything else we have seen. More than the wasteland. More than Koreh. More than even my dreams.

I may have been miserable, all pent up while healing

here, but Haven was always a place that felt safe. Protected. Untouched, somehow. This attack from the inside feels like the very deepest violation.

If the divide of this war can break apart even Haven, what can't it destroy?

Koreh cannot win. Abazel cannot.

"But what next?" Jordan asks. "We just walk into the village, and then what? They will send us right back again. If the people want me to—"

I pick up the sword lying limp next to one of the guards.

"The people? Gods-damnit, Jordan. This isn't a time to stand around and wait for something inspirational to drop from the sky and validate you. They only send us back here if we let them. They only take Haven if we let them. And you know as well as the rest of us that they have no claim to that. You are Haven's leader, and it's what you were meant to be."

"Look at us, Rona. We can break out any time we want. It's not about that. We need a plan."

"No! No more waiting. No more planning." My voice is shaky and sharp. "This is how it was the first time. Don't you get it? The war doesn't only come at us from the outside. It was never just about the Gods versus the Firsts. It seeped into everything like poison. And it's doing it all over again."

It is all so clear now. How has it taken me so long to understand?

All the discord—Theia and me, my family, Kythiel, the entire town, and well beyond it. It was all exactly what the rebelling First Creatures wanted. I did not know then what was coming. But this time, I do. I have seen all of it before.

But can I stop it? Is it enough, even if I can?

I have to try. I refuse to stand by and watch as the war breaks apart everything I have come to care about.

"You can't perpetuate the division. That's what they want."

Jordan squints, confused. "It's what *who* wants?"

I don't know how to answer. I don't know who exactly. It is just a feeling. A strong feeling, a feeling I know to be true down to the depths of my broken soul.

"The war. The thing in this realm that is broken."

I know as soon as I say it that it is the truth. This is bigger than Koreh, bigger than Abazel, bigger than all the rebel creatures. The true evil behind these wars is a creature all its own. A monster, lurking in the wasteland as sure as any other. It waits for us to show our weakness, and then it pounces. Its poison spreads through everything, person to person, until its hate is in everything and we are all divided.

"Yes." Lena steps forward and takes the sword from the second guard. "It is time things were set right again."

Xamson steps forward too, and places a hand on my shoulder. "Yes."

Calipher is already near where we stand, but he shifts to close the gap and stands with us in solidarity. My body fights the rush of peace that comes with him. But the gut-level fear he triggers in me is losing its pull. Adem joins us too, the box now safely tucked away, and more like his usual self.

Jordan stands alone, facing us. His hair is limp and his eyes dark with exhaustion. Hidden in morning's shadows behind the light reflected off the water, he seems small.

"What if Avi and Helda are right?" he asks. "What if I am unfit to lead?"

"How can you say that!" I demand. His hesitation burns, the worst kind of betrayal.

He pulls his hands away from his face. His eyes are bloodshot, tears hovering at their edges.

"They just stopped. All of a sudden, nothing. It is more than a quiet. It is like a vacuum in the realm. I have never felt anything so terrible in all my life."

"What stopped?" I ask.

"The Gods. They stopped speaking to me."

I study him. His horror at losing the Gods' words is the exact opposite of how I felt when Theia finally left me. But then, it is different for him.

Jordan has heard the Gods' whispers around him his entire life. He has never been without them. And now that he is, it seems he does not know what he is without them.

A whisper nudges from inside me that I immediately resent—maybe Avi and Helda are right. Without the Gods in his ears, what is Jordan? He is practically still a boy. And that is all he is. He has no experience. No special skills. Just a broad smile, and an even larger heart.

"But the worst part is that I cannot figure out what it *means*," Jordan goes on. "Now that the Third War is here, did the Gods decide to choose someone else? Have They fled the realm? Did I do something wrong? It has been driving me mad, trying to understand it."

His shoulders quiver. Xamson rushes to his side and

wraps his arms around him.

"Shhhhhh."

I turn and look to Adem, Calipher, and Lena. *What do we do?*

I have no idea what to think, what to say. But we can't afford for any of us to break apart right now.

Why didn't I see it? While I was busy seeking my adventure, Jordan was taking on everyone else's burdens like a sponge. But in times like these, the troubles are like an ocean. No matter how much he takes in, there will always be an unbearable amount still there.

"You can't quit, Jordan. Not now. Forget the Gods, if they're going to abandon us like that. Do it for all the people out there. They still believe in you. And they are waiting for you to take Haven back and claim them."

He shakes his head. "I don't know. I just don't know. Maybe Avi and Helda really are the better leaders for these times. Maybe I was a leader for easier times. Maybe I am no longer fit to lead."

"Not fit to lead?" I am surprised at how angry the suggestion makes me, like boiling water surging through my veins. He may be all heart, but that is exactly what Avi and Helda lack. And perhaps, it is just what a people need most in a time of war. "I have never met anyone more qualified. There is no one more prepared for what is about to happen than you. You have been preparing for this exact moment your entire life. We've all invested in you, Jordan, in the faith that you are the leader that is supposed to get us through this war."

I step closer, grab him by his shoulders. He needs to

hear this, to *really* hear it and believe it. Maybe *I* need to believe it.

"I have seen what the wars will do to this world. And I am telling you, there is no hope for any people who are not completely united when this war breaks through. You've got to extinguish this flame, and now." I take a deep breath. "You need to hear the Gods? Fine. I can be your connection to them now, with Theia back in my dreams. Let me help you. But you have to keep leading, Haven needs you. The entire realm does."

And in that moment, I truly, finally, believe in him.

Something shifts on his face as I talk, taking on sharp resolve, like someone who has made a decision.

"Yes, you're right. The people need us. They need someone who is confident, and can *inspire* confidence. These times are too dangerous for anything less." His eyes drift, then harden. When he steps forward, he does it with resolve. "Let's go."

Everyone gets up. They look as energized and ready to claim our freedom again as I am.

"One more thing." I grab Jordan's arm and pull him back. "You can't tell them, Jordan. You have to let them keep believing you can hear the Gods."

"Yeah." He shifts uncomfortably, shaking my hand away. "I know I can't tell them."

"It's not just that you can't tell them, Jordan. You have to be prepared to lie. I know you don't like it, but you're going to have to this time. They won't understand. They'll be terrified about what it might mean, just like you. And after all this—" I gesture around the cave "—they *will* ask."

Jordan may know people, but I know fear. I know

war. I know how a village falls apart.

When he turns back to me his face is a mask. "I got it. I'm ready."

I study him. His gruff expression lights a terrible fire in his eyes. He has never looked so old as he does now, taking on this burden for his people. It makes me uneasy how quickly he agreed to this, but if he is lying now, he is doing it well. And that is what we need from him.

"Good, because Gods help us, you're the only one who can do it."

CHAPTER 27

WE STEP OUT into the cool sea breeze. It has never felt so good.

The water speaks to me in hushes. The moon, a swollen gibbous, glimmers in broken beams over the water. Thick clouds cover most of the sky, hiding the stars.

The others file around me. Xamson steps out front and nods toward the village. "We stashed some weapons. This way."

I hesitate, glancing back to the guards. They lie with limbs sprawled awkwardly, their weapons splayed next to them. I pick up one of the swords.

"Should we..."

I can't bring myself to say it, so I gesture with my sword, stabbing at the air.

"No!" Jordan and Xamson exclaim almost in unison.

"Fine, fine." I hold my hands in surrender, sword and all, and step away from the guards.

Who am I kidding, anyway? I don't even have the

heart to kick them a third time to keep them unconscious longer. It wasn't their fault really. They were only following orders.

Jordan must be getting to me.

"Let's do this, then."

It won't be dark like this for much longer. We need to move.

But first, Xamson leads us around the village to the bluff, stopping in front of a small sapling tree. He paces three steps to its side, and then drops to his knees to dig.

"Weapons," he says. "We've been stashing some, when we could. We're going to need them."

About a foot into the sand, the gleam of metal begins to show. Xamson slows, and Jordan joins him, brushing the sand away. Adem and Calipher hang back while we choose.

I squat down to survey them: long blades and swords, mostly. But then a dark hand stretches into my line of vision, holding a short blade, like mine.

"Thought of you," Xamson says from over my shoulder.

I take it from him and stand. He holds out his other hand, handing me its twin.

"Thanks," I say.

I let their shafts settle into my palms and take a few swings through the air. It feels good. Not quite the same, but close.

Xamson and Lena each choose a sword. Jordan takes only a line of rope.

Which, it turns out, is the most important thing. We go back to the hut Avi and Helda burst from yesterday, and slide the door open as quietly as we can. Scrolls with maps and drills and plans are scattered over the floor. Against the wall, they sleep pressed against each other on a single cot.

Jordan pauses, watching them. "I...I had no idea."

"Me either." Xamson pushes past him. "But it doesn't change anything."

He hauls Avi up and pushes him my way. I pin him to the ground before he is even awake, his arm coiled behind his back. Xamson grabs Helda and does the same. They grunt and twist against the ground.

Jordan kneels so they can see him. The usual sparks in his eyes are smoldering embers. He binds their arms and legs with the rope.

"You struggle. But you do not call for help. Do you even know why?" he asks them.

"You scum," Helda snaps at him. "You will pay for this."

"You thought you would get away with this?" I sneer. "How did you think this could possibly end?"

"I didn't consider the odds, only what was necessary to protect my people," she fires back.

Her eyes are hardened and full of conviction. Finally, I have to look away.

"Don't be a fool, Jordan," Avi warns, trying to break free of the ropes. "It's over."

"It *is* over," Jordan agrees. "Do you know why you have not called for help? Because you know that no one will come to help you. You have not earned a place with these people. You stole this village. But you cannot steal its people, and you know they will not fight for you."

Avi tugs away from Jordan, rolling so his back is to

him. Helda spits, barely missing Jordan's foot. We drag
them outside and wait for the village to wake up.

In the village center, Lena waits.

She turns to Jordan, then to Avi, tied and sprawled
on the ground. She comes forward, lines deepening
across her forehead, and leans in to stroke Avi's face.
But he pulls away with a grunt.

Lena watches him a moment, her hand still
outstretched, a tear glistening in her eye. But she refuses
to let it fall. She stiffens her expression and blinks it
away.

For a moment I remember my own mother, the way
she used to brush my hair from my face. How
impossible this must be for Lena, watching her sons
turn against each other.

"Why?" she asks.

He does not answer.

The first hint of light is graying the dark sky from
beyond the wasteland. It won't be much longer until
Haven's people begin to rise to start their day, and find
us. But for now, we wait.

All is quiet. The first true quiet we have had, I
realize, since we last left this place. Now that I am
finally still, all that happened in the night catches up
with me, and my limbs start to feel slow and heavy.

I pace in a circle to keep alert, fighting against it. As I
turn, something catches my eye between huts, a small
girl with gleaming dark skin and wide solemn eyes.

"Nabi!"

She runs toward me, and at first, I think she is
scared. I kneel to meet her, but as she nears, I begin to
see her expression is not fear, but regret.

"I'm sorry," she says. "Theia says you must dream. Now."

She draws forth her thumb, which is smudged with some kind of bright red powder, and presses it into my forehead.

Then, everything goes dark.

Exhaustion comes over me like a thick curtain almost as soon as I settle onto the ground. Haven fades away, replaced by the familiar, terrible darkness of the dream.

***

I am huddled on the ground. I always am. I push to my feet as quickly as I can. The scratching is still there, persistent and even closer than before. But I do not fear it now.

I trace my steps from last time, heading for the Host. *Perhaps this time I will see Her,* I think. Hope flutters in my chest in a way I have not dared allow in ages.

But before I reach it, a terrible rip echoes through the dark empty sky and shudders through my body, as if this in-between dream world were tearing apart, and tearing me apart with it.

The familiar thudding in my head returns, and my hands quiver, wishing for my blades.

A steady tapping moves closer in the darkness, echoing from all around—footsteps. I turn in slow circles, trying to protect myself from all sides until I find the source—a faint light, growing larger and taking shape as it nears.

At first I welcome it, sure it is a creature of the Host. But as it nears, its form becomes clear. Panic freezes me to the spot where I stand.

It is Kythiel.

It cannot be. It is impossible. Adem took care of Kythiel, and he is gone now.

But gone where? My head rushes. Into the void between the realms. This.

Terror turns me cold from the inside out.

He is getting closer. Too close.

He is mangled almost beyond recognition, more animal than angel. The feathers of his wings are riled and awry, in some spots broken and even missing. The perfect form he held on Terath has withered away, his body shriveled and starved, bones jutting out and exposed tight against his once-perfect flesh.

But worst of all are his eyes. Always lost in chaos, now they are hardly eyes at all. Where there should be irises, whites, focus, there is only a blank darkness.

The only thing that is the same is his aura, more out of place than ever. It forces itself into me, a mismatched peacefulness that is like sunshine in the middle of a terrible storm.

He comes toward me like a vulture, unsteady and hungry.

"It was you? It cannot be you," I say.

"And why not?" He speaks to me as one might to a small child.

"It...it was Theia. She was calling for me."

"Theia? Here? Absurd."

"But, but, but..." My mind trips over the thoughts crashing through my head, and I scramble to catch one. "The Host. I was there."

He grabs my arm and squeezes tight, pulling me in to close the gap between us. His aura bursts within me, flooding out everything else but the terrible blankness of its calm, and the trembling terror that comes with it.

"The Gods are gone. The Host is empty. You want a savior? You're looking at him."

"No."

I try to pull away, but he squeezes tighter, sending a thousand fine lines of pain through my wrist. I give in, afraid he will crush my bones to pieces.

"Where do you think you are going?" he sneers, a grim smile baring his teeth. "There is nowhere to run to here. Only me and you."

My head clouds with fury and fear.

"No, only you. I can leave this place. You cannot."

It is a guess, but a good one, judging from the way the edge of his mouth quivers.

"Go? You are not going anywhere." He shakes me. "You think you can turn against me and go your own way? I gave you my heart and you crushed it. I gave you what no human gets, a second life. And now you owe it to me."

I take in a breath to retort, not sure what words, what thoughts, I will catch next from the torrent inside me to throw at him —

***

And then I am flung from the dream and awaken with a sharp gasp.

Darkness is replaced with bursting light. The vacuum by a gentle breeze. My arm is free, and a gentle hand presses into my shoulder.

I shake my head and look around to gain my bearings.

It is Adem. The sun is up, and all the people of

Haven fill its center. Past the crowd, between the huts, Nabi watches me.

My heart pounds, my entire body on full alarm. Cold sweat films my face and palms.

Adem studies me and frowns. "Are you all right?" he asks.

"I..." The memory of the dream is loud in my mind. My wrist throbs, and I look down to see four finger-shaped bruises already forming on my skin.

The realization washes over me in slow motion, like watching yourself fall.

It was real. I finally got to the terrible truth. I thought I had it before, but I was fooling myself.

Kythiel. He's back, I want to scream.

I had it all wrong, and now he has finally broken into my mind.

Again.

But the words are trapped in my head and will not come out.

It wasn't Theia at all. A most terrible mistake. A horrifying one. How could I get so confused? How could I be so naive and stupid? Why would Theia come to me, now, after all that I have done? Of course She wouldn't.

"Of course," I stutter.

Adem stands there a moment more, studying me, but I hold his gaze as steadily as I can, and he lets it go.

"It is time," he says.

CHAPTER 28

It is time.

The threat of Kythiel is still loud and loose in my mind, and it takes me a moment to remember for what.

But of course...Haven, Jordan, the village. We have to set things right.

Things will never be right. Not while Kythiel is out there.

But I cannot deal with that now. With the war rising, this is too important.

The Gods—I can't hear them at all. I can't do anything to help Jordan. My stomach twists.

And then I realize something else, and my stomach drops completely, the Gods aren't in the Host. If they have retreated even from their home, where are they?

I stand and shake, trying to break free of the gripping fear wrapping around me.

Adem is still watching me.

"Great. Yes. I'm ready."

He nods, and gestures for me to lead the way. I walk

past him toward where Jordan stands in the middle of the crowd, Avi and Helda on the ground in front of him. I try to force everything else away. At least for now. This is too important.

The village has gotten so big—bigger than when we left, and not only because of the new people from Ir-Nearch. Where have they all come from? They crowd around the village center and back in between the huts. Some standing near the back lift others onto their shoulders for a better look. Buzzing and curious, they stare at Avi and Helda bound on the ground.

No one speaks for them.

Jordan steps forward.

"I know you have a lot of questions. And I know many of you have doubts. It is okay to doubt. It is okay to fear. But when we have lost our ability to speak to each other, when we resort to violence and just destroy, just take, that is a whole different thing. That is going back to the hateful, fearful lives we have all chosen to leave behind in the dust of the wasteland. And we do not live like that here. We have chosen a better path."

Jordan looks down at Avi and Helda. He frees his sword. An anxious murmur churns through the crowd. Jordan pauses, letting the tension grow.

"Now. We have ways in which we deal with traitors here, as do all societies. Betraying your village is a very grave offense. But we cannot cast these two into the wastelands now—for that is where our enemies are. What would become of us if our enemies find our other enemies, and work together against us?"

He pauses and looks around, letting the thought digest.

"So we must find other ways."

He raises his sword for all to see, and then pulls Avi to his knees and holds the blade to Avi's neck. Avi holds his head high and proud, refusing to show fear, though his cheeks burn a vicious red. In this moment, I have to admit, I hold grudging respect for him — at least he owns what he has done, and faces the consequences bravely. Helda too, is stony-faced next to him, though she does not seem to be able to look to her lover and ally, and instead holds her hardened stare straight ahead.

The people begin to shout. No, they begin to cheer.

They have turned from people into a mob, angry and eager. Eyes bloodshot, faces twisted with rage.

A thick haze of fear closes in around me like clouds on an overcast day. Haven has always been a village of warriors, but the heart of this place has always been still. Always peaceful. I did not think these people had it in them to contain such hatred.

Kill them. Kill. They really want him to do it.

I want him to do it.

My blood runs hot with hate and my body is hungry for action. All that we have done to fight against this terrible growing thing slithering out of the Underworld, and it only gets worse. And then we come back to betrayal and a village divided.

They do. They deserve to die. Send them to the Underworld, my mind urges. It's where their side of this war is anyway.

Jordan moves back the sword as if to swing it. Avi closes his eyes. Behind them stands Lena, a pale face frozen like stone amidst a sea of red, heated anger.

Jordan speaks, "Is this what you would have me do? Would you have me turn betrayal into murder? Two murders?" he gestures to Helda.

Even as I want to join them, the people's cheers turn my stomach. I would never have guessed that the peaceful people of Haven could be so vengeful and bloodthirsty. Jordan is right; this is not about politics. This is about fear.

Jordan raises the sword, then casts it to the ground and stomps on it. "I will not. I refuse to add to this cycle of poison."

The people shout.

Some are outraged. Some are cheering. My heart pounds, hardly knowing whether I am relieved or incensed.

"Enough!" he calls sharply over the anger. The shouts drop away. "I hear you. I know that these restless times have left you hungry. Fear is staving us, and we crave action. But action must be driven by thought. By understanding. And this is what we will fight for today. There are no exercises this morning. Instead, you will listen to us speak. And if you wish, you will speak yourself. But we start with these two."

He points to Avi and Helda.

"Stand up, Avi. Helda," he orders. "Speak for yourselves."

Jordan cuts them free of their bindings. The village is silent and completely still, waiting to hear what they have to say. Even the sea breeze, ever-present in Haven, holds its breath.

Avi and Helda look to each other and stand up. The demand that they defend themselves not with swords,

but with words, has them at a loss. Jordan was right.
They have been stripped of their momentary power.
Helda looks so thrown that I wonder if she would have
preferred to face death—at least this she would
understand.

Avi nods to her, and stands, scanning over each
person in the crowd, disbelieving they would all go
against him so easily.

"These are dark times. We all know this," he starts.
He does not have his adopted brother's presence. His
voice starts soft and quivering, his tone pleading. "I am
scared. Gods, we all should be. And I refuse to stand by
while someone who is supposed to lead us, to protect
us, invites strange creatures to live among us,
disappears for fortnights and refuses to lift his sword in
our defense."

Avi whips around and gestures to Jordan's blade,
already back in its sheath. I can feel the warmth rise
over my cheeks as I blush, embarrassed for him.

"We need someone ready to react to these troubled
times. Someone willing to do anything to protect us.
Isn't that what you want? Isn't it? Don't tell me you
stood by and let us take over out of fear of what *we*
would do. Every man and woman here is a warrior. I
have heard the whisperings that have been passing
through this village since the battle that played out on
our shore a few terrible weeks ago. You are afraid, but
not of me."

My heart races at the reference to Adem's fight with
Kythiel. *It didn't even work,* I want to scream. *He is still
out there, waiting to hunt me.*

Avi is gaining confidence now, force building

behind his voice like the gusts of a rising storm.

"And you should be afraid. Anyone with their eyes open in these times will be full of fear. We need someone willing to protect us to lead. Isn't that what you want? Isn't it? We may not have fought a battle with our own hands yet, but we are already in a war. All that is left to do now is to keep as many of us alive as we can for as long as we can."

He is shouting now, though at what, or who, is unclear. At Jordan? The people? The Gods?

"This is no game for boys, and this is no time for us to choose leaders by how well they speak. Words will not help us now. You have grown up on the stories of the First and Second Realm Wars, same as me, and you know their horrors. Where will his charm get us when we are up against an army of angels and demons and sprites? Are you willing to die for that, for the idea of a ruler who is your friend? He will not mean to, but he will lead you to your end if you let him, in the name of what is noble. And why would you follow him? Because he is a friend? Because he says he can hear the Gods? If that is true, let him prove it to us."

At this, I look to Jordan to gauge his reaction. He manages to keep himself still, the only sign of anything wrong a quick glance toward the ground, but then he is back again. Maybe he can uphold this illusion better than I thought.

Avi steps back, having said his piece. Helda comes forward.

I cringe. What more is there to say?

"We know what we have done is ugly," she begins. "We know this is not what many of you would want.

But that is exactly why we needed to do it. We can make the hard choices, the bitter choices that war requires. And war demands many of these. We are willing to let war turn *us* into villains, so that *your* conscience will let you sleep when this has passed. Will this naive, young boy do that for you?"

She steps closer to the people, emboldened by their silence.

"We are not made of prophecy and mystics and smoke, like the Gods are. We are flesh and blood. When we fight, we put our lives on the line. Why would we sacrifice our lives for the Them? What have They done for us? They have done plenty for this boy." She gestures to Jordan. "It is easy to understand why this blessed child, who escaped the dictators young, who never had to fight himself, would chose to stand behind them. But the rest of us? Those of us from Ir-Nearch, we have seen things, and we have done things. We have suffered. And what did the Gods do while we suffered?"

A lump swells in my throat. I underestimated Avi and Helda. They make some compelling arguments. But Jordan still appears calm, at least on the outside. What is he thinking? I would give anything to know.

"They did nothing," Helda continues. "And now you want me to fight for them, when they have not once fought for me? I say no. I say let us find a better way than the Order they have pushed onto us. The tides are changing, a war is here, and we all have the power to choose, to help shape our futures through it."

Helda steps out of the center, back to Avi's side. A silence sets in as their words settle over us. Some of what they said was painfully true. What *have* the Gods done for me? They were quick to abandon me at my first mistake, and have done nothing for me since. Even now, with Kythiel hunting me in my sleep, the Gods have not only watched idly. They have left altogether.

Anger rises around my heart. It feels good, it feels strong.

I am not the only one who feels it.

The people are murmuring to each other, fists clenched, brows pulled low. They are heated, seething, edging to fight.

"I know you are scared." Jordan's voice rings out over the murmurs, and the voices die down. "I'm not going to lie—these are troubled times, and there are good reasons to be scared. I am scared too. But we cannot be ruled by fear. That is how dictators gain power, the kind that so many of us have fled." He takes a breath, gives his words a moment to sink in. "I do not claim to be a solution. I do not claim to be chosen, or to know anything special that you do not. I never have. You know me. Each and every one of you. I have looked you in the eye and made you promises. We have traded jokes. We have prayed for each other. And you know I would never lead you into the wrong battle. I would never put you at risk for anything that was not worth putting my very own soul on the line for."

He moves from the center and paces the edge of the crowd, carefully looking each of them in the eye.

"It is easy to let fear choose for us. It is easy to close in and hide from the terrible things happening around us, to say that we have no part in it, to join the side that seems bigger and safer. We want to make the choice that seems will best protect us, individually."

He purses his lips, pausing to let the words settle over the crowd.

"What is hard? Choosing for ourselves. Choosing what is right over what feels safe. But this is what we do in Haven. We have chosen this already. We chose it generations ago when the first hut was built in this village, and we choose it again every single day when we rise, pray to the Gods, and train for a war we cannot yet see."

He continues to walk among them as he talks, touching shoulders here, the heads of children there.

"I cannot take away your fear. All I can do is try to follow the advice I have given you. I must stop allowing my fear to rule me, and make the better choice instead."

Jordan heads back to the center, and turns until he finds me. He holds my gaze for a pause, his brows folded with repentance.

"I must confess something to you, my friends."

What is he... *oh no.*

"I did, once upon a time, hear the Gods. They whispered to me from the leaves of the trees and the stones on the ground, they urged me with each wave of the ocean, and through others here in this very village. They were close to me, and I could see them everywhere, because they showed themselves to me."

Don't you dare do it, Jordan.

I want to cry out, throw something, anything to stop him, but it is like I have been frozen where I stand. I try to will him to look back at me, try to somehow throw my anger into his being, but he won't turn back. He keeps going.

"But they do not anymore."

Too late I find my breath, and there is no point anymore. The crowd begins to shift and whisper again, restless and uneasy.

"I do not know why it changed. But I know the Gods are still here, still among us. If there was one thing I learned from hearing them, it is that they are part of this realm the way breathing is a part of us—inextricably."

Gods, Jordan, it is too late for that. People are listening, but their eyes are wide with fear.

"I have also learned from the Gods to listen to what is around me. And I have listened today. Perhaps, with all that has passed, it is time for new leadership in this village."

A thick rage pulses through me, pulling me into its unstoppable current like an undertow.

He can't. He *can't* turn power over to Avi and Helda. Not with how they went about it.

A strange rushing sound fills my ears, and before I can think, my arms are pushing people out of my way and my legs are taking me toward him. I have to stop him, and I no longer care how.

"And that is why I am stepping down and handing my power over to Rona."

I burst through the crowd, tumble into the open space, and stumble to an abrupt halt. What did he just say?

Jordan's announcement is met with stunned silence. Heat builds in my fingertips and behind my ears, rushes over my face.

He goes on. "I know she is new to you, and many of you may not even know her by name. But she has seen these wars before. She knows the signs to look for, what to expect as the barriers between the realms break down."

This much is true. I know the terror that lies ahead.

I know how unprepared I am to face them again.

"Time and again she has demonstrated a willingness to make the hard choice. The ones that stare fear in the face, and then forge on anyway."

Seeing that I am frozen, he comes to me, and takes my hand between his own. Even as he approaches me, even as he holds my hand in his, he does not look me in the eyes.

My fist tingles. I could slug him across the face, I am so filled with rage. But I know I cannot, not with so much at stake in this moment.

Maybe later.

"And," he says, "if we are going to fight for the Gods, you deserve a leader who can hear them and share their messages for us. Rona is that leader."

Oh Gods, oh Gods, oh Gods. I have to stop this madness. I have to tell him.

Except that, now, I can't.

The rage cascades through me in ripples, fighting with all it has against the cage Jordan has put me in. I let it burn away at me from the inside out, and do nothing.

Because someone has to take on the burden of this. Someone has to be willing to bite her tongue and let the lie stand. One of us has to let these people believe we can hear the Gods, and Jordan took a pass. There is no one else left to pass it to.

"A council will advise her. It will include the leaders from our cities, both governing and religious. It will include me. And it will include Helda and Avi."

Jordan's voice feels far away, even as he stands at my side. It is as though I will float away, and his hold on my hand is the only thing keeping me here.

"That is all for now. There is still a lot to figure out. We will have more for you this evening. For now, go in peace. After our midday meal, the normal schedule will resume. Rona will have words for you when the day is done."

My mind whirls. My heart races so fast I can feel its pulsing through my chest.

I have a few choice words for Jordan already.

CHAPTER 29

The crowd disperses.

I wait until the last of them is gone, and then I yank my hand away from Jordan and shove him.

"Are you out of your mind?" I hiss.

He finds his footing. "Look, Rona. I know you're —"

I shove him again.

"What? You know I'm *what*, Jordan?"

He steadies himself, this time throwing his arms out to guard from my next move.

"I know you're angry."

"*Angry?*" The word is too small. "I am furious. I am…"

But no word seems big enough for the churning chaos inside me.

Adem is the first to reach us. He puts a steadying hand on my shoulder, whether it is to comfort me or to protect Jordan, I do not know.

"What is wrong with you? I can't be responsible for these people. I am no leader."

"Not a leader?" Jordan lowers his guard. "Of course you are. At every turn of all this, you have had an answer. You have what we need next. And at every turn, you have had the resolve to see it through. You don't choose what's safe. You don't choose what's easy. You choose what needs to be done. And then you go do it. Rona, you already have been leading us, out there in the wasteland. And your judgment has been right every time."

I can feel Calipher's aura edging into me, blurring my thoughts, before he comes up from behind me. I fight to stay focused.

"No, you don't understand. I am not what you think I am."

The truth hurts all the more, knowing what he thinks he sees in me. How do I tell them?

"No, you're not what *you* think you are," Jordan says, fighting back. "That girl from the Beginning, in your first life? You're not that girl anymore."

"But—"

"It doesn't matter," Calipher says. "It is done now. These people cannot handle any more instability. Not in wartime."

"Stop!" It comes out loud and high-pitched. "You don't understand. I am not what you think I am. I don't have any special connection to the Gods."

Jordan laughs. "What? Of course you do." He isn't listening. "You said—"

"I know what I said," I reply. "I was wrong."

I tell them about Nabi and what happened in my dream, watching their expressions melt from eagerness to dread. Jordan frowns and shakes his head, rejecting what I say before I am even done.

Usually I would hate to shatter Jordan like this — he is so young and hopeful — but right now I am furious, and he needs to know. The darker side of me feels warm with vengeance to crush him with the truth he did not save room for in his secret plan.

"Kythiel?" Jordan is puzzled. "But no, Rona, you're confused. It can't be."

Why does someone always tell me I am wrong when I tell them something they don't want to hear?

"I'm not confused. I was confused before. Or maybe I didn't want to admit the truth. But it was him all along. Trying to break back into my dreams. And he finally found a way in. I didn't have a chance to tell you."

"But we destroyed him," Adem says.

Jordan nods. "All that was left was his robes and a pile of ashes."

I shake my head. It all feels so empty, so meaningless. "You're forgetting that angels aren't corporeal."

"Our true being is all soul," Calipher adds. "The bodies we take on in Terath, they are like a robe we put on to fit into this realm."

"I told you then, he was still out there in some form, somewhere. I just thought we were through with him."

Jordan nods thoughtfully as I speak, his eyes drifting off to somewhere far away. He keeps nodding after I stop, as if caught in a cycle of thought he cannot escape.

"Jordan?"

He jolts out of it, and forces his expression into a small smile. "It will be okay. We will help you lead; you are not in this alone. And we will find a way to end Kythiel for good."

"No, you are not listening. It will not be okay. It is already not okay. He is out there, and he has access to my mind. I have no idea what to do about it, and eventually, I will have to sleep again. And now, on top of that, you want me to lead your people for you?"

Jordan's eyes plead with me. "I couldn't do it, Rona. I couldn't lie to them."

My heart starts to melt, feeling for him, but then the anger churns again, and I harden against him again.

"So you want me to lie to them instead. You want me to do the thing you could not. Do your dirty work, so you can go on being pure and beloved."

He hangs his head, brilliant red curls shaking into his eyes. "You're better at it than me," he mutters.

This much is true.

"I am going to need help."

"We will give it to you!" Jordan cries. "Whatever you need."

I wrap my arms around myself, and stare at the sea. The shore is dotted with tents of those who have come here from sister cities for protection against whatever is out there. Someone has to do the protecting.

So I guess this is what happens next. Me, responsible for all of these people. A girl who made such bad decisions for herself that the only way out was to send herself into the Underworld.

The rage simmers to a determined resolve, hard like ice.

"What now?" Calipher prompts, breaking the quiet.

And it is as if the answer were already there, waiting

for me.

"Jordan, you are leading my army. Get them ready."

"Right away," he says. "Ready for what?"

"War," I say. "We head back into the wasteland at dawn. All of us who can fight."

"Wait," Jordan stutters. "But—"

"We can't wait for them to come to us, Jordan. We have to get to Koreh first."

CHAPTER 30

Jordan and Calipher stare at me.

"We know Koreh will come for us. She already has," I urge. "We can't let the rebel First Creatures choose when they get to fight us. Abazel and the others already have too many advantages in this battle. We have to get to Koreh first. Before she is ready for it."

I stare back at them, watching their expressions shift as they consider.

"She's right." The words are rough like grating rocks—Adem. I turn around, and there he is, just behind me.

"I know." Jordan frowns. "I guess we need to hold our first council."

"Then round them up," I say. "But I will get Avi and Helda."

"I'll go with you," Adem says.

He flexes his fists, and I know what he is thinking. Gods only know how angry they still are. Or what they might do about it. It's the very reason I need to be the one to find them. But all the same, they have already tried one wild, desperate thing.

I nod, and head off to their hut, Adem on my heels like a guard dog.

My face flushes with heat as I tap at the door. Helda answers, half-dressed and hair in wild tangles over her chest. She doesn't smile. But she doesn't frown.

"We were just burning you off," she says.

"Well," I hold my expression stoic, remembering her penchant for shock, "you'll have to finish later. We have blood to spill, and we need the council to finalize the plans."

Avi peers from the door behind her, naked except for a blanket around his waist. He looks past me to size up Adem, then drifts over the blades in my belt.

"But first, let's get some things straight."

Pointlessly, I wonder if this is just sex for them, or if they actually love each other, whether they have been keeping this quiet for a long time, like Jordan and Xamson, or if they only found each other when Helda brought her people to Haven.

"You lost," I continue. From the corner of my eye I can see Adem inching closer to me. "Jordan may want to forget and move on, and I will honor that as long as you allow me. But do not mistake this as weakness. Try anything like that again, and I will kill you. I do not have your brother's capacity for kindness."

Avi leans forward, baring his teeth in a grimace. "Who do you think we are? Have we not shown yet that we will do anything for these people? Even stay and fight."

"We will be there," Helda says.

She closes the door on us.

I turn and sit on one of the logs around the main fire pit, Adem on my tail, and wait.

Jordan returns with the others—two I do not recognize, but who must be the leaders of Haven's sister cities to the south. One is a man with a bald dark head and a full white beard. The other is a woman with short blond curls that spring every which way from her head.

"Rona," Jordan says. "Meet your new advisors."

Avi and Helda's door opens again, and this time they emerge, fully dressed and in battle gear. I do not know if Helda knows any other way to dress.

I tell the council all we have seen on our journey, all that has happened. I tell them we must go fight.

"But tomorrow?" the man says, tugging at his beard. "How will we prepare that quickly? How will we have enough food ready?"

"Leave that to me," Calipher says. Is he part of the council? Or has he simply continued to follow us? Either way, he has powers we need on our side, so I push aside the anxiety he stirs in me. "All we need is a small portion of fish and water. There is a charm that will allow it to feed any crowd."

Suddenly, I understand how we managed to keep enough rations for the long trip back from the helmuth. Calipher is even more useful than I realized.

"We already have all the weapons we will need," Jordan adds.

"Wait." Helda brings the momentum to a halt with her command. "What of our enemy? Those soldiers that struck down upon Ir-Nearch were not human. And rumor is that there was a woman there with even greater power. Do we have the weapons necessary to fight this kind of enemy?"

I bite my lip and heat rushes over my face. It is an important question, and one I am not prepared to answer.

Jordan jumps in, offering a quick explanation of what we learned of Koreh, the necklace, and their powers to lure men in.

The council pauses, some frowning and looking to the others. Helda's frown seems to curl at the edges with smugness.

Something small pushes past me into the center of our meeting—Nabi, who seems to ever be at my side when my answers run dry. She drops to the ground and draws in the dirt.

"This," she says, stepping away to show us. It is a dot, bounded in a triangle, encompassed in a simple curving wave—seed, shield, and fire, the symbols of the Three. "This will protect them. It must go on the shields."

After that, convincing the council is easy. It seems Nabi's abilities are known throughout all of Haven's network. All that is left is to tell the people. As Jordan promised, after dinner, we gather so I can address them. They watch me with wide eyes, murmuring to each other and waiting to make their judgments.

I stand next to Jordan, my palms sweating.

"Go on," he says. He smiles.

I nod and step onto the log. The buzz of conversation dies, and they all watch me, curious and eager to hear what this new leader, unknown to most of them, has to say.

I stare at them, my mind blank. I know I have to say something. I have to explain what we are doing and why. I have to make them understand why this matters.

Avi and Helda are not the only ones here who would rather fight with the Firsts. I am sure of it. But all I feel is empty and tired. And scared. Put a blade in my hand and place me on the front lines any day. But this? I look out at them all, trying to find the right words within me, the ones that will win them to my side.

Gods, this is why Jordan was leading these people. This is why I never do this.

They're all watching me like I have the answers they need, like I have everything. If only they knew I cannot even face sleep—and why—let alone whatever lies ahead of us out there.

But here we are. These people need a leader to talk to them. And I am the one in front of them. So I'd better start talking.

"We have seen what is out there," I say. "And I am not going to lie to you. There are fearsome things in the abyss, and they are becoming more fearsome every day."

I do not have to look to Jordan to know he will think this is a terrible place to start. I swallow, searching frantically through my mind for something better. My heart pounds in my ears and it is impossible to hear my own thoughts over its thick rhythm.

"The rebels are out there. And they are building an army. I have seen this with my own eyes. They are stealing to get their soldiers, from the dead and from our very own, fighting against their will, in a trance, so that the cowardly Firsts don't have to put themselves on the line."

Something shifts in the air. The quiet turns tense.

"And it is worse than that. They have opened a helmuth. They are releasing creatures of the Underworld into this realm—*our* realm. Are we going to sit here and let these monsters overrun our Terath? This realm was bestowed upon us by the Gods at the Beginning of time. The Firsts were never more than guests in this realm."

My eyes drift to Calipher and a knot twists in my gut.

"These rebels have already encroached on us enough. It is well past time that we sent them back where they belong."

An energy builds over the people, and I take it in. My pulse shifts to a new pace, excited and hungry, feeding off of them. It is a buzz I have never known before. I can feel each of them, and they are excited. They are angry. They are ready for a fight.

The only question is, do they have something worth fighting for?

"I know the Gods have done little to instill loyalty in any of you. Maybe you are even angry at them. And maybe you should be. The Gods have left you in a deserted wasteland of a realm, and they have done nothing to help heal it. As the war beings, it will only get worse. Storms will grow stronger, torrents will tear up the ground, and waters will flood past the shore. I have seen this before."

The crowd is turning from still to restless, shifting and kicking at the sand.

"But I have also seen all this realm can be. I was

there in its earliest days, when the Gods, the Firsts, all of humanity came together in harmony, before everything became so broken. And I believe that we can have that harmony again."

I am not sure where I am going with this. I am not sure I even believe what I am saying. But the people, *they* seem to believe, so I will myself to believe it too, because I have to.

"But we won't get it the way we did before. Those times have passed. So you want something to fight for? I'm not going to tell you to do this for the Gods. The Gods have abandoned you. The Gods should be begging for your forgiveness."

Cheers from the crowd. An excited buzz rolls over me. It's working. I can hardly believe it, but this is no time to stop.

"Instead, fight for this. Fight for your children. Fight for your lovers. Fight for your parents. Fight for what should have been — so we can make it what *is* again."

Some of them are beginning to cheer now, and it sends a thrill quivering up my spine.

"Fight for yourself, for what your life should have been instead of this scene from a nightmare, fight for the basic humanity every ruler you fled from should have provided and didn't. Fight for the lives you should have had, if the Gods had been here."

The cheers rise again, stronger this time. They're all cheering. Except Jordan. Right in front, he does not jump and light up like the others. He frowns, arms folded, shaking his head at me.

A pang of guilt tugs at my core. But then I remember, Jordan is not in charge anymore.

I'm in charge, and we're doing things my way. And it's working.

"We are not pawns for the Gods and Firsts to play around with as they please. We do not enter this war taking one side or the other. We come to this in our own right, for our own gain."

They want more. I can feel the crowd's hunger boiling in my veins. I take it farther.

"We will banish these rebels from this realm, and then the Gods will come back. And when they do, we are going to have some demands ready for them. We will start a renewed agreement to protect our realm. We are going to make things right again — better, even."

They cheer and whoop, clap their hands.

I do not look to Jordan.

"But first," I call over the cacophony. "But first, we must go into that damned wasteland and send these rogue Firsts back to the Underworld where they belong. First, we have to close the helmuth. I'm not going to lie. It won't be the end of this. This war will be long and hard. But it will be a damn fine start."

I let the crisp tension build, scanning over the crowd.

"Are you with me?"

"Yes!" The cheers burst free, a rolling roar rising over them like a cloud.

"Are you with me?"

"Yes, yes!" The roar builds, curling into itself and becoming its own beast.

"Whose realm is this?" I shout.

"Ours, ours!"

I let the people cheer themselves out, fueling from

each other until they finally begin to settle.

I hold out my hand and the sound dies down.

"Then," I say, my voice shaky with excitement, "we leave at sunrise."

I step down from the log amidst a final wave of cheers. Then the crowd begins to break away and they being their preparations, packing and sharpening their weaponry.

Jordan marches to me and grabs my arm.

"What exactly do you think you're doing?"

I tug away from his grip. "Leading."

"This isn't leading! Leading is offering the inspiration to do what must be done, for the greater good. *This* was... it was making up what you think people want to hear, so they'll do what you want."

His eyes are wide, and their orange flecks burn, reflecting back the setting sun at me.

"Quiet!" I order. The others will hear him. "If you want to discuss this, I will hear you. But not out here. I will not have you spreading dissension all over again."

"Where, then?"

"In my quarters."

He gestures, and I lead the way. Once the door has closed behind us, he lets loose.

"Just what do you think you are doing?"

"I'm getting your people ready to do what must be done," I snap back.

"You mean you're lying." His eyes are wide and sad with boyish betrayal.

"No. I am not *lying*." I fold my arms and stare at him. "I am saying what should happen. What I intend to try to do."

"You can't do that. They're all depending on you. They trust you," Jordan cries, his hands tugging at his hair. "You can't just say what you think *should* happen, when you know that it won't."

My heart hardens with resentment and resolve.

"I *do not* know that."

"Rona," he sighs. "Come on. You're going to look me in the eye and tell me you really think you are going to renegotiate terms between man and the Gods? You think they will just hand over an entire realm to you?"

"And why not?"

Tiny twitches of muscle quiver over his face, threatening to break him. I press my lips together and wait for it.

But he suppresses whatever emotion is fighting to get free, flattening out all expression from his face, his eyes hardening.

"I was wrong," he says. "You are no leader at all."

My fists clench, and rage gathers in a tight ball in my jaw.

"Enough. You are the one who put me in this position. You did not ask if I could do it. You did not ask if I wanted it. You just shoved your mess onto me. And here I am, doing it, managing to unite your people in a way you could not, and you are telling me I am doing it *wrong*?" I step closer, so that we are inches apart, and spit the words right into his face. "No. I am in charge now, and just because you put me in this precarious position does not mean you get to dictate terms. I will do as I see fit, and you will obey like the rest of them."

Silence swells between us. Jordan steps back, toward

the door. He takes in a breath and opens his mouth as if to say more, but I cut him off.

"Go," I order. "Get our soldiers prepared for morning."

He nods, his head drooping low onto his chest, and does as I say.

I slam the door behind him so hard the entire wall shudders.

CHAPTER 31

A BURNING RESENTMENT fueled me through my argument with Jordan.

But now that he is gone, I keep hearing his words over and over.

I did what I had to do. But was it the right thing? I truly do not know. But what could I have done instead? Perhaps there is no right thing left anymore. Maybe all the choices are wrong.

Either way, my mind will not stop cycling through it all, questioning what I told them, echoing the horrible words I threw at him. My feet will not stop pacing from wall to wall and back again. All the old feelings I used to feel in here—caged, crowded, trapped—start to come back.

I cannot stay here and keep questioning myself; it is too late for that. And I cannot go to sleep. Not until I can figure out what to do about Kythiel.

I have to get out.

So I do.

It has been dark for hours, but outside, the fire is still bright and roaring, and the people are awake and busy, transforming themselves into an army. The sharp night air is full of sparks, the clanking of sharpening blades and the lugging of equipment.

The air is crisp and smells of smoke.

I keep to the shadows, preferring to be by myself. My feet lead me out of the village and down to the water.

Oh, how I missed the water.

Out in the wasteland the horizon was dry and empty, and my soul was constantly parched, constantly aching for something more, something healing.

The shore offers endless water. Endless peace.

I must be in it, despite the air's damp coolness.

I undo my robe and drop it to the ground, not caring for the gritty sand that will catch in it later, and walk right into the waves.

The water's chill shocks my skin, makes me feel alive again, drives away all thoughts except for the moment. The cold shivers over me and washes it all away, at least for a little bit. As it reaches my waist I stop walking and lean back into the sea's rhythm, letting it close around me, over me.

Just like the last time I came to it.

Except it is not the same. The sea has not changed. But I have. Every sway of the water reminds me of all that has happened, each decision whittling away and shaping me into something new.

I've lost the force that came back from the Underworld with me and pulled me back to life. But I am stronger without it. More focused. More in control. I belong to this world now, even if I still can't bring myself to love it.

I lie and float. Take in the cold, take in the pull of the waves and the stillness of the stars. Despite all that has happened to this realm, the stars are still perfect. Looking at them is almost like being in the Beginning again, almost like nothing was ever broken. Though somehow the stars seem farther away than I remember.

I close my eyes and let the whoosh of water in my ears fill my mind.

When I open them again, there is something large hovering over me.

"Adem."

I open my eyes and stand upright. There he is, standing on the shore, waves rolling around his feet.

"Your speech tonight," he says. His tone is inquisitive.

"Yes, well." A breeze blows and goose bumps rise over my exposed shoulders. I sink them back into the water for warmth. "That is what they needed."

Adem purses his lips. "And that's on you? To provide what these people need?"

I look to the twisting reflections of the stars on the water.

"Seems like it is."

Adem nods. He fidgets, the way he does sometimes when his thoughts make him too anxious, wringing his hands around each other.

I wait. Allow him the time to find the words.

"I am older than old. I watched the rise and fall of the last of these wars, and all that has happened in between. And now..."

He sighs. People call to each other in the village. The breeze rustles. Waves rise and fall. The moon shifts.

He does not go on, lost somewhere in his tangled thoughts.

"Why are you telling me this?" I prompt.

He blinks and pulls back, drawing again to this place, this time.

"I do not know. Something is different," he says. "Something that matters."

He looks around, as if he will find what it is before him.

"I feel different," I say.

His focus comes back to me again. He tilts his head. "Different how?"

"It is as though my mind has been blown open. Like a door was kicked down."

His brows pull low. "Open to what?"

"I do not know. That is what scares me. Just..." I don't know what to say.

It's only that my unhinged former lover is caught between the realms and has broken into my mind.

I am so on edge I could burst. I cannot keep carrying this around alone like I did last time. I know this much. Maybe letting Adem carry some of the burden will help.

"Kythiel. The angel I used to..." I can't bring myself to say it. Adem's shoulders rise as he tenses in response to his name. "He can reach me in my dreams again."

It occurs to me that if anyone can understand the depths to which I have messed this up, it is Adem. He is has made disastrous choices of the same scale.

The night swells between us. Waves roll. Crickets chirp up to the sky. Adem stares at the stars. I can feel my lip quivering like it does when I am about to cry. I bite it to make it stop.

"I don't know what to do," I whisper.

A pause swells between us. Adem studies me. The panic creeps from my chest into my limbs.

"I can't go to sleep. Not until I can figure out a way to defend myself in there."

"Humans need sleep. You need to sleep."

"I've gone without it before." I don't want to talk about the details of how it was last time, when Kythiel went mad, how close I came to losing my mind, trying to avoid him. "This sleep is no kind of rest, anyway, with these dreams."

How far will I go this time? The answer comes deep from within my bones. *As far as I have to.* There is simply no other choice.

"But I don't know what to do about the rest of it. These people—we're leading them into a war. Not even a war against other humans, a war against the supernatural. They're all trusting me, just because Jordan said they could."

Suddenly the tug and flow of the waves is too much, like I will be swallowed into the tide. I stop floating and rise again.

"And they can't. I can't even recognize my own enemies inside my head. How can I lead them against the enemies all around us?"

Adem growls, and at first I think he is agreeing with me. But then he balls his hands into fists and turns around toward the bluff. A chill prickles over my shoulders, and I brace for a fight.

But then, he slowly forces his muscles to relax. He

calls to the dark. "Might as well join us."

And then, in a blink, Calipher appears beyond the sand. "I did not want to disturb you," he says.

Adem responds with a guttural sound.

"How long have you been there?" I demand.

"Not long," he says, stepping up to the waves. He tilts his head, and I realize he is studying me. Looking me over.

"What are you doing?" I ask.

He keeps staring for another moment before answering. "What do you mean when you say you feel *open*?"

I don't know how to explain it. "Why?"

"It's like I could reach right into you, if I were to find the right place among the planes."

Adem shifts, inserting himself just a little more between the angel and me.

Tension tightens my shoulders. "I don't like the sound of that."

Calipher frowns, and his wings spread slightly from tension, ruffled so that each feather stands alone. He leans in and frowns, seeing something around me I cannot.

"I have never seen anything like it," he says.

"What is it?" I demand. I try to choke back my fear, but the words come out broken anyway.

"Let me show you."

It is not Calipher who answers. It is a higher voice, light and sweet. We both turn toward it.

It is Nabi.

The one who started all this and made me dig deeper into the dreams. The one who pushed me back to Kythiel and let him finally get to me.

"You!" I exclaim.

Apparently all the people adding burdens to my life are out and wandering tonight. Anger crackles through me like stormy waves bursting against rocks. Before I know it I am on the shore, wrapping my robe around me and stumbling on a mess of angry words.

"Listen closer? *Listen closer?* What were you trying to do, get me killed? Do you enjoy messing with people's heads?"

Her head tilts up to me and her expression wilts. All of a sudden I remember what it was like, being the one bringing people the Gods' messages, never knowing what they meant, and always at the bad end of their anger and frustration when I could not tell them more.

A giant hand drops gently on my shoulder, and I realize Adem is behind me. The anger drowns under a flood of guilt.

"Sorry," I say. My robe is soaking up the water off my skin and sticking to it uncomfortably. "I'm sorry. It's just...what you did. It has put everything wrong. I do not understand. Why would the Gods want me to listen closer to *him?* To *that?*"

I know that she does not understand what I am talking about, and really, she does not need to. She understands that damage was done, and I understand that is it not really her fault. It is the Gods' fault. They gave her that message, and they are the ones who led me astray with their damned puzzle.

Her wild curls blow and bounce in the wind. Her little hands ball into fists, like she is trying to gather up all her courage.

"Draw out the power."

"What?"

She stands tall, emboldened by something within her. "You forgot. *Draw out the power.* The other part of the message."

It is like flint grating against itself, a sudden burst of light within me. She is right—there was more to her message. I forgot.

But...

"What does it mean?"

My voice is harsh. Ever since I was brought back to this realm, there is something new, something terrible at every turn. I am fed up with not understanding. With this feeling that the walls are closing in around me.

Nabi offers a slight smile. "I will show you." She reaches for my hand and waits.

I shut my eyes and think for a moment. Do I want to know anything else from her, from the Gods? It has served me poorly so far. It seems it hardly ever goes well when the Gods try to tell us something. How many times over did I see this when I shared Theia's word with others who had not asked for it?

But...she is offering me help. And I need all the help I can get right now.

"Fine. What do you have to tell me?"

"It is not words this time," she says, prompting again for me to give her my hand.

I give it to her. Then, she reaches for Adem's too.

Nabi takes each of our hands and guides them so that they press together, palm to palm. The touch of his rough hand is calming, and my eyes flit over to his face, hoping to read whether he minds my touch, if he might feel the same way.

Nabi presses her own tiny hands outside of each of ours. She closes her eyes and her eyebrows pull together in strain, a small crease forming between them. Her hair begins to rise around her, though there is no breeze.

And then I feel it. A great stirring. A rush through the open hole at the back of my mind, like a gust of wind billowing through me. A gust full of glowing, humming power.

I gasp and pull my hand away.

I blink and stare at my hand, then to Nabi, then to Adem. He stares back at me, flexing his fingers, his expression echoing my own feelings of utter surprise.

He turns to Nabi, finding words before I can. "What was that?"

There is something quivering behind his words. Is he frightened?

Am I? I hardly know.

"She gave some of your magic to Rona," Calipher cuts in. He steps closer. "I can see it in her."

I know he is right. I can feel Adem's power pulsing under my skin, throbbing and hot. The very earth below my feet is humming with it. I am energized and awake, so awake I could go for days without rest and never feel the strain of exhaustion. Everything feels as though it has fallen into place, and I understand.

"No," Nabi says. "She took it. I only showed her how."

Adem lifts his hand and stares at it. "I felt it. Like a drain, pulling my energy out." He takes a step away, as if I will steal more from him if he stays too close.

"But how?" Calipher asks. "How could it be

possible?"

It's true. I want more. But I am also wary of the want, and what it could mean for me. I know this kind of want. It is addictive and bottomless, and it has run me into the ground before. Following this kind of want is exactly how things with Kythiel spun so far out of control. How much of another being's power could I bear? I don't want to ever find where the breaking point is. I do not know that I could come back from that.

Nabi points to me. "Her mind—it was opened when the angel broke through. She is connected to everything now."

Calipher squints and looks me over. I understand now what he is looking for. I can see the magic in tiny sparks all over him, and I know that he is searching for something similar in me. I glance at my hand and see the magic dancing through me.

When I turn to Adem, he appears completely different through the veil of magic coursing through me. New.

I am used to Adem seeming dull and dusty, shrinking to the background despite his size and power. But now, his presence is alive with sparking light. It is not anything like the steady, full glow of the angels. It is *alive*, dancing through him in lines and flashes. Like lightning bugs, or lightning itself.

"That's what it is," Calipher says. "That is what was different about you."

I nod. The entire world is glowing at the edges, sending humming vibrations my way. It is like I am listening from within an invisible bubble—I hear them, but they seem somehow far away.

"What do I do with it?" I feel as though I could blow the very sea away, if I willed it so.

Nabi shrugs. "That is not for me to say. It is only for me to show you."

"Thank you," I say. I force myself to stop staring at my hands and look at her. Through Adem's power, she looks different too. Her power is beautiful, like a brilliant rainbow of glowing color. But through that, I can still see her as she usually is too — small, young, and wide-eyed.

I am not sure which version of her is the truer one.

"Go," I say to her. "You should be in bed."

"I will walk her back," Calipher says. He is uncomfortable around me too. "Do not leave. Someone must teach you to control this power, since you have it. And I have seen enough from the golem to know it cannot be him. I will return."

I turn to Adem. The way his mouth pulls tight makes me think maybe he is as shaken as I am. Maybe more.

***

I wait.

I stand perfectly still, Adem by my side, taking in the realm. All is strange and altered and new seen through the power now pulsing within me. The stars, the sea, the sand, it all speaks to me. The beads of water seeping from my skin into my robe, trickling down my back from my hair. The shore, sticking in grains between my toes.

It is all too loud and too big. I feel wobbly, like a calf testing its legs for the first time.

It is so big it quiets everything else. Kythiel may be

looming just beyond consciousness, waiting to ambush me as soon as I fall asleep, but I am so filled with boundless energy I cannot imagine ever wanting to sleep again. The Gods may have fled from me, from the realm, but the power I hold feels like enough to fill Their void.

All is still, and the things that prey on me feel far away and irrelevant. The whispers of the universe are telling me to be still, be at peace, and all will be fine in the end. I tilt my head to the sky, close my eyes, and absorb it, giving myself permission to believe it for a little while.

"We're going to start with some simple exercises for control." Calipher's voice bursts the bubble of my meditation. How long have I been standing like this? "What's he still doing here?"

It does not feel long enough. But I force myself to let go and focus. Learning how to manage this power—and before we march into the wasteland this coming morning—is too important.

He's glaring at Adem.

"What do you mean? We share the same magic. Can he not learn too? Do we not need him in the battle?"

"Fine, then." He is completely focused and business-like. We have no time for shock or discomfort, only for preparation and what *is*. "Now do exactly as I do."

He levels face to face with me, leaving Adem to peer in from the side. Then, he stretches out his hand, palm flat and fingers taut, spread wide.

"We will start with what you know. *Aaeros*," he says. At first I do not see any kind of response to his spell.

But he turns his hand over as if presenting something to me. "See?"

I lean in to look closer, and I see that he has called up a single grain of sand.

"Is this really going to help in a battle?"

"Control first. Then power. When you can call up a single grain of sand like this we will move onto bigger things. But great power is more dangerous than it is great if you cannot wield it with precision."

I sigh. I have seen Adem lift full boulders. "But we don't have time—"

"No, we don't." Calipher's words are crisp as the night air. His eyes cloud with the dark wrath only angels can project. "There is no time to argue about this. There is no time to explore what happens when magic is left uncontrolled. If you want my help, you will learn how to wield it the way that I deem fit."

His sharpness bristles under my skin, and the magic hums in response. I want to yell back at him, to shove him. I want to let the pulsing magic burst free and throw it at him.

Uncontrolled magic.

I hold too much power in me now to go on expressing myself in tantrums, like a child. Maybe he's right. Maybe I do need more control. I will myself to hold my tongue, and simply nod.

Then, to show him I mean it, I put my hand out and do my best to imitate the positioning of his hand and the word for the spell. An entire fistful of sand leaps from the ground and high into the air, some of it flying into my face. I turn away, spitting and rubbing at my eyes to get it out.

"You are using too much power." Calipher grabs my hand and poses my fingers, correcting their positioning. "It is not about force or will. It is about precision and focus. Again."

We keep going all through the night. Over and over, this one single spell. By sunrise, I am able to lift a small number of grains and control them enough to hover under my extended hand. It is not perfect yet, but is a great improvement. Adem stands near us, listening and practicing on his own.

The power still throbs and pulls through me, but already I feel more in control. Stronger.

The first hints of light are rising over the wasteland. People are beginning to stir, and the village is fueled with a thirst for battle. We need to join them.

I turn to Adem and Calipher. "Tomorrow night, again," I tell them.

They nod in agreement.

I start to head toward the village. On second thought I stop and turn back to them.

"And this stays between us, at least for now. All of it."

My skin hums with a strange glow, and though I know no one else can see it, I feel strange, still reeling from all I have felt and experienced on this night. The way Kythiel's trespass into my mind has blown it open has made way for power, but it has also left me exposed and vulnerable. And there is no room for vulnerability. Not now, when I am about to lead all of Haven into battle.

Calipher throws a hard cut of laughter. "I cannot imagine breathing word of this to anyone."

CHAPTER 32

THE SUN IS not even fully up, but all of Haven is awake, a writhing bustle of focused energy. Each of us concentrates on the final actions we must complete before we depart, like an arrow taut against the bow and ready to fly.

As morning rises a fog sets in, as if the realm is reading our mood. The thick air sparks with tension.

For a moment, through the bustling soldiers, I see Jordan. He appears to be at ease, his usual calm and smiles, laughing and slapping soldiers on the back as he makes his way through them, making sure they are ready, checking the symbols on each shield painted to copy what Nabi drew for us. The exact opposite of the wild tugging mayhem that wrestles through me, a mix of this strange new power and wild nerves.

He turns, and our eyes find each other for a pause through the crowd, and then in a flash he spins away. It is like a knife twisting in my side.

I have always thought myself to have a warrior's

heart, but I have never truly gone to war. I have never felt this strange mix of dread and hunger before. War is not only the battles; it is the terrible pauses between them. This is the part I did not stick around for last time.

Somewhere deep inside me, below the energy of the morning and the buzz of Calipher's power pulsing through me, nerves trickle like a stream in drought, uneven and unsure. Do I really have what it takes? I am about to find out, and suddenly I am not sure I want to know. Perhaps the idea I have had of myself all these years — tough, wild, bold — is not what I am.

"Eat," a gruff voice urges from my side. Adem.

I turn to him and he holds out a bowl of steaming stew. I take it and spoon some into my mouth. The fish stew is warm and moist, but it might as well be sand. My senses are too overwhelmed to take anything else in.

"I am not hungry," I say.

But I take another big bite anyway, and we stand in quiet while I chew. Adem stands as still and stoic as ever, a true warrior. Does he feel as calm as he looks?

Just then a hut door opens with a creek, and the soldiers fall silent as Helda and Avi emerge. Helda's spear gleams.

The morning bustle stills for a pause. The soldiers all turn to watch what they will do.

Helda takes them all in, and then thrusts her spear into the air with a tight fist.

"Who can rest when there is blood to be had?" she bellows.

The soldiers cheer.

Jordan is quick to build on the energy she ignited, jumping onto one of the logs with a sharp whistle. As he leads them in a series of cries, followed by wild cheers from the soldiers, I sink into the bubble of the power pulsing through me, and it is like I am watching it all unfold from very far away.

Jordan howls. The people go wild, fierce hollers burst from them, spears and bows wave overhead. They are not just a village anymore, not just soldiers. Jordan has transformed them into an army.

But I don't stay to listen to the whole thing. I make my way through the crowd to Helda, and between the army's cheers, I ask her, "Are you always this pleasant after losing, or do you just love the fight that much?"

She turns and sizes me up, folding her arms over her chest, the spear leaning against her.

"I am a warrior first, not a leader. I have no desire to lead if not necessary," she says. "Whatever his intentions, Jordan was misleading us. He has stepped down. Your speech last night...we are satisfied with your terms."

Her words wrench through me. Maybe Jordan was right. Maybe I have taken this too far.

Another wave of cheers bursts over the soldiers.

But what did he expect? I am no leader, either. He put this on me without asking. I am simply digging out of his mess. Someone has to make the hard choices, he wouldn't.

I decide to take what I can.

I nod at Helda, and turn away. Nabi is so close at my heel I almost trip over her.

"What are you doing here?" The children, elderly,

and pregnant are staying behind.

Another cheer rises over the soldiers and Nabi pulls me down to her level. "I'm going with you."

She is not asking, she is simply letting me know.

I glance at Helda. She and Avi are already bellowing with the others again, but I won't take any chances.

"Not here." I take her hand and lead her out of the crowd by the huts.

She waits until I am ready and then insists again, "I'm going with you."

I hesitate. Something in me longs for her to be near, like a security blanket. "Haven't you seen enough adventure already in Ir-Nearch to know it is not adventure at all?"

"No, it's not that," she says. She leans in and half-whispers, "It's the other thing. You're going to need me."

She gestures, mimicking the way she pressed my hand and Adem's together last night, and looks at me with wide, significant eyes.

I snatch her hands and put them back at her sides, looking around to see if anyone is watching, though my mind tells me no one could possibly know enough to understand.

"Okay, okay. I know you're right." I glance ahead to Jordan, who is marching at the lead and does not bother to look back any more. "But stay as hidden as you can. Especially from Jordan. Especially the first day."

After that we'll be too far from Haven for Jordan to do anything about it, even if I can't explain to him why I let her come along.

"And if anyone asks, you snuck away."

If Helda knows what her young citizen can do, Nabi's presence will be a great risk, tipping her off that we still need someone else to reach the Gods for us. But going into battle without her may be an even bigger one.

Already a little of the power she siphoned to me last night is beginning to fade, and for every inch the power gives, exhaustion floods in to fill it. I know this craving, and fear it, but any battle against addiction I may need to face is moot until the real battle is over. I won't be able to keep this up for too long, not without her and Caliper near to help me through it.

Somewhere in the background Jordan's voice rises, fierce and tense. One more great burst of cheers explodes from the army, spears thrust high and armor clanks. Then, the soldiers begin to disperse.

It's time to go.

I sling my pack over my shoulder, check my blades in my belt one last time, and make my way to Jordan's side at the front as we march toward the sunlight, into the wasteland.

CHAPTER 33

IN THE WASTELAND, it doesn't take long for our spirits to begin to wear down. The sun is hot overhead, with no sea breeze to cut its power. The sheer blankness of the landscape, the debris of wars past reminding us what we soon face with every step, is inescapable.

Even one day of marching takes its toll. I see it in my soldiers, and I feel it in my bones. Already I think of them as mine. I am not sure if this is a good thing or bad. In the morning the soldiers start in high spirits, singing marching songs, but by sundown they are too drained to keep it up anymore.

The power I have siphoned from Adem continues to wane, and more quickly than I would have guessed. To think, all the last few days, just this morning even, that power pulsed through me so strongly I thought I could never be tired again.

I try to shake the weariness off like dust and stay alert. I have to. These people are counting on me. This in itself brings its own weariness.

Finally, the sun drops and it is too dark to push on any further. Jordan assigns shifts for guarding the camp. I am happy to let this duty of ordering and organizing a strategy fall to him. Pallets are laid out, and we eat our dried fish and pass the water. Calipher stands toward the wasteland ahead of us, Adem facing where we have come from.

The soldiers sprawl out in quiet exhaustion, and it is like the sun has already defeated us.

How many more days of this do we have ahead of us? I try to remember, but the walk back from the fortress to Haven is a blur.

After we have eaten, Jordan stands up. He wanders around until he finds a smooth flat stone. He tosses it in the air, catches it, tosses it again. As he does this, he moves in a circle so the others can see. He's smiling like a child.

"Who's in?" he says.

Soon he has rallied some to play. They kick and pass the stone between them. Even those who prefer to rest get in the spirit, and soon they are laughing and bantering with each pass. The weariness in the air lifts, and the army takes on a renewed spirit.

I had forgotten just how good Jordan is. He is young, but he knows people. It stuns me, the ease with which he connects.

The game calls to me. I could use a little lightness. But I cannot play just now, and I do not know that I should, anyway. Perhaps this is what made Jordan so easy to take down—he was too approachable and easy. Instead, I roll my pallet and lie on it. Not to sleep. Just to rest my body for a time.

The residue of the power I siphoned from Adem still twists through me, the way muscles sometimes ache after an illness. As I lie there, my body pleads with me: *no more.* But it is the only way.

I tell myself it is just until after the battle. Then, I will figure out a way to take down Kythiel and banish him from my mind forever. Until then, I have to stay awake. The bruises on my arm are fading from where he grabbed me, but I can only imagine what might happen should I cross his path again unprepared. *Just a few more days,* I promise. Then, I will deal with Kythiel, and my body can rest for a time. I do not let my mind think on all the times I have promised this before.

When the others have gone to sleep except for the first night's guard, I will meet with Calipher and Adem under the guise of checking in.

Until then, I will lie here and get what rest I can without sleep.

As I wait for the play to end, the voices fade to the background, and then away.

***

The darkness slips into me, and when I open my eyes, I am not in the wasteland anymore. I am surrounded with the terrible darkness of the dream.

Beyond the darkness' curtain, I hear the slightest padding of steps through the brush, the erratic strain of his breaths.

The old, stale fear courses over me. I have felt it too many times, for too long, and it is too comfortable in my bones.

I force myself to my feet. I cannot keep playing this cat-and-mouse game with him, waiting for him to come to me. I may not have wanted to face him now, I may not be ready for it the way I want to be, but here I am. Running and hiding isn't something I do anymore.

This is *my* mind, *my* corner of this strange in-between, and he will come face me, by the Gods, or I will hunt him down.

"Kythiel!" I shout. My voice is shrill and small in the vastness of this place. "Get out here."

My hands are already shaking, and I secretly hope he doesn't show. What will I do once I have him here?

One step at a time.

When he doesn't show, I pick a direction and start off, unwilling to stand still and wait.

Just as before the darkness fades into an overwhelming brightness, the glory of gold and white and polished marble. But this time I am not so enchanted by its beauty. This time the Host's emptiness is what presses upon me, and it lights within me a rage too great to contain.

The marble is cold under my bare feet.

"Kythiel!" I cry again.

The sound throws and echoes through the empty rows of columns and into the mist beyond. The quiet here is a terrible one, accented with the rustling of Kythiel's prowl. A place so grand and beautiful should never be so desolate.

How dare the Gods leave us? How dare they leave us *now*? Are they truly so frightened of what is coming? How could they leave us in Terath all alone to face it?

"You wanted me?"

Kythiel's velvet voice is behind me, and I gasp before I can stop it. I whip around to face him.

He appears as awful as the last time I faced him here, maybe even worse.

The dark feathers of his wings are awry, his curls tousled and wiry. His cheeks are hollowed and sharp, and his eyes have hardened, the skin around them sunken and dark.

But none of this is why he sends a tremor of terror through me.

Something is different about the way he looks at me. He no longer gazes at me through the misguided adoration that drove him to violate my mind before. Now he glares at me with raw hatred.

I stumble a few steps back. "Yes."

Kythiel grits his teeth, baring them at me. "Well, here I am."

He lunges for me, and I barely pull back in time, raising my arm to shove my elbow into his neck. It feels sluggish and weak, but even so, he stumbles and coughs, giving me a moment to think. My breaths turn thin and come too fast.

This was a bad idea. I should not have called to draw him out while so weak and unprepared. I should never have lain down to rest at all.

I try to turn and run, but Kythiel moves faster this time, clamping a hand around my forearm and tugging me back. I pull and squirm, fighting to be let loose. My heart pounds loud and fast in my ears. But my struggles only make him tighten his grip, and the bones in my arm strain against the pressure.

Panic seizes through my body, and I thrust forward and shove my other hand into his face, pushing hard, twisting his neck back at an unnatural angle. He tenses, making a strange gurgling sound, but I know I have only seconds before he reacts. My muscles ache and my body shakes, too weak and depleted for this fight. But I will not give up. Deep in my gut, I miss the overwhelming energy that came with the uncomfortable healing I held when I first returned to Terath.

I need energy. I need power.

And that is when my mind bursts open with a gasp, like the uncontrollable force of release after holding your breath for too long, and *draws in.*

Before I know what I am doing, Kythiel's power fills me. It is different from Adem's, like the difference between saltwater and fresh. It is murkier, thicker, and holds a bitterness in it. But it fills me with energy just the same, and that is all I need. As I siphon it from him, his grip falters and his eyes widen.

His mouth opens with a quiver. He is about to say something, when I am jolted out of the dream.

***

I wake up with a shudder. Jordan's face is inches from mine. The rest of the camp is still, the soldiers sleeping.

He blinks. "Shh. The wasteland."

I nod. He leans back, allowing me space to sit up.

I struggle to orient myself after the abrupt lurch between worlds. My head throbs, burning hot with energy from the inside, my skin chilled by a cold familiar sweat. The new power pulses through me. I feel dizzy, much as through the earth were shifting below me.

I take deep breaths, staring at the bruise swelling

again on my wrist in almost the same place as before. My heart beats ferociously, and I fight to calm it. As I begin to settle, I become more aware of a hot hum coursing through my body in currents.

The power goes between the realms, I think to myself. *It came back with me. Kythiel's power.*

I didn't get as much this time, on my own without Nabi's help, but it is enough. It barrels through me.

I want it out.

But there is no question about it, I feel reenergized. Awake.

"Are you all right?" Jordan asks.

His voice is patient, and I almost think he has forgiven me, until I pull my gaze up and see the stiffness of his expression.

"What?" I blink, shake my hair so that it comes forward around me. "Yes. I am…I am fine."

Jordan frowns, studying my face. I pull back my shoulders and straighten up, trying to look more confident than I sound.

"Are you?"

Kythiel's power lacks the peace usually associated with angels. Strange, it always had it before. Now it throttles through my veins with hot anger.

I try to push my face into a smile. "Of course."

I expect this to be enough, for him to roll over and go back to sleep. But he is still watching me.

"You could have told me, you know."

"What do you mean?"

"About Kythiel. You could have told me. Did you think I would not stand by you, just because the Gods are not in your mind? I am hardly in any position to judge."

I look away, up to the sky, trying to hide the tears fighting to break free. Why is this swell of emotion crowding my chest from this small gesture? It is as if everything lately has been too big, too loud, too much, and Jordan's small gesture of grace has brought it all to a standstill, and it is catching up with me.

"You could have told me too," I reply.

"I did not want to put that on you," he said. "I did not want that on anyone."

"Me neither," I confess. "Especially when you put so much faith in me, for these people. Gods. It did not even matter. We are not even to the battle yet, and I have already failed you."

I cannot help it. A tear escapes and rolls down the side of my face.

"No. No," he soothes. I turn and raise an eyebrow at him. "Well. You did not do as I would have wished. But I stepped down for a reason. Who is to say what is right, or how we should carry ourselves, in times such as these."

I know he believes otherwise, and is only trying to comfort me. But the smile he gives me is so pure it works anyway.

"Well." And with that, I am out of words. I settle back on my pallet, and Jordan does the same.

I wait until Jordan's slow deep breaths tells me he has fallen sleep. Then, I push around the early morning guard to get to Calipher and Adem. Calipher stands with his back to the camp, wings half-spread and tense, as if to shield us from whatever may lie out there in the darkness. Adem stands next to him, facing the opposite direction.

He turns his head to me as I approach. "You came."

"And I'm ready," I say.

"Finally. I was starting to—" Calipher stops talking as he turns and looks at me, his smile disappearing from his lips. "What's wrong?"

I shake my head, hardly sure how to explain.

"Once Adem's power wore off, I was more tired than ever. I fell asleep. And it was so strange..."

I tell them how it started like all the other times, but this time, I went hunting for him.

"He grabbed me, and we fought. But I was just so tired."

The words feel empty, unable to capture the depths of exhaustion I felt.

"It is all right," Calipher says, coming forward to place a hand on my shoulder. His peace bursts over me. "It is over."

"It's more than that, though. I siphoned power off of him."

"Like you did from Adem? Inside your dream? By yourself?"

"Yes. I didn't even mean to do it—I didn't *want* to do it. I can still feel him inside me. Here in the real world."

Calipher stares at me in disbelief. "That's amazing."

"No, I do not want his power inside me. It feels like him."

His dark predatory rage is a part of me now, throttling through my veins. I have never felt more trapped by him. I can only hope it will leave me as his power dies off.

"But think about what it means. It means you can

protect yourself from him."

It is true. The look on his face when I drew his own power from him...

But this is hardly a time to have the rage of a crazed fallen angel coursing through me. I need to keep my head cool. For my people. For the fight ahead of us.

"Did you get what you needed, then? Do you need any more?" Adem offers his hand.

Guilt swells in my chest like water into a leaky boat. Have I not asked enough of him already?

"Maybe a little," I say.

I don't think I got all that much from Kythiel, really. I still feel drained behind the power, more like a thin trickle than the waterfall's torrent Nabi drew for me from Adem the night before. If nothing else, I need his calming presence to balance Kythiel's energy inside me and quiet it.

He steps closer, and I press my hand into his. The relief is immediate, a rush that surges in response to my touch like a breeze. I close my eyes to concentrate, and then, I try to pull it from him, try to imagine the power as currents in a river, to reroute its flow toward me. It comes slowly, unwillingly.

The effort is draining. I pull away.

"I cannot."

I drop my arm to my side. It was so easy in the dream. Was it because I was in the dream world? Because it drew from desperate need, rather than thought? I can only begin to guess.

"Let me help."

I turn around, and there she is. This little girl with so much power within her. Her hair is mussed from laying on the pallet, curls flying every which way, and sleep still crusts her eyes. She may be wiser and tougher than I was when my powers started, but she is still only a girl. I should never have allowed her to come. It was irresponsible and selfish.

But she smiles, and comes to us. She presses our hands together again and puts her own alongside them, and I am reminded of how much power she carries. Adem's power bursts into me like it is knocking down a wall. What I took from Kythiel was a drop in a bucket; what Nabi pours into me now from Adem is an endless sea.

Who needs the Gods when you have this?

***

"Not quite. Try again," Calipher says.

I sigh, letting the sand drop to the earth.

It frightens me, how little control I have over this power. Not that Adem is too much better. But I have to get this right. I feel more likely to go mad from the repetition first.

"There are other spells, right? Please. Tell me they at least exist."

"They exist."

I flail with frustration, swinging my fists to my sides. "So why can I not try something else?"

He closes my angry fist in his large calm hands.

"You're getting better. Keep trying." He smiles, and it is so beautiful it makes my fingers tingle. "This is the simplest of spells. Perfect for beginning to master control and power. It is how we all start."

I sigh again, and shut my eyes.

"Come now. There is no time for this. When we get

there, you must be ready."

I nod and open my eyes again. He is right. There is no time for self-pity. It simply has to be done.

I put my hand out again. "Aaeros."

"Better. Again."

We train through the night, and just before dawn, Nabi helps me siphon more from Adem to keep me going through the day ahead. As the sun rises and the army begins to stir, we bring our training to an end.

Adem bends down and scoops Nabi into his arms.

"Sleep," he says.

She settles her head into his broad shoulder and is once again a small girl instead of the Gods' last known prophet.

CHAPTER 34

ANOTHER DAY OF marching. Another night of learning to control my power.

And then another.

I am getting better, can draw more from Adem without Nabi's help.

I take different guard positions through the nights, changing it at each shift to avoid drawing attention to my lack of sleep. Even so, some of the soldiers eye me when I send them back to their pallets to sleep. But they follow orders and do not ask questions. For now.

Calipher, Adem, and Nabi are always near, and together we try to hone the power I take into a weapon.

As we march, the fortress begins to take shape, a dark speck on the horizon. The energy begins to mount. We are all hungry to take it down.

Early into the next day, streaks of pink and orange still staining the sky, a guard near the front of the line shouts and points. Far in the distance, a whirling torrent is winding its way toward us.

I do not waste time wondering on it.

"Army approaching! From the East!" I shout. The other guards turn to see, and then all of us begin shouting in a chaotic choir.

Jordan echoes after me, "Approaching! Battle posts! Look alert! And remember, shields up. Don't let them go."

The camp, a scene of perfect quiet just moments ago, bursts to life like a wildfire. The soldiers drop their breakfasts, grab their weapons, and take their positions for battle. I feel the action whooshing around me, but still I stand and stare at the torrent, churning closer and closer. Are they prepared to take on the supernatural? Do they understand what they face? There is no way to tell, and nothing to do about it, if they are not.

Jordan rushes to my side to see for himself, his eyes wide and dilated, and then turns to his soldiers and shouts more orders.

Where is Nabi? In the midst of the chaos the question pounds at my mind. When I brought her with us, I knew she could fend for herself—after all, she fought at my side the last time we faced the Unnamed. She is the only reason I survived. But now, when it is too late, it feels so wrong to ask her.

I spot her with Adem across the sea of the army, but there is no time to go to them. The torrent is already almost upon us, and beginning to break apart. Just as in Ir-Nearch, the sand and wind twists into shape, forming arms legs, swords, and shields, spitting the Unnamed into the wasteland. First it is only a few, and then more, and more, until there are too many to count and they fill the sand all the way to the horizon, the tower barely beyond them.

The Third Realm War is here.

They look as monstrous as before, helmets coming down over their stoic faces, their limbs streaked in chalky white. But now through the veil of the magic pulsing through me, I can see what lies within them, too—and it is nothing. A terrible vacuum, an utter emptiness that hungers to pull more into itself.

As the last Unnamed take shape, the torrent shrinks into nothing with a burst. From the kicked-up dust and swirling sand, Koreh's spindly figure emerges.

"Did you truly believe you could sneak up on us?" she calls over. "Out here in the wasteland?"

Her voice rolls over the barren and crackled earth that spreads between our armies.

"Did you believe we would wait for you to come for us in our homes?" I call back. "Doesn't matter if we do it at your fortress or right here. We're going to destroy you. And then, we will destroy your fortress, and your helmuth with it. Send you all back to the Underworld where you belong."

Through the magic, I can see the mingling powers that Koreh is made of. I can see the demonic darkness, and how it mingles with a lightness like the sky—her sprite half at work. There is so much of it that I do not know how she contains it.

My hate for her burns through my veins.

From behind me, Jordan calls out. But his words are directed to our own soldiers, not Koreh.

"Are you ready?" he cries. The soldiers roar, clang on their shields and helmets. "They may look like they outnumber us, but these are not soldiers of flesh and heart, like you and me. They are dust. They are nothing. And let's make sure they feel it."

Another roar breaks free. Shields are lifted high, brandishing Nabi's symbol. Something in the air shifts. When I look over them, they are no longer the men and women of Haven, or Ir-Nearch, or of anywhere. These are soldiers chosen by the Gods to uphold their Order, soldiers who will protect their realm above all else, who have been training and waiting for just this moment for generations.

Jordan may not have powers like Calipher or Adem, but he holds an undeniable sort of magic within his words that I could never begin to touch.

"No more talk, Koreh," he bellows. His hair is a wild crown over his head, and the sun catches and glows in his eyes, drawing out their orange and yellow specks. He has never appeared so otherworldly. He thrusts his sword into the air. "Charge!"

A bold warrior's cry erupts from him, and the army bursts forth around me like a tidal wave of fury.

I rush forward with the army, with Calipher's power, Kythiel's rage, the rumbling energy of the war-hungry thing inside me reverberating with the tremors of battle. My blades set confidently in my hands, and with them, I am ready for anything that lies ahead. Suddenly, the entire realm narrows down to one thing: get to the necklace and kill anything that tries to get in my way.

The Unnamed charging toward us are the same as before, the same strange chalky skin, the same warriors' patterns streaked over their faces, the same slack soulless stares underneath. There must be at least three times as many of them than there are of us.

They charge us from the front and close around us from the sides. Not all of us will make it out of here, no matter how many of them we take down with us, no matter if we take them all down.

Some of us are going to die.

I look to Jordan leading the charge, to Calipher at his side, to Adem scooping up Nabi and clutching her to his chest. And right then, as the Unnamed close in on us, is when I realize...*this*. This is what I fight for. These people. This community. It is a home unlike any I have ever had, and it has crept into my heart and made it theirs.

I buckle with fear, afraid of all I have to lose, and then double my resolve. Whatever horror we see in this fight, well, that is war. But I can at least make sure the sacrifice is not wasted. I can make sure we get the necklace. That we end this.

That is the last thought I have before the armies collide. After that, everything is simply a blur of chaos.

CHAPTER 35

THE CHARGE MELTS into chaos as the armies crash into each other. I am tossed and shoved from all sides, a mob of soldiers eager for the next kill.

My blades are tight in my hands, slashing through Unnamed after Unnamed. With each stab, their dust bursts like a cloud, thickening the air and making it harder to see.

To my side, a soldier stumbles to the ground, and my first instinct is to get to her before she is trampled. But judging by the pool of red that expands rapidly beneath her, it won't matter for long. I turn away and look for another enemy to destroy. I need to fight my way out to where I can see. I need to find Koreh. I know she is near. The necklace mingles with the magic pulsing through me, calls to me to come to it.

A pivot and another swing of my blades takes down two more. The entire battlefield is a haze of floating ash and bobbing soldiers and glints of sun off blades.

A luring hum floats over the battleground, drifting

and luring. The same song that I heard in Ir-Nearch, weaving its way through the air.

I pull up short and turn to chase after it. I shove my way through the soldiers, ducking blades and dodging swings, taking out an occasional Unnamed when it is faster. The action makes the magic within me go wild, pounding to break through me.

Slicing my blade through one, I look up and find a familiar face under the war paint, just in time to see it crumble to nothing. It takes me a moment to place it and then the realization crashes over me: it is one of the men from Ir-Nearch, who was delirious under the necklace's spell at the fortress.

She killed him. She killed him just so she could add him to her ranks.

Rage flares through my limbs. How many others has she lured in this way?

I grab hold of another Unnamed closest to me, wondering if I will recognize its face too, but as soon as my skin presses into his, a strange feeling overcomes me. Like from a crack in a bucket, the power is leaking out of me and into the Unnamed. I let go with a cry, but it is too late; there is a vacuum where the Unnamed sucked out my power.

I stab the Unnamed to end it. Flecks of ash fly out of the soldier as I pull my blade away, but then it doesn't disappear. The Unnamed grimaces and hisses, and swings his sword at me. In my disbelief, I am not fast enough, and he cuts into my forearm as my reflexes kick in and I pull it up to guard my face.

My head reels. Warmth spreads over my arm as the blood begins to ooze, and my boots feel like they are filled with heavy wet sand.

Is the power the Unnamed stole from me keeping him alive?

But there is no time for questions, not here, not now. A warrior's hunger pulses through me. *Kill. Destroy. Fight.* I embrace it.

Mustering my will, I lunge in to stab again, this time in the heart, as I would in any other enemy. The soldier staggers back. I stab him again and pull down through his chest, splicing him open. He howls, and finally, breaks apart and disappears.

I pant, relieved to be rid of him. How did he steal my power from me? But there is no time now to think. I must stay alert, and I've lost the hum's trail. Without a lead, I keep pushing on in the direction I was going before, stabbing and slicing, carefully dodging Unnameds as I go, until I break through the mob into open space.

From the outside, the battle is a mad mob, a mess of floating ash and terrible cries, writhing arms and glinting blades. I make my way around the battle's edge, eyes and ears strained for any sign of Koreh, trying to help all I can as I go, and careful not to touch any more Unnameds.

A few bump into me anyway, each one stealing a bit more of my power away. Each time my heart pounds faster, my body seems to move slower.

But I cannot give in. I cannot stop. I cling to my blades and put them to task, mercilessly thrusting them through each new enemy. I pull a blade out of one and turn, ready to take down the next. But the next one is caught in its charge, freezes as if it has hit a wall.

I blink, startled.

"Get him!" Nabi is at my side, her hands tense in front of her. She is so covered in ash that she is hardly more than a ghostly white shadow and a brilliant dark pair of eyes.

I do as she says.

"You are supposed to be with Adem."

She ignores me. "This way."

Nabi turns and runs, leading me around the side of the fighting, not bothering to look back or explain. I run to catch up and follow her as fast as I can, the vacuum in my stolen power weighing me down.

Then I hear it, the hum is back, with the same haunted tune as last time, painfully familiar and terribly sad. We've got her. I tilt my head towards it and strain, trying to find her amidst the chaos. It tugs on my chest much like the feeling of having been away from home too long.

Nabi stops abruptly and finally I catch up. As I pant at her side, Nabi points. I follow her directive, and there she is. Koreh is weaving through the fighting like an eye in the storm, a small gap of stillness amidst the chaos. Around her neck rests the large emerald necklace.

As she makes her way, some of the soldiers nearest to her stop their fighting and turn to follow her — a trail of Haven's own soldiers. They drop their weapons, their expressions turn slack, and suddenly, they have eyes only for her. Some are instantly cut down by the Unnameds they were fighting. Others trail behind her through the mob. Just like in Ir-Nearch.

Every so often Koreh turns and whispers to them, and then they turn away, their pallor turning ashy, and

begin to attack their own army, their friends from
Haven. Gods, we warned them, and we tried to protect
them. But how do you truly prepare someone to fight
their neighbor, their friend? No one can take the time in
battle to see how their faces have changed, how their
souls seem to have left them.

Watching it unfold chills my blood.

"Stay here," I say to Nabi. Now that she brought me
to Koreh, I don't need her in any more danger.

I fight my way through the battle, keeping one eye
on Koreh all the way. I block attacks with my blade as
needed, but don't bother pausing to make the kill
anymore. The longer this goes on, the more of our own
Koreh will turn, and it will go on and on until we have
killed ourselves off. Stop Koreh, and the entire army
will break down to nothing.

I finally reach her, my arms feeling the weight of
exhaustion from the struggle. Koreh whips around as if
she could sense me there, her eyes alive and burning
bright.

"Finally," she says.

CHAPTER 36

KOREH WAVES HER slender hand, and a bubble expands around us, casting the fighting away through a film.

"I wasn't expecting it to be *you*. I thought it would be one of the angels. Or maybe the golem. The ones with the inhuman powers," she says. She raises an eyebrow, looks me over. "But it seems you have acquired some for yourself."

Soldiers are out there dying. I will not waste time with — or give her the satisfaction of — an explanation.

"Give me the necklace."

"This?" she says, her fingers tracing the gold chain. "It is far too pretty to give away. Don't you think it suits me exceptionally well?"

She sways her shoulders, catching the light in the gem. Its magic calls to me, wild and hungry, eager to be unbound from its cage.

"Besides, you have seen how they dote on me," she continues, looking out over the army. "They would do whatever I ask of them, with this. You think I will just hand it over?" She laughs, and it is a delicate, sweet sound that does not match the cruelness detailed across her face.

Searing heat explodes in my stomach and spreads like lightning over my body. Pure, deep hatred. Is this all just a game to her? A way to feed her ego?

My body throbs with the power I have taken. It begs to be used. I obey.

"*Aaeros,*" I command, throwing some rocks at her from my feet. They fly at her as if they were tossed. Gently. One lands near her feet, and she kicks at it.

That's it? My fingers burn where the magic coursed out of me. I have to do better.

"You have not had this power very long, have you?" A smirk presses into her thin lips. She doesn't wait for an answer. "Where did you get it? Careful now. Play nice or I will have to send you away."

Play nice?

"Do you think this is a game?" I shout. The magic buzzes in my ears, aches in my palms, begs to be used again. All around, soldiers are fighting, men and women are dying. "That thing is no toy. Take it off. Give it to me."

She pushes her hands out and shoves me back with her power alone.

In a wave of anger I muster all my power up and shove back, trying to emulate what she did.

Nothing happens. I blink and stare at my useless hands.

"Really?" Koreh asks. "Don't you know *anything* about the magic you took? The Gods' powers work differently. Only Gloros's magic will obey emotions. See?"

She frowns and swings her arm in a hitting motion, and I am knocked to the ground.

"You'll need spells for that angels' magic you've taken." She comes and stands right over me, watching me struggle to get back up.

Gloros's power is what I need then? I reach out my hand and grab onto her leg, and try to *pull, pull, pull* the power from her. She shrieks and tries to kick me off but I grip into her hard with my nails, feeling the power course into me like a stream. I'm not drawing at full power, but it's stronger than when I tried on Calipher last night.

Koreh's power is entirely different from what I have taken from Adem or Calipher or Kythiel. With their angels' magic, it was like a light was inside me—even if Kythiel's light burned and stung. What I am taking from Koreh now is cold and darting, like a flurry of ash and embers, singeing me in small bites from within. I recognize it, though it has been ages upon ages since I have felt it—the aura of a demon. With it is something free and rushing like a wind, her sprite side at work.

She finally breaks free, but it was long enough. I can feel it, a mix of her auras inflaming my emotions and darting through me in chaos, her two halves cutting through the angels' power already in me.

There, I think, now we are more equal.

When Koreh looks back to me, a monstrous scowl darkens her face, and hair is falling loose from the elegant pins all over her head. I throw some of her own magic at her. It lands on her shoulder and shoves her back. Then, with a strange, spindly contortion of her hands, a thread of blue twisting light grows in front of her, and she shoots it at me like lightning.

It wraps around me and seizes my chest. Then, it drops me to the ground with a painful shock.

It is then, as I fight to pick myself back up from the sand, that I realize how foolish I have been, how egotistical. How could I believe a little stolen power could make me a match for her? I hardly know what I am doing at all, and she has had ages of practice, and much greater power that is all her own, in her very nature.

As soon as I am on my feet, she strikes me with the lightning again, and I am back on my hands and knees, numb from the shock.

My shoulders tremble with panic. I have failed. I am no match for this wrathful creature. My best chance is to keep her distracted long enough to let our soldiers take out hers, and stop her from creating any more. If I can hold out long enough for that, the others will come. Maybe they can make up for what I lack.

But then it comes to me, almost as if the magic itself were speaking to me. *If we can't overpower her, we can at least drain her of it.* Just like the Unnamed did to me.

Is it possible to take it all from her, at least for a little while? I have to try. It may be my only chance.

I launch forward and pounce at her. She yelps and pulls back, but too slow. I place my hands on her and hold on tight, try to tap into the desperation that allowed me to take from Kythiel and *draw* her into me. As her power courses into me, Koreh screams, a great bellowing scream as if she were in pain.

Does it hurt, what I do? Right now, I hope so. I dig my grip into her arm and focus on drawing all that I can from her.

Finally, Koreh twists free and begins a chant, and a dark mist forms over her open palm, growing larger and larger, and then, she throws it at me.

The ball of shadow rushes through me, overcoming me with a chill colder than ice and stealing my breath. As I drop to the ground, it propels me back, back, back, almost like flying.

Except my own body is still crumbled at Koreh's feet as I fly away from it.

No.

No, no, no.

Koreh will not take my life from me. With an overwhelming, primal urge, I want it. I am not done yet here.

And I refuse to leave it.

I muster all the magic I still have in me and throw it out toward my empty body like an anchor, and *cling*.

I do not know how it works, other than sheer will. I do not care. Slowly I manage to pull back into myself, my body aching deeply in every crevice, emptied of all its energy. But at least it is still mine.

Get up, I order it. *Now.*

It obeys with a struggle.

But something is wrong. My soul is back in my body, but they don't feel like *one* anymore. I stretch out my arms to test them, and they move just as they should. I shake my head, trying to break free of the feeling. I blink.

And in the flash that my eyes are closed, I see not the

normal darkness of my mind, but the barren landscape of the in-between.

I open my eyes again, stumbling back from the shock. *It can't be.* But when I close my eyes again to check, there it is. When I look down to my body, it is vibrating and blurred, like it is struggling to hold onto its place in this realm.

"You're... you're back!" Koreh cries. "How?"

I blink again, and am briefly thrown into the in-between and back. A thousand thoughts close in on me at once, and not one can make sense of what it happening to me. My hands begin to shake with fear. I try to transform it into rage.

"What did you do to me?" I shout. My voice sounds as though it comes from somewhere else. "What did you *do*?"

"You cannot be here still!" She yells back. Her voice is fractured and sharp, like an unevenly sharpened blade. "Go!"

She shoots sparks at me, and I dodge them.

"I knew you would come back to me again."

It is a voice I would know anywhere. In any time.

But how?

"Kythiel?" I cry. "Kythiel! Show yourself, you bastard."

"I am right here." His voice is hot in my ear. I whip around, but still there is nothing.

I turn toward the voice at my side, but there is nothing there, only the floating ash and sea of fighting going on all around us past Koreh's bubble. I keep turning, searching frantically all around. Koreh shoots sparks at me again, and in my distraction, I forget to dodge this time, and my side bursts with pain. Instinctively I shut my eyes against it.

And there he is. Right at my side. On the other side, in the in-between.

My heart pounds so hard I am sure it will burst free. Bald panic overtakes me. I'm awake—how did I get trapped in this terrible dream again?

But, I realize, this time it isn't a dream. In my dreams the darkness of the in-between is blurred and distant, and I cannot see beyond it. But here…it is all the same, but everything except me is in sharp focus.

"What is this?" I demand.

I can hear my own voice echoing as if from down a tunnel, feel the words coming from my own throat back in Terath. Somewhere very far away, the ring of Koreh's chuckle floats toward me.

Right in front of me, Kythiel stares, as if he can hardly believe it either.

"You're here. You're here for real," he says. His expression is mystified, eyes wide. But then it darkens into a scowl. "Now I will show you the pain you have caused me all these years."

I am so startled I open my eyes, and am thrown back into Terath, with Koreh before me.

She is smirking. "I suppose it did work, in a way."

I blink, and Kythiel flashes before my eyes.

"You tried to cast me from the realm!" It is starting to make sense. She tried to cast me out, just like we did to Kythiel, and now I am caught in both planes.

"It should have worked too." Koreh frowns. "What are you?"

Koreh paces around me, and I can imagine Kythiel

doing the same in the in-between.

What happens to me here if Kythiel does something to me there? How do I pull myself back into one again?

In a panic, I demand of Koreh, "Put me *back*."

But Koreh is circling me, her arms spread out as if feeling the vibrations of the air. Her gaze is intense, thoughtful. It feels as if she is trying to pull something apart in my being.

Koreh is too curious not to try to figure it out.

"It is your own fault, fighting back against my curse. What are you?"

At the same time, Kythiel is also speaking to me, also responding to my demand. "Me? Why would I want to do that? I don't know how you got here, but I wouldn't send you back now even if I could—not when I finally have you here with me."

His threats from before race through my mind, and I panic. I run.

I open my eyes and throw magic at Koreh's bubble, bursting it in time to run through it into the wasteland toward the fortress. In the in-between, I am racing past the barrenness into the Host, and through row after row of lovely columns and clouds. In both realms, my enemies are close on my heels.

I race through the wasteland's sand, hearing my steps echo on the marble floor of the Host, emptier than ever and leaving me hopeless.

Through the cuts of my panting breaths, I beg, "Oh Gods, oh Gods, oh Gods."

"The Gods aren't here, Rona. Just us," Kythiel replies. "The Gods are gone."

It looks that way—too empty—but it can't be true. It

can't. Not when we are all out here fighting for Them, sacrificing life after life for Them. Would They dare turn their backs on us like this, at the first sign of trouble? How could They? It is unthinkable.

But then...where are They?

At the back of my mind, my lies to Haven's people gnaw at me.

"The Gods do not care about *you*." The voice is far away, in a different realm—Koreh. Her taunting, assured voice reverberates over the sky from Terath.

Its closeness startles me, and my body brings me to a jolting halt. Something crashes into me and sends me tumbling to the ground, my eyes shoot open. We are a tangle of limbs tumbling over the sand. I tug at her loosening hair and grab around her neck as she claws at me, and order my fingers to *draw* from her again. Weakening her is my only chance.

Her power begins to flow into me. The more she struggles to get away, the harder I cling to her, and the longer I hold her down, the greater the flow of her power becomes inside me. I don't dare stop for fear of what she will do if she breaks free.

As I do it, I pray a fierce, raging prayer for help, dare the Gods not to answer me. They came before, for Adem. Surely they will come for me now. For all of us.

The rush of power I have drawn from Koreh is filling me, making my very skin hum. It is too much, and yet I have no choice but to keep at it, to keep draining until she is dry. But not even this new body of mine was made for this. At least, I do not think it was.

This is not the first time I have demanded too much of it. I can handle this. I have to. A great grunt forces its way out of me, and I will myself to draw harder.

A swift kick to my back makes it explode with pain. The magic coursing through me flutters to life and I turn and shoot toward Kythiel without closing my eyes to find him. Koreh's sprite power pulses through my fingertips. But the great light it casts off simply flies toward the film and burns to embers against it.

I shut my eyes and transport myself into the in-between. I am huddled up on the Host's marble floor. As I adjust to this realm, his foot meets me again, this time right in my side. It explodes with pain, shuddering in waves over the magic like ripples in a pond, distorting my vision. I keel forward, forgetting Koreh, and Terath, and everything but the pain.

I fight back the only way I can. I shoot a messy orb of power at him. It flames at the edges and turns to cinders, but it manages to hit its mark. Kythiel arches his wings and cries out. When he looks back to me, his eyes are fiery and bright with rage.

I shoot another orb, but do not wait to see if it hits. I run again.

But I do not get far. A hot force knocks me to the ground, I do not know which enemy, which realm it came from. All I know is that I am on the ground and Kythiel is over me, kicking. Back in Terath I can feel slender hands closing over my robe and lifting me up, a fist arming into my face.

The magic rolls through me in angry waves, begging to be used. But I do not know how.

The auras of angel, demon, and sprite fighting against each other within me overwhelm my senses, leaving me dizzy and disoriented. Hits come from all sides, and I simply take them.

What is the worst that can happen? They kill me? I go back to the Underworld? It was not so bad there. It is where I am supposed to be anyway.

No, that is not the worst thing.

Deep down something inside me resists, refuses to give in and accept this fate. I might have welcomed such a fate a few short weeks ago, but now a stubborn kernel within me refuses it. For Adem. For Calipher. For Nabi. Even for Jordan.

The worst that could happen has nothing to do with me at all. The worst that could happen is that Koreh wins. That Kythiel somehow breaks free. If the rebel creatures gain so much against Terath's only defenders so easily, the realm's time will be limited. The war will be over before it has even begun.

It does not matter if I am worn down and beaten and outnumbered and outpowered. I have to fight. I have to *win.* It does not matter what it costs. I have no other choice.

I curl up tight, accepting the attacks, and muster all the energy I can manage. I set it free in a pulsing wave from my core, and I can feel the ground reverberate with its force, from both realms.

I take my chance and force myself to my feet, turn quickly to take in the Host and again to take in Terath. Kythiel and Koreh were propelled away by my attack but it has not slowed them down. They are both already coming at me again, from opposite sides, Kythiel a ragged beast of loose dark feathers, Koreh's slender beauty giving way to a gaunt monstrosity, exposing her truer nature. They come at me with eyes dark and teeth bared, hands poised to deliver pain.

The power I have taken in weighs on me, pulsing and twisting and stealing my energy away. I let it burst free again, this time not bothering to aim it at any purpose, simply trying to get free from it. It bursts from my chest and my hands, through my legs and over my back, my fingertips and the top of my head. But the amount released is not nearly enough to break free of its weight.

Koreh stumbles into my tipsy vision. She pants, throwing her head back to get her hair out of her face. She wings back her arm and I brace for the magic she will throw at me, but instead the fists keep coming, and she hits me in the face.

She grunts, then hits me again.

It is startlingly *human*, coming from her.

Another punch. And another.

The hits throw stars in front of my eyes, blocking my vision, knocking me to the ground. When I shut my eyes against her attack, Kythiel is there. His wild churning eyes brim with pure hatred, and though he does not understand it, he smiles to watch my struggle. Then he joins in, kicking me.

"What happened to us, Rona? Why did you leave me?" he asks. The questions throw me, and amidst the attacks I have no answers for him. "Why would you ever hide from *me*?" he goes on as he kicks at me again.

Guilt rushes over me. I did what I had to, but in his crazed state, I never stopped to think how it might be hurting him.

"You," I choke as Koreh tugs at my hair and punches me again. "You weren't yourself anymore."

"Not *myself*? But how could I not be me?" Kythiel stumbles back, as if I have hit him across the face. He frowns, too lost in trying to understand to see my ongoing struggle with an invisible enemy. My face and arms are pulsing with swelling pain in hot splotches.

My pounding heart melts a little—Gods, he really had no idea, all this time. He truly has gone mad. The Kythiel I fell in love with never would have raised a hand to me. Never would have stalked me in my dreams.

I open my eyes and focus on Koreh, pinning me to the ground with her knees so I cannot draw from her, as she hits me again and again. I twist and writhe until my arms are free and then hit her back, knocking her off of me.

I close my eyes and return to Kythiel.

"It is my own fault," I say. "I drew you away from Theia's path. And it broke you, and everything I loved about you."

Kythiel smiles. Even with his battered wings and drained face, it is beautiful. "Oh, my love. How I have missed you."

But as I speak something deep within me, something buried so deep under my layers that I can barely reach it, resists. It buckles at every word.

From Terath, Koreh's fist slams into my head, and it is like the truth has been shaken loose.

It is *not* my fault.

All this time I have pulled this guilt tight around me like armor. Why? To keep from seeing this creature I used to love as too monstrous?

Now the armor has been ripped away. When did

this happen? Is it the power I have taken in? The healing force from my return from the Underworld? All that has happened in between?

I open my eyes and blast Koreh away with a burst of power from my palm. I stand and stare out past the bubble to the fighting soldiers. By instinct I begin to search for Adem, for Jordan, for Calipher, for Nabi. *They* are what happened to me.

Because beautiful or tattered, sweet or hardened, a monster is just what Kythiel has been all along.

An abrupt shake pulls me back to him in the in-between.

"Rona."

I close my eyes to find him inches from my face. Despite the soft tremor of his voice, his eyes still burn with a bottomless hate, and I know whatever he has in store for me, it is no longer motivated by what he called love.

"Rona, my own, come back to me."

I frown so hard my head begins to ache.

Kythiel is a First Creature. Directly connected to Theia's Will. He knew exactly what he was doing, every step of the way. He chose a girl over his own Goddess. And then he took me down with him and trampled over me until I was no more than a puddle in the mud. Even after he fell, he should have been able to hold onto himself—Calipher did. If he had not so lost himself in this singular idea of *us* that consumed him...consumed both of us.

I made my own terrible choices—plenty of them— but I will not bear his too. Not one moment longer.

I draw up all the guilt I have carried for him in my

chest, bundle it into a great burning ball and thread it into the stolen power within me. The combination burns and throbs, begging to be released.

Then I imagine thrusting it back onto him.

And it obeys. It surges, bursting right out from my skin with stinging brilliance, and knocks him back.

The relief is immediate, a lull in the building power, but it is not enough. Already Kythiel is getting back to his feet, his wiry wings spread wide, and back in Terath I can hear Koreh muttering something that is sure to hurt if I do not stop her before she finishes.

This has to end. Kythiel. Koreh. All of it.

The rage crackles through my body and bleeds into the magic inside me, latches onto it. My mind turns strangely blank. I stop trying to tell the magic what to do and listen to it instead. I grab Kythiel by the wrist, and then open my eyes and take Koreh's contorted hand, aimed at me mid-spell, and I *draw*. I draw their power in the way a waterfall pulls in the river—with effortless, undeniable force. I let myself plunge over with the pull and fall over, fall into it deep, let it swallow me in its tug and pull until I am no longer sure which way is up. I soak in it until I feel myself coming back together into one.

And then before I lose hold of Kythiel in the fading tie between the realms, I stop the current, and I *push*. And the power bursts free from me, angelic, demonic, sprite, all at once. It is freedom, it is obliteration, it is drowning and it is desert, it is total stillness, and it is a wildfire that burns me into embers. It is splitting me apart from the inside.

Except it is not. I *push* and I *push*, willing to break

away into nothing if that is what it takes, the magic's fury whirling around me, but somehow I hold together at the eye.

Eyes open, I watch as Koreh's flawless face begins to pale, as the veins darken then begin to crack and break her apart. Eyes closed, I see Kythiel's glow begin to fade and flicker, to move through him in uneven bursts that burn right through his perfect marble skin to break free of him.

Both of them scream, terrible animal cries that cut right from the gut. But I take it in and let it fill me and keep on *pushing*.

And it works. The screams stop, and when I close my eyes, all that is on the other side is darkness. When I open them, there is only silence and ash. Ash on the ground where Koreh stood. Ash strewn through the battlefield mixed with patches of red-brown blood in the sand where her Unnamed soldiers once were. Ash all over my hands, splattered up my arms and, I suspect, my face.

One by one the soldiers turn to me and stare. A mystified mumble starts near the front and travels through them. Calipher, Adem, and Jordan shove their way toward me, but when he sees me, Calipher gasps and holds them back.

"She is not in control." He speaks only to them, not to me, and I realize that though Koreh's bubble is gone, I still feel as though I am reaching into the realm through a film.

It is the magic. The fight is over, but its current is still growing. And it hurts. It hurts like it will tear me apart from the inside and burst free, like it will burn me to pieces, like it will drown me and bury me in its depths. I try to shut myself off and reel it in. Calipher is right. I am not in control of it anymore. I have taken too much in and the magic will do whatever it must to fight its way free again.

I do not remember seeing her approach me, but suddenly Nabi is right in front of me. She kneels to the ground and sifts through the ash, pulling out of it something brilliant and glistening. It is the emerald. She picks it up and brings it to me, places it in my hand and wraps my fist closed around it.

"Go," she urges.

As soon as she says it I know what I must do. I turn toward the fortress and run as fast as I can, taking the growing torrent of swelling power with me.

CHAPTER 37

WHEN I COME TO, I am pinned under a great fragment of onyx stone, surrounded by even more of it, a whole mountain's worth. The last thing I can remember is the feeling of being blown into oblivion, of staring down the vicious throat of the helmuth.

It was like being ripped apart, the way the magic burst from me. The walls shook, the ground split in two. It purged me of all the intermingled power, purged me of the fear, of the anger, of all the ugliness that had piled up on me. All that is left is deep emptiness, and it is a true relief. I am too exhausted for anything more than this nothingness.

The rocks begin to pull away from me, and Adem's stoic face peers in my view.

I blink up at him, and he drops to my side.

"I have her," he calls out.

He reaches down to take my hand, and pain stretches over it. I gasp and pull it away to see. Seared over my palm is a deep burn, marking the imprint of small links from a chain, stretched all the way across it.

The necklace is gone.

Relief floods me, and emotion swells forth so great I cannot contain it. Tears begin to drop from my eyes. Adem wipes them away.

"Thank the Gods," Jordan says, leaning into my view. "What was that?"

Calipher leans over me too.

"I don't know. I have never seen anything like it. But it destroyed the helmuth," he responds. His face is lined severely, all worry. Without taking time to explain, he stretches his hands over me and chants. A soft warm light showers from them and into me, and I can feel shifts through my body as it begins to heal. "She needs rest, lots of it."

Adem scoops me into his arms and my head rests on his shoulder. He smells like dirt and sand and sea.

"Let's get you home."

I want to tell him I already am. But as my body relaxes into him, a blackness swims over me.

CHAPTER 38

I WAKE UP amidst a fog of memory and dreams that quickly dissipates. Nothing haunted me. My sleep was quiet. The realization is a shock and a relief. When I open my eyes, I am in a wooden hut. Which means I am back in Haven. How long did I sleep? It must have been days.

I still feel a little achy, a little drained. But so much better than before. And satisfied with what I bought with it: protection from the Unnamed, and Koreh, and the necklace. A little more time, before the war begins in earnest.

But oh, the battle. The war has indeed begun. There is no mistake about it. Much worse things are bound to come, and we're going to need a lot more men to fight them. They will not all be Unnamed. It will only get worse. In the First War, the Gods themselves walked the dirt of Terath and took on the Firsts themselves. I do not see that happening this time.

Should we be fighting so hard for them, when they

will not do it for themselves? Maybe Avi and Helda and the rest were right. Maybe Haven has been training for so long for nothing, only to be killed on the battlefield like an ant.

It is a question too big for me and I cannot cope with it, not now without more strength. Instead I try to sit up.

The room spins as I do it.

"Careful!" comes Calipher's voice. "You need to take it easy."

I look up to see him on the far side of my hut, sitting right on the ground next to the door. No wonder I feel so peaceful.

"You don't seem like you're quite at one hundred percent yet," he says. "Don't try. Your only job is to rest."

I stop trying to get up and stay sitting in my cot, wrapped up in blankets. It feels good.

"How long has it been?"

"Four days. Drink some water." He points to a large basin at the side of my bed. "Are you hungry?"

"No."

I am not thirsty either, but I drink a little anyway.

"How long have you been here?"

"The whole time. Ever since we got back. About a day and a half. I have to ask you something, if you're up for it," he says.

I nod. "What is it?"

"Koreh. What did her power feel like?"

It is a strange question. But there is a desperation in Calipher's eyes. It is not the crazed desperation that consumed Kythiel, but rather a sad, pained variation.

He needs to know.

I shut my eyes and think back, though I would rather not think of that time at all.

"It was...busy. Chaotic. Like a horde of bees."

"Oh." He offers a halfhearted smile. "Demon, then. Not angel."

"But you already knew, did you not?"

"No, no well, I don't know what I wanted to hear. I just wanted to know the truth. Thank you."

He forces a gentle, perfect smile over his beautiful marble face.

"After all that's happened, I don't even know if I wanted her to be mine. I just...I still look for that connection to Nia. Even now when I know I shouldn't."

I nod. "Now that Kythiel is gone—*really* gone—I miss him. It is like a small part of me was destroyed along with him. I do not want him back, not after all that has happened. But I miss him all the same."

Calipher nods.

For a moment we just sit there, both staring off to whatever lays in our minds beyond the walls of the hut.

The door opens, and Adem peeks in. "You're up." I have never seen him look so expressive. His entire body perks up when our eyes meet.

"Here I am," I say. I feel maybe I have been staring at him too long, and look to my hands in my lap. The battle was terrible, but it's no small silver lining that along the way I was able to mend things with Adem. I don't want to break it again.

"Can we talk?" he asks.

"Yes. In fact, let's go for a walk."

Both of them look like I have just suggested we burn

down the village. But I hate to be confined like this, and despite my shakiness, I am feeling strong. Neither of them says anything to stop me.

The sun is high. It is harsh on my eyes, but its warmth on my skin is bliss.

I shield my eyes and look around. The sun splays between huts and gleams off the ground. People are gathered throughout the open center, repairing armor and weapons. But it is too quiet. Empty.

I am almost too afraid to ask. "Just how many of us died in the battle?"

He hesitates. "More than survived."

When the people see us coming, they stop. They turn to us and watch us approach. More of them than not are wounded and bandaged. There are so few of them left that it breaks my heart. How can we possibly keep up the fight when rebels next try to attack whoever that might be?

As we get close, they kneel.

"What are they doing?"

"They are honoring you," Adem says.

"What? Why?"

"They saw your powers," Adem adds. "We all did. The power you wielded. You were like a God."

And then it all clicks—that's what they think I am. Some kind of demigod. Like the Firsts. Like Koreh, or even Calipher.

"No! No. I am nothing of the sort." I stop trying to explain to Adem and turn to the people. "Stop!"

They continue to kneel.

Adem shrugs. "That's not possible. We all saw."

I did not come out here for a fight, but for new

beginnings. "Let's just go."

We both head toward the sea without even talking about it. When we reach the water, we come to a stop together at the waves' edge without speaking, and let the water lap over our feet.

We stand together in silence, and everything is perfect. Everything except this valley of empty distance between us. We grew something so good, Adem and I, without even meaning to. And then I messed it all up.

"Can we go back to how it was?" I realize as soon as the words have escaped me that it is not what I want. How it was before this all started, it was like a lifetime ago. What I really want is what we became through all of this. Before I ruined it. I try to clarify.

"Can we be friends again? Like it was before I...before I ruined it all."

"Yes."

I wait to see if he will say anything more, but it is no surprise that he does not.

Instead, he takes my hand.

And this is everything. Like the water brushing gently over our feet, his touch is gentle and soothing. Healing, even.

There is still a lot ahead. I know what I did has not stopped the war, only put it off for a little longer. But for once, finally, I am at peace.

"Rona?" It is Jordan, calling from behind us.

I lean back to look at him.

He is not alone. With him stand three petite beings, so lithe they almost seem to float. They edge a little closer as I watch them, and the tinge of an aura, a surge of buzzing emotion, washes over me. Sprites.

"Who are—"

"They have a message for you." Jordan cuts me off.

The sprite next to Jordan steps forward and bows. "I am Nissa, sprite of Gloros, Goddess of passion. She has sent us to you. To fight by your side against the rebels in the war ahead."

"But…" I hardly knows what to think, let alone what to say. "The Gods. I was in the Host myself. They were not there. They are gone."

"They have sent us to you," Nissa insists. "More will arrive in the days and weeks to come."

My heart swells. I look to Jordan, then to Adem. They look as bewildered as I feel.

"Thank you." It comes out in a small whisper. I am too overwhelmed for anything more.

Nissa bows again, with a slight smile, and steps away. Jordan turns back toward Haven, taking the others with him.

I turn to Adem. He forms a rare smile, and squeezes my hand tighter as we watch the tide go out.

Maybe there is hope yet.

THE END

Thank you for reading! Find book one, MUD, and the prequel novella, RAIN, in the Chronicles of the Third Realm War available now.

Please sign up for the City Owl Press newsletter for chances to win special subscriber-only contests and giveaways as well as receiving information on upcoming releases and special excerpts.

www.ejwenstrom.com

@EJWenstrom

All reviews are welcome and appreciated. Please consider leaving one on your favorite social media and book buying sites.

For books in the world of romance and speculative fiction that embody Innovation, Creativity, and Affordability, check out City Owl Press at www.cityowlpress.com.

Turn the page for a sneak peek at prequel novella, RAIN, in the Chronicles of the Third Realm War

BY: E. J. WENSTROM

Available Now from City Owl Press

IT HAPPENED BEFORE I could stop myself — my hand reached out and stroked the angel Calipher's wing. It seemed perfectly harmless.

As my fingers reached into the soft feathers, a surge of peace broke through me like an unexpected breeze. When I pulled away, the vacuum it left behind flooded with shame. I realized, too late, I'd stolen something I had no right to.

Now, Calipher turns around, searching.

"Who did it?" he demands. His wings, like great founts of silver sprouting from his shoulders, bristle. "Who touched my wing?"

My heart pounds and my chest floods with panic. I want to run and hide, but my feet are planted to the ground as if roots have sprouted from them and bind me here.

What is wrong with me? I should never have touched him. But his aura gives off what I crave most — more today than ever. Deep peace pours out of him, like the quiet trickle of a forest creek.

Heat rushes to my face, and I am sure a deep flush will give me away.

"Who touched my wing?" Calipher repeats.

Tousled golden locks fall onto his face, which is cast in shadow under his furrowed brow. The feathers of his wings quiver and pull away from his back.

He is glorious and beautiful and terrible. For the first time in all the years since the goddess Theia sent him to us, I am afraid of him.

I have always been jealous of the way he could fly away and soar through the skies any time the realm of Terath might become too much for him. When I was a young girl, his wings seemed like the most magnificent things that could ever be, the way they spread around him, bright and gleaming. He seemed like the most magnificent thing that could ever be. He still does. I wanted that magnificence for myself.

Calipher's great shadow casts about as he turns to look for the culprit. He is larger than any human, and perfectly lean and tall. His skin glows pale as the moon, and his great silvery wings spread wide, the tips catching the morning sun with an orange glint, like embers at the edge of a fire. He is wild and alive, and he has never looked more enthralling.

It makes me want to touch him all over again.

The busy morning villagers—Shara, who I just traded with, Taavi, our closest neighbor and fellow farmer, all of them—step away, creating a halo of space between him and the crowd. As always, they are afraid of him. Afraid of his large-ness. Afraid of his magic. Of his wings and his glow and all that makes him beautiful. They are afraid of his other-ness, and all it implies.

"Come forth," Calipher urges. "Who was it?"

The others back away more, murmuring among themselves in fear. I'm the only one who doesn't, transfixed by his ire.

He turns slowly, looking over the gathering crowd. He looks right past me into the mass of faces.

He is so close, close enough to reach out and touch again, and yet still he barely even sees me. I can't bear it anymore.

"It was me." I have to force the words out. They crash around me and shatter like clay pots.

In their wake, the most painful kind of silence falls over the village center. Calipher stops his pacing. He stares at me. They all do.

My face burns with shame and I can't bear to hold his gaze. What is wrong with me? Why, this day of all days, could I no longer bear it?

After all these years, with day after day of pain piling onto my soul, I could not stand to *not* touch him any longer.

I woke up this morning to find Mother had disappeared again.

Mother does not disappear in the typical way, where a person cannot be found. For her, it is more as though she drowns inside herself, and her body becomes an empty shell. Even after all these years, my father's death still festers inside her like an infected wound. It is as if she spends her life treading water, fighting to keep herself at the surface. And then sometimes she gets too tired, and the pain overcomes her, and she drowns.

When she drowns, I am not even there in her eyes. Nothing is there, except my father's absence. She fumbles through her days barely seeing the next step in front of her, blindly stumbling through her routine.

I try to let it be, when Mother disappears. There is nothing to be done about it. It simply is, like the tides. But I feel my father's absence, too. It burns at me like coals trapped in a furnace. When she drowns, the silence she leaves behind burns inside me, each time a little deeper into my soul.

The release of touching Calipher's wing was one I needed desperately.

And now?

I do not know what now. But I cannot imagine I will have the courage to get close enough to him ever again to feel even the periphery of his aura.

But I cannot bear to be here anymore, facing the bewilderment that wrinkles Calipher's brow.

I turn and shove my way through the collecting crowd. It is too much, and I have to get away, a stinging shame coursing through me.

Could I have held back, if I had known the chaos my small moment of indulgence would lead to? If I am honest with myself, I am not sure. Even with the harsh glares and mystified glances people give me as I shove past them, that small moment when his peace rushed over me—it was just what my soul needed.

My feet propel me away from Calipher, away from the village, into the forgiving cover of the forest. Only when I am enclosed in its depths do I stop and catch my breath.

As my breathing steadies and I begin to walk again, a shadow rushes around me, then pulls together into a figure at my side.

"Not now, Bastus."

I glance at him. His icy blue eyes are completely blank—the only thing that gives him away as a demon, rather than a human—but the rest of his face is solemn.

"Nia," he greets me. He studies my face and tilts his head. "What troubles you? Is Liora at it again?"

Bastus knows more than most what my mother is. He was there when my father died years ago, and he watched with me as something in her died along with him.

"Yes," I reply. "But this isn't about Mother."

Standing so close, I can feel his aura vibrating off of his skin. He's a creature of Shael, god of chaos. While Calipher's aura is so soothing, Bastus' strains me with restlessness.

"What is it, then?"

He means to help, but his aura goes where he goes, like a shadow. It is like a poker shaking up embers from the coals, waking up the things inside me that I try to suppress.

"It's nothing." I sigh.

I lie to him reflexively, even though I know he won't believe me.

He folds his arms over his chest, accentuating his strong, square shoulders, and waits. Loose locks of thick, dark hair frame a brooding face. His brow steeps heavily over his eyes, casting them in shadow.

Some call him handsome, but to me he seems so typical, so human. He is nothing compared to Calipher's glowing perfection. Why would a demon, who could choose any form he imagined, choose to be something so typical?

And yet he is never anything but kind to me. It's not fair, the way I keep him at arm's length.

"Did something else happen?" he presses.

The heat rushes to my face again. I can't bear to say it out loud.

"Don't you have something else you could do?" The sharpness of my voice stops him in his tracks. He looks down to the dirt, and guilt floods me. I take a breath, ready to apologize.

"Nia?" a velvety voice interrupts from behind us.

My chest seizes. It is Calipher.

My bottom lip trembles as I turn around.

"I didn't mean to," I plead.

At least, I did not mean for him to notice.

For the first time, the peace emanating from him isn't enough. I am distressed beyond its comfort. My fingers beg to touch him again, to let the rush of peace blow away all the bad things inside me. I clutch my hands together to stop myself.

"What is going on?" Bastus steps half in front of me. He has never trusted the angels, not even the one he has worked alongside in this village for so many years. He looks to me. "Nia, what happened?"

He has that look on his face again—an expression that is so much more than concern, a mix of empathy and longing and a strange kind of hunger. It is a look that makes me embarrassed for him, though I have no reason to be.

"Bastus, go."

Bastus glances at me one more time, a reproachful look full of injury. His unsettling aura buzzes through me, competing with Calipher's peaceful one.

"Please," I say. It takes some effort to keep my expression steady while his blank eyes study my face.

He considers, then nods.

He breaks apart into shadow and whooshes away. When the last of his aura stops buzzing through me, I turn to Calipher.

***

We make our way through the woods side by side. This is all I wanted, to soak up his aura and feel this great calm again. To be close to him. But now distress hums underneath it.

"Why did you do it?" he asks.

My heart races. I can't bear to say it, it is so terribly embarrassing.

"I am so sorry," I whisper.

A tear drops down my cheek, heightening my embarrassment.

But then, Calipher smiles. It is as if the sun has chosen to single me out, of all of the people of the realm. I soak it up as if I have been freezing in the darkness of night all my life.

"There is nothing to apologize for," he says.

I let out a sigh, my throat catching on it from the stress. My mind spins—I am not in trouble? What does he want from me, then?

"But I do wish to know why you did it. Please. Tell me," he says.

I will my eyes to look up again and get lost in his gaze.

When a person is with you, they are right there with you, in that moment only. But angels—it is as if the time and place they are in do not bind them. As if they see something beyond them. Even as Calipher smiles down at me, he seems far away and distant, his eyes are relaxed and unfocused.

Is he listening to Theia? Or to the realm shifting under our feet? The whispers of the trees?

"I...."

How can I possibly explain to him? I am not fully sure myself. I just needed a small piece of his aura so badly. I can't bear his gentle expression any longer and drop my gaze to the forest floor.

"I just needed the peace you give off."

Calipher's smile melts away into a thin, straight line. "Do you not have peace of your own?"

It is like being stripped naked. "No."

"And when you touched me, did you get the peace you sought?"

"Oh, yes." The unexpected enthusiasm in my voice sounds crass. I bite my lip to stop myself from saying more.

His eyes drift off and his great wings bristle, as if he is lost in great thoughts.

He opens his mouth to speak, and I am afraid of what he will ask next, afraid I will have to explain to him the things in my life that keep peace away. But he doesn't ask.

"When you touched me, I felt something, too," he says. "Something I have never felt before."

My mouth drops open. How could I possibly stir anything in him, this great First Creature of the gods?

For a moment we just stand there, staring at each other.

"Has no one touched you before?"

I realize as I say it just all that means—not one hug, not a friendly stroke of a shoulder, no pressing of hands. And yet, it is not so surprising. Most of the people have feared and distrusted him since he arrived. Even the ones who have nothing against him are wary of his other-ness.

But right now, Calipher seems less like a great First Creature and more like a broken bird. His wings are pulled into him tight and his shoulders are tense.

His gaze drifts off, traveling to somewhere far away. I grapple for something else to ask, something to keep him here with me.

"What did it feel like for you, when I touched your wing?"

"It felt like...." He frowns. A sweet crinkle forms between his brows, a single imperfection so beautiful it makes him even more perfect. "It stirred me up. It was like a craving. It was a hunger of the spirit."

It sounds so much like the strained currents that flow through me most of the time. A restless sense that there must be more out there, somewhere. Something better, something good, if only I knew where to look.

I look down, my hair falling from my shoulders and around my face. "I'm so sorry. If I had known my touch would make you feel this way, I would not have done it. I—"

But he stretches his hand out in a gesture to quiet me.

"You misunderstand. This feeling, it was strange. But it was like waking up."

"You...you liked it?" I stutter.

"It was almost as though I had my own Will, outside of Theia's. As if I could become my own being."

I've never fully understood the angels' tie to their goddess. They are individual beings, and yet somehow Theia's Will is planted within them as if it were their own. Is it possible that they do not like it that way?

Confusion clogs my thoughts. I am completely bewildered by this turn of events—the entire morning.

Caltpher takes a shy step toward me. "Would you do it again?" he asks.

His request is hesitant and unsure. But his eyes are bright with a fire I've never seen before. It sends feelings coursing through me that I never would have dared to let free.

Would I do it again? If only I never had to stop.

I nod.

He reaches toward me, his palm up. I lay my own over it.

The peace washes over me in a rush, shooting up my arm and nestling into my core. As it fills me it softens, bringing all my anxiety and tension to a standstill, dissolving it into a gentle, pulsing warmth. Underneath it, there is the thrill of touching *him*, this beautiful strange creature that I have longed for, for so long. And this time he is touching me back, craving it as much as I do.

I look up to find he is watching me. I smile. He smiles too, a perfect angelic smile revealing perfect pearl teeth.

And then I do something I had not realized I even wanted.

I don't know what makes me do it, whether it's the relief that he is not angry, or the intense pleasure of his aura, or the giddiness of being here, with him, touching his hand.

But before I can think, I am stretching up to him on my tiptoes, and he is bending his neck down to meet me, and I am pressing my lips into his.

As we connect, his aura hits me so hard I can't feel the ground beneath me. It is utter perfection.

ACKNOWLEDGEMENTS

First and foremost, thank you Chris, for making the year in which this novel came pouring out of me possible. Whereas MUD came out in painfully slow drips and drops, one word at a time, this one came out in a flood. Some of this is likely the mystery of the creative process, but much of it is due to the freedom I had to work from home for a period, and I did my best to use this time as wisely as I could.

Many thanks also to Heather, my incredible editor. Your feedback is always kind but unrelenting in its pursuit to polish a story to its most optimized form. If Rona's story resonates with readers, it is in no small part to your notes, and your efforts to reel me in before I fell over the edge into her dark side.

And, of course, to Tina and Yelena, the heart of City Owl Press. I am ever grateful for your quick responses, helpful recommendations, and ceaseless hustle to bring the stories I pull out of my head into the world and into readers' hands.

Thanks also to my family, who has never had anything but absolute faith that if I said I was going to be a writer, then that's what I would be.

ABOUT THE AUTHOR

E. J. WENSTROM is a fantasy and science fiction author. A D.C. girl at heart, she currently lives in Florida with her husband and their miniature pinscher. Her first novel, MUD, received the Royal Palm Literary Award for Book of the Year and First Place for Fantasy. When she's not writing fiction, E. J. drinks coffee, goes running, and has long conversations with her dog. Ray Bradbury is her hero. Keep tabs on E.J.s writing and other antics at

www. ejwenstrom.com

ABOUT THE PUBLISHER

CITY OWL PRESS is a cutting edge indie publishing company, bringing the world of romance and speculative fiction to discerning readers.

www.cityowlpress.com

CPSIA information can be obtained
at www.ICGtesting.com
Printed in the USA
FFOW02n0514301117
43820143-42751FF